To C.
The world [is] a dark pla[ce]
without your
humor. I pray
lose it.

Black Magic Woman

by Connie Lynn Webb

Connie L Webb

This book is dedicated to my friends, my family and my tribe, without whom this book would never have been possible.

Prologue

Looking back on all that had happened, Daniel was amazed that he and Lauren had survived at all. It was only after several long discussions that lasted late into the night that they agreed not to tell anyone about what happened. Lauren was right when she questioned who would believe them. On the other hand, he really knew nothing about Rue's past, it is possible that the wrong people would believe and seek retaliation. Daniel looked over at the two other people sleeping in the king size futon, his wife Lauren and his son Luke. Reaching out, he gently touched each one of their sleeping heads. Lauren had her arms wrapped around Luke as if to protect him from the world.

Quietly he slid off the bed and made his way to the door. He watched as the light from the hall briefly lit their peaceful features before stepping into the hall and closing the door silently behind him. He went to his study and turned on the tiffany desk lamp. Wondering again if what he was doing was the right thing, he hesitated for only a moment before opening his top drawer and sliding leather bound journal from the drawer. They had agreed not to tell anyone what had happened, not even Luke...at least until he was ready to know. With another glance at the door to the study, he took a pen from the desk and he started to write. This is an accounting that will probably never be believed, I Daniel Everett Warwick of sound mind and body do write this tale. For my own sanity, and for you Luke when you are ready to know, I am writing the truth of what happened to bring both you and Lauren into my life. May God and you forgive me for what I have done; know that I am not the man I once was. This all starts on May 23 2014...

CHAPTER ONE

In the small tourist town of Bethesda Massachusetts, it would be common during 'tourist season' to see men in breeches and waistcoat and sporting a tricorn hat strolling up and down the cobbled streets. You might even see Mrs. James the baker's wife wearing a woolen dress and petticoats, her hair pulled back and covered with a lace cap as she set out trays of fresh baked pastries. The tourist season lasted from March to July then died down until September where it again picked up until the end of November and then was through for the holiday season. The people of Bethesda enjoyed a roaring tourist trade and seemed to never tire of playing to the masses. The few restaurants and businesses that did not fit the 'Colonial' image were relegated to the outskirts, leaving the town proper a town 'lost in time'. One of the most popular restaurants and sadly one that did not fit the tourist image was Angelo's Ristorante Italiano. Angelo's was a pizzeria where you could order just about anything on a pizza crust or choose from 13 menu choices. Besides

Pizza, you could also order several varieties of Pasta, soups and salads all made fresh on

demand. If you were interested in Bethesda's darker subculture there was a nightclub

called The Pariah's Nest which could be found on the opposite side of the town from

Angelo's and was relegated even further from town as if Bethesda were physically

distancing itself from those attracted to that sort of thing. The Pariah's Nest catered to the

Gothic, Emo, and pseudo vamp crowd. Basically, anyone who fantasized about living in

the world of True blood or Twilight was attracted to the club.

For the last eight years Daniel Warwick had been the head Chef, baker and Pizza

Slinger, his roommate Jason Lorenzo worked at the Bethesda petting zoo (yet another

tourist attraction where families can pet an ancient draft horse, a few goats, some

chickens, geese and cows). Together they shared a 4-bedroom bungalow situated right

across from James House O' Bread. It was a pretty nice place if you ignored the quaint

white picket fence out front; it also had a small walled courtyard out back. Jason had

been trying for nearly a year to get Daniel to come with him to 'Pariah's', which just

happened to be one of Jason's frequent haunts. So far, Daniel had found a way to politely

sidestep all invitations and had kept to his room with his olde English sheepdog Kirby on

the few occasions when Jason had brought someone home with him. Kirby was ten years

old and enjoyed sharing the Futon with Daniel and watching old movies. Daniel only

played black and white movies when he and Kirby were stuck in the room, the way

Daniel figured since Kirby could not see in color that he would not be missing anything.

Kirby had been a gift from Daniel's parents when he had graduated from the Boston

Culinary Academy but instead of starting his own restaurant or traveling abroad, he moved just 33 miles north to Bethesda. Bethesda lay equally between Middlesex and Essex. Jason loved to say Bethesda was perfectly located, with Middlesex on one side and Essex on the other side; you had sex on either side of you. Tonight Angelo's seemed to be more packed than usual, mostly with the high school homecoming crowd coming back from a game against Salem. From the sounds of things, Bethesda had won. Jason leaned on the counter his pleas for Daniel to join him at Pariah's tonight becoming whiny. Daniel attempted to ignore him as he brushed another coat of seasoned olive oil on the bruscetta and added fresh feta and green olives to the Caesar's Delight pizza he was working on. Sliding the pizza into the oven, he placed the plate of bruscetta on the pass through for the waiting server and tried to come up with yet another award winning reason he could not go with Jason tonight.

His mind was blank. Daniel waved Jason back off the counter as he placed more plates that are finished on the pass through and smiled as they were quickly whisked onto trays and the servers made a beeline to their tables, tips would be flowing tonight. Jason snapped his fingers in front of Daniel's eyes. "Come on Danny, the girls that go to Pariah's are hot enough to make even YOU forget your conservative upbringing and get a whole new outlook on life!" Daniel shrugged and though he was sure he would regret it, heard himself say, "What the hell, one night can't kill me right?" Jason laughed and cheered. Some of the jocks thinking Jason was joining in the celebration started singing their school's anthem as Jason danced his way to the front door.

Jason and Daniel stopped by the house to shower and change before heading to the club. Jason came out with his dark hair gelled flat and wearing a black sleeveless muscle shirt and black leather pants. Daniel laughed, "You look so gay!" Jason made a

scoffing noise and rolling his shoulders, did his best Derek Zoolander impression as he

pursed his lips and strutted from one side of the living room to the other spinning and

flexing his biceps. "This is my Goth gear, Danny boy." Daniel lacking any "Goth gear"

had put on a clean pair of jeans and a blue t-shirt that the girls at work claimed brought

out the color of his eyes. Jason took one look at his outfit and marched him back into his

room. Leaving Daniel standing confused in the doorway for a minute, Jason sprinted into

his own room and came back with a black t-shirt that he tossed at Daniel. "Wear this,

there is no way I am going to a club with you looking like a virgin farm boy." Daniel

stripped his shirt off and pulled the black one on. He stepped in front of the mirror. "What

the hell is Evil Dead? Girls like a guy with a chainsaw hand?" Jason slung an arm over

Daniel's shoulder as he joined him in front of the mirror. They were as opposite as

possible. Jason with his Dark hair and eyes and his olive complexion, and Daniel "the

Golden-boy" with his honey blonde hair and baby blue eyes and a California tan that had

never seen a beach. Where Jason was slender, Daniel was broad in his shoulder and chest

adding to the Iowa farm boy impression.

Jason smiled at their reflection "You do realize if this becomes a regular

thing for you we are DEFINITELY going to need to get you some new threads bro."

Daniel knocked his arm off his shoulders and grabbed his keys. "Lets get this over with,

and then you'll stop bugging me." After much debate, they decided to take Daniel's crew

cab instead of Jason's 1970 Barracuda. Daniel's truck lacked the flair of Jason's car but if

they took the truck, they would not have to park on the main road and walk to the club,

owing to the fact that the club despite being fairly popular was also down a dirt road that

Jason's car had a hard time navigating.

Daniel and Jason passed more than few couples on their way to the club and the one thing they all had in common was black clothes and lipstick. Daniel was beginning to wonder if this was a mistake when they came around a bend in the road and he caught sight of the Club. Someone had taken a beautiful Victorian style house and turned it into a gaudy nightclub. The front of the club was covered in ivy, with garish neon pink letters spelling out the name of the club. Two barely clad "vampire girls" danced in cages suspended five feet from the ground on either side of the entrance. The pulse-pounding beat could be felt through the soles of their feet as they made their way towards the front doors. Daniel paused twice on the way to the doors and both times Jason pushed him forward. The third time Daniel stopped Jason gave an annoyed huff. "Really Jason, this is the place? This place looks like it is straight out of one of your Tarrantino vids."

Turning back towards the door, he noticed the doorman was dressed in a moth-eaten velvet tuxedo and tails with rose-colored 'Lennon style' glasses. Shaking his head at the raspy voice the door attendant was using, Daniel handed the door attendant his $20 cover charge and his ID that the natty door attendant only gave a cursory glance before pocketing the cash and handing the ID back. Daniel waited for Jason to retrieve his ID then opened the door and immediately felt a headache start behind his right eye as the volume nearly made him take a step back. He had to wait a sec for his eyes to adjust to the darker atmosphere inside; he stepped in and to the side as people pushed past him. Jason immediately pulled him farther to the side, whipping his head around to look past the crowded entryway; he was obviously searching for someone when he suddenly tugged Daniel in the direction of one of two bars positioned on either side of the sunken dance floor. Daniel glanced at the dance floor as Jason tugged him through the crowd, it seemed like everyone was wearing leather, chains or velvet...and lots of black makeup. Daniel suddenly found himself in front of two beautiful and heavily made up girls. Jason slapped him on the back. "Daniel I would like you to meet Belladonna and her sister Hecate."

The woman introduced as Belladonna had her red and black striped hair pulled into two pom-pom looking ponytails and her sister Hecate had hair too black to be natural done up in a thousand tiny micro braids. Belladonna was wearing a burgundy and black velvet striped dress that matched her hair and ended just above her thigh high boots. Hecate was wearing a leather bra, low-slung leather pants with her knee high leather boots, and when she smiled at Daniel, he could see she was also wearing cosmetic fangs as well. Jason leaned in and whispered something in Belladonna's ear and she snorted and gave a high pitch giggle that Daniel instantly remembered hearing several times when Jason had brought a 'friend' home. The girls seeing Daniel was not really 'into the scene' dragged Jason onto the dance floor leaving Daniel leaning against the bar watching the many wraith-like dancers grinding against each other to the loud music.

Turning his back to the dance floor, Daniel ordered a beer and then hopped up on the vinyl barstool and let his eyes wander over the black mass. David laughed as he caught sight of Jason's 'moves' which looked more like a cross between an epileptic fit and a chimp's mating dance than any dance Daniel had ever seen. Daniel let his eyes slide past to some of the other dancers and finally over to the secondary bar against the far wall, he noticed two women were staring in his direction. One of the women was a buxom blonde-haired woman in an abbreviated black dress with draping sleeves. Even from across the room he could tell she had full lips painted Fire engine red. Her companion was more on the petite side and had dark hair buzzed short in the back with long bangs that fell in front of her face. Daniel lifted his beer in a silent salute and was dragged away from staring at them by the laughing and shoving return of Jason and the girls.

Jason got the bartender's attention and ordered drinks for the three of them. Turning with drink in hand, Jason hopped up on the stool next to Daniel. Daniel looked over at Jason and an idea suddenly came occurred to him. "Hey Jason, you know the girls that frequent this place right?" Jason took a drink and shrugged, "most of them, why?" Daniel jerks his chin in the direction of the other bar. "What do you know about the blonde eyeballing me?" Jason followed his gesture and smiles lasciviously "Not much but just give me an hour or two, because I sure wouldn't mind getting to know ALL about her." Belladonna must have heard part of the conversation because she suddenly slapped Jason upside his head. Jason winced and laughed "Just kidding sweetheart." Belladonna raised on plucked eyebrow as if in disbelief than looked across him at Daniel. "So which little vamp tramp are you two drooling over?" Jason pulled her close and pointed across the crowded dance floor to where the blonde-haired woman and her friend now had their heads bent close in conversation.

Both Jason and Daniel jumped as Belladonna gasped and the glass in her hand exploded. Jason spun around and got a clean rag from the bartender to wrap Belladonna's bleeding hand in. Not seeming to notice her hand, Belladonna grabbed Hecate "She's back Hecate." Hecate spun to follow where Belladonna was pointing and let out a string of curses before starting to muscle her way straight across the room. Belladonna gave a helpless look at Jason before following her sister. Jason followed behind her. Curious to see what was going on, Daniel followed and apologized for the groups jostling of fellow patrons.

Hecate shoved through the last few people separating her from the blonde and her friend and just as the blonde turned to see who was approaching her, Hecate threw a right cross that caught the blonde just below her left eye and knocked her off her feet. The blonde-haired woman got to her feet hissing and wiping blood from her corner of her eye. Her friend had shrieked and hopped to the floor to help her but was shoved back as the blonde-haired woman approached Hecate her eyes hot enough to burn. "Fucking bitch how dare you strike me!" Hecate spat in the blonde-haired woman's face and lunged forward but was stopped short as the blonde's friend jumped in between them. "Fuck you Rue, my brother committed suicide two years ago after you used him and spit him out!" Rue's friend (who he later found out was named Kate Rochester) shook her head at Hecate. "You must be mistaken, the last guy Rue was with broke her heart and left her for someone else." Rue glared daggers at the back of Kate's head and Hecate laughed, "If you believe that then you have been huffing too much nail polish sweetheart, no one ever leaves Rue...and lives!" Rue laughed a low throaty chuckle "That almost sounds like you are accusing me of something little girl, you may want to be verrrry careful whom you slander." There was a distinct edge to Rue's voice and her eyes were narrowed dangerously. Hecate reached past Kate to shove Rue's shoulder "Or what you'll hex me?"

Hecate snorted and turned to walk away then spun back around and flipped Rue off. "No one around here believes that whole 'all powerful slut of Satan persona you are peddling, you are just as much of a poser as the rest of them so take your broomstick and shove it where the sun don't shine!" Rue's eyes briefly widened in surprise then she suddenly grinned, "Oh you are so very dead vamp tramp." Kate dragged Rue off with whispered conversation. Belladonna grabbed Hecate's arm hard "What do you think you are doing, you know what she is!" Hecate pulled her arm free and headed back through the crowd towards her abandoned drink. Jason glanced from Belladonna to Hecate's retreating back. "Anyone want to enlighten us what just happened?" Belladonna gave a worried look around then gestured them both close "Most of the regulars here play the part, dress in black and assume Gothic names and personas but Rue Bishop..."

"Many of us are of the Wiccan faith and despite local belief, being a Witch has nothing to do with worshiping the devil or being evil. Our gifts work WITH nature not twisting it for personal gain, heck our core belief is 'do no harm'." Belladonna was passionate about her beliefs and defending them was something she had gotten used to but being in a club surrounded by posers was neither the time nor the place for this discussion. "Needless to say what she does is very real and a dark perverted version of our beliefs, she walks a twisted path and there is a price for power such as hers."

Jason started to smile like he as waiting for Belladonna to tell them she was pulling one over on them but she just stopped. "Hold on sweetheart, are you trying to tell us she is the real McCoy?" Belladonna shrugged and shook her head as if to say she could not answer that. "I've never seen anything, but everyone that gets on the wrong side of her gets hurt, sick or has a string of bad luck." Daniel rolled his eyes and left Jason and Belladonna talking and wandered over to where Hecate was sitting with her hands wrapped around a tumbler of Jack and Coke. "Guess you think I am an idiot for taking on the 'bitch queen' too huh?" Hecate shoved her braids out of her face and stared into her drink. Daniel sighed and gestured in the direction Rue and Kate had headed, "whatever is between you and her is your business and none of mine, but I sure am sorry to hear about your brother." Hecate turned and smiled at Daniel that is sweet to say, even if he WAS an asshole. You want to go someplace else?"

Not wanting to jump to conclusions Daniel asked, "Go someplace else like..." Hecate laughed, "Down tiger, I meant someplace we could have coffee and chat...and maybe after that we can discuss going 'someplace else'". Daniel let Jason know they were taking off. Jason gave him an ear-to-ear grin and after checking with Belladonna, stated he would stay at her place tonight so Daniel and Hecate would have the house to themselves. Daniel shook his head and waved off Jason's catcalls as Daniel followed Hecate to the doors. Neither of them noticed Rue and Kate watching them as they passed their shadowy alcove. If either had seen the look on Rue's face, they would have known that things were far from over.

Daniel held the truck door open for Hecate much to her bemusement then jogged around the front to open his own door. He noticed her trying to stifle laughter as he slid behind the wheel. "What's so funny?" Hecate beamed at him, "I thought gentlemen had made a mass exodus from Massachusetts or had gone the way of the dinosaurs anyway." Daniel laughed and plucked at his Evil dead t-shirt. "Guess I just blew my 'Goth' image out of the water huh?" Hecate smiled "Don't worry about it; spending time with a gentleman will be a refreshing change of pace from what usually tries to pick me up." Hecate dug through the tote bag at her feet and pulled out a black T-shirt and slipped it on over her leather bra. Daniel started up the truck and took her to Deja' Brew, Deja Brew was a cute little retro coffeshop that vaguely resembled something from the Happy Days

TV show. Daniel slid into the booth, the vinyl bench protesting loudly, Hecate had skill sliding into the booth without the embarrassing noise. Their waitress Sally brought them menus but in the end, they both just ordered coffee. Daniel asked about her t-shirt and got a raised eyebrow in response "You have never seen Split Second?" Daniel shook his head "I recognize Rutger Hauer but that is about all I know about that movie." Hecate shook her head as if he had suddenly grown two heads. "I hesitate to ask what kind of movies you DO know about."

Daniel took a sip of his coffee and added more sugar, "Mostly black and white movies, Kirby and I spend a lot of time holed up in my room when Jason has a date." Hecate snorted. "Kirby is your...boyfriend?" Daniel shot her a horrified look. "NO! Kirby is my dog! You thought I was gay?" Daniel looked around to see how much attention his raised voice had gotten but everyone seemed to be minding their own business. Hecate apologized for the comment and they moved into safer conversation waters, favorite movies, colors, actor/actress etc. When he finally looked, at his watch, it was just after midnight and Sally was giving then an annoyed stare from behind the counter. Hecate noticed the impatient stare being shot their way and leaned forward on the table giving Daniel an eyeful as her t-shirt pulled tight. "OK tiger, now you can take me...'someplace else'."

Daniel suddenly felt his face go warm and his throat felt very dry. Hecate laughed as Daniel went red faced. "Aaaaaand he blushes, you just get sweeter and sweeter Danny." She slid out of the booth and held her hand out for his. Slowly taking her hand, he slipped out of the booth and escorted her back to the truck. All the way back to his house, he kept a running list of worries; did I remember to pick up the laundry on the bedroom floor? How badly trashed is the house, I have been working many extra hours, maybe I did not notice.

Daniel parked his truck out in front of the house and hesitated then quickly got out and went around to Hecate's door before he could think up an excuse to not go through with this. He led Hecate up to the front door then hesitated again as he heard Kirby barking on the other side of the door. Turning to Hecate, he asked, "You are ok with dogs' right?" Hecate smiled "Unless it's a rabid Saint Bernard on the other side of that door I'll be fine." Daniel laughed as he unlocked the door "nope no Cujo, just Kirby." Daniel shoved Kirby away from the door so Hecate could enter. For once, the house did not look like it was being rented by mindless Neanderthals. Out of the corner of his eye, he spied something red sitting under the lit end table lamp. Crossing the room he picked up a note written in Jason's handwriting saying simply "Have fun", beneath the note was a three pack of Trojan condoms in red wrappers. The note and condoms had not been there when they left the house earlier, which meant that Jason had snuck in while he and Hecate were at Deja Brew and cleaned the house and left the note and 'gift'.

Quickly he stuffed the condoms into his pants pocket. He turned back to the room and smiled. Hecate was sitting on the couch with a 70-pound sheepdog sitting in her lap and thoroughly bathing her face in dog slobber. Most women would be grossed out by Kirby's breath let alone his drool but Hecate was laughing and twisting her head from side to side to avoid getting Kirby's tongue in her laughing mouth.

Daniel crossed his arms over his chest and laughed at Kirby's antics and waited until Hecate actually called for help before stepping in to pull Kirby off her lap. Taking Kirby by the collar, he led him over to the cedar filled dog pillow in the corner and told him to stay. As soon as Daniel joined her on the couch, Hecate excused herself to the bathroom to go wash the dog drool off her face. When she re emerged from the bathroom her face was scrubbed clean of all traces of dog drool but also of all the dark makeup she had been wearing at the club.

In Daniel's opinion, she looked twice as beautiful Au natural as she did with all that makeup on her. She crossed the room and then sat cross-legged on the couch facing Daniel. Daniel let the awkward silence linger for a minute then blurted the first thing that came to mind. "So Hecate and Belladonna, those are unusual names..." Hecate scrunched up her face in an expression of distaste. "My real name is Kendra Starling and my sister is Courtney Starling, we go by Hecate and Belladonna at the club and with the local Goth community." Daniel smiled "I think Kendra is a beautiful name." Hecate smiled back "Maybe someday I'll let you use it, but for now it's Hecate." Reaching up she popped her fangs off her teeth and set them on the coffee table nearby. Then leaning forward she started nipping at his lips.

Daniel wrapped his arms around her and leaned back until he was lying on his back on the couch with her stretched out atop him, then tilting his head he playfully slipped his tongue between her parted lips and deepened the kiss. Hecate sat back, straddling his hips for a moment as she slid the shirt over her head and dropped it to the floor next to the couch. Stretching back out on top of him and purring as he ran calloused hands up and down her back. Suddenly she jumped up with a shriek. Daniel sat up confused for a moment then looked over to where Kirby was standing close to the couch panting. Giving Kirby a scowl as the dog shoved his cold nose in Daniel's face, he realized that cold nose on Hecate's ribs was probably what made her shriek. Looking over at Hecate who was now laughing, "I think we better continue this is in another room." Grabbing Hecate's shirt from under Kirby's prancing feet and her fangs from the table, Daniel led Hecate to his room and closed the door in Kirby's face. Hecate looked around the room curiously.

A king sized futon bed with a deep blue oriental patterned comforter dominated the room, there was also an old fashioned wooden dresser, an antique desk and a door to what was presumably either a walk in closet or another bathroom. Turning back to Daniel, Hecate saw he had dropped his shirt onto the dresser and stood barefoot in his jeans. She admired his broad chest with a dusting of red gold curls, toned abs and muscular thighs encased in tight jeans. Yup definitely a 10, not that I will tell him that. Daniel put an arm around her to pull her to him and began nibbling the side of her neck, his other hand stroking down her arm and then skimming back up her ribs until he cupped her full breast through her leather bra.

She reached behind her to unhook the bra and let it slide off her to the floor. Stepping in front of her, he cupped both breasts in his hands and recaptured her lips, his thumbs brushing back and forth across her hardening nipples. Hecate felt light headed at how wonderful his lips and hands felt. Pulling back, he looked deep into her passion-glazed eyes and then smiled. Then trailing his lips down her body he slowly knelt in front of her, his rough hands sending shivers down her spine as he trailed them done her ribs and then caught them at the waistband of her leather pants. Kneeling in front of her and looking up her body at her, Hecate for the first time in a long time felt nervous.

Daniel reached up and unbuttoned her leather pants and then hooking his fingers in the sides, slowly slid them down her legs and helped her step out of them. She was wearing a black leather thong that matched the bra she had been wearing earlier. Slowly he slid that down her legs as well. Then pulling her closer he rested his forehead on her abdomen his warm breath fanning the curls between her legs. Daniel could feel her quivering and smiled as he slid a hand up her thigh and cupped her cleft in his hand. Hecate let out a low moan as he nudged her legs further apart. Dipping his head Daniel removed his hand and sliding his hands up to cup her firm butt, he began using his tongue to suckle and stroke her quivering center. Hecate gripped his hair in her fists as she bit her lip and cried out. Wave after wave of pleasure ripped through her. God I could easily fall in love with this man!

Gently he nudged her backwards until her knees bumped the edge of the bed and she was forced to sit down. He placed a hand on her abdomen and indicated he wanted her to lie back on the bed. She laid back and then gasped again as he reburied his face between her thighs. Her hands fisted in her braids as she lay there feeling like she was going to explode. Suddenly Daniel was beside her on the bed kissing her; she could taste herself on his lips. She rolled towards him and slid her hand down to cup him through his jeans. The front of his jeans strained and he caught his breath at her touch, proof she was not the only one in agony right now. With a hand on his chest, she gently pushed him onto his back and sliding down the bed decided it was HER turn to torture HIM. Hecate unsnapped his jeans and grinned at the groan he bit back as she slid the zipper down. Amazingly, enough he was not wearing any thing under his jeans. Gee and I thought he would be a boxers type. His hard cock strained at the opening to his jeans until she pulled his jeans past his hips.

With a wicked look at his face, she took as much of him as she could into her mouth, my they do make them big in Boston don't they? Hecate chuckled, as it was his turn to grip her hair. He groaned at how good her mouth felt. She continued sliding him in and out of her mouth, then with no warning at all she slid up his body and lowered herself onto him making them both hiss with pleasure. He gripped her hips with strong fingers as she moved on top of him. Several times, he heard her cry out and felt her thigh muscles starting to shake while he continued to grit his teeth to keep from joining her too soon. Her movements were slowing as her legs got tired, taking that as a sign to take over, her rolled her beneath him and began thrusting first slow and deep then hard and fast. Again and again, he heard her cry out loudly, her nails raking down his back with delicious pain. With a final deep thrust, he allowed himself to join her, his voice strained as he cried out and shook with the force of his orgasm. His arms shook with weariness as he held himself above her, then leaning forward he tenderly kissed her lips.

Daniel shifted his hips to pull free of her then rolled them both to their sides facing each other on the bed. Hecate propped herself on one elbow and he did the same "Where have you been all my life Daniel?" He laughed, "I was going to ask you the same thing." She leaned forward and kissed him again tenderly, his hand came up to tangle in her braids again and she smiled against his lips. "If we keep this up we are never going to leave this room." Daniel started to say something when Hecate's stomach abruptly gave a loud growl. "That tells me we need to get you fed, but first we need to shower." He slid off the bed and went to the door in the far wall, which did indeed lead to a large master bath with a sunken tub and walk in shower. Daniel hopped in the shower and quickly cleaned up, then came out with a towel wrapped around his waist. Handing her a towel big enough to drape her whole body in, he gestured for her to use the shower next and kissed her forehead as he headed to the kitchen to make them something to eat.

Hecate took her time showering, enjoying the hot water on her tired muscles. She might have stayed in there even longer if the smell of Belgian waffles had not wafted into the bathroom making her stomach growl even louder. Quickly she towel dried her braids and then wrapped the towel around her and headed back into the bedroom. She passed on putting her leather undergarments on and just slipped into her pants and t-shirt. Emerging from the room, she was overwhelmed with the mingling scents of waffles, bacon and eggs. Daniel was setting out two plates, each containing two Belgian waffles three strips of bacon and scrambled eggs with grated cheese. He also placed two bowls on the table with fresh strawberries and blueberries, then snapping his fingers as if he suddenly remembered something he skipped back into the kitchen emerging with two steaming cups of coffee.

Hecate stood in the kitchen door amazed "You made all this?" She gestured to the breakfast-laden table. Daniel gave a half shrug "I went to the Boston Culinary Academy, cooking is kind of a passion of mine." Hecate beamed "I ask again, where you have been all my life?"

Daniel laughed and pulled her chair out. "You go ahead and get started while I finish getting dressed." It was only then that she realized he still had a towel wrapped around his waist. He went back into the bedroom and closed the door behind him, when he came back out he was wearing a pair of whitewashed jeans and a blue t-shirt that matched his eyes. Daniel joined her at the table and Hecate had to concentrate not to moan at how good the food all tasted, the bacon was chewy, the eggs were perfectly seasoned, even the waffles were light and fluffy not hard and chewy like the toaster waffles she was used to. "Anyone ever tell you that you are too good to be true Danny?"

Daniel smiled and nodded his thanks while shoveling more food in his mouth to avoid

answering. "So what about you, what do you do for a living?" Hecate considered lying to

make herself sound more interesting, after all, he was an academy trained Chef and they

had just met last night. "I am the assistant librarian at the Bethesda Public

Library...mainly I run toddler story time and spending a lot of time re-shelving books that

people happen to leave lying around the library." He nodded and wiped his hands on the

linen napkin next to his plate "So that must mean you do a lot of reading right?"

She polished off her bacon and eggs before answering. "I have so many books

that Courtney is making me have a garage sale to get rid of some of them, otherwise we

will have no room to walk around in our living room." He grinned and took his plate to

the sink, turning; he leaned against the counter and crossed his arms. "So what does

Courtney do?" Hecate finished the last of her waffle and sat back with a satisfied groan.

"She is a beautician over at the Essex Beauty Boutique." Daniel laughed "Yeah I can see

her being very into her appearance." Hecate joined the laughter then got up and set her

dishes in the sink. Standing close to him, she looked up at him and felt herself staring.

Shaking her head, she stepped back "This could get awkward real fast, maybe we should

call it and you can drop me at the club so I can pick up my car." Daniel pressed his lips to

her forehead again and nodded, "let me just go grab my keys." Daniel pulled on shoes

and socks and grabbed his keys off the hall table. Hecate did a quick peruse and pocketed

her fangs before following him out the front door but not before ruffling Kirby's ears on

the way out.

Daniel once again held the door open for her and waited until she was buckled

before trotting around to the other side and sliding behind the wheel. The ride back to the club was silent, each one locked into their own thoughts. When they got to the club, the only vehicle was a yellow 1974 VW bug, which she pointed out as hers. Daniel pulled up alongside and opened her door for her; Hecate fidgeted with her keys for a few minutes then looked up at him. "This may sound like a cheesy line but ...I really did have a great time last night and breakfast was amazing" She shuffled her feet for a second feeling like a teenager again. "Jason has our number, maybe we can go out someplace ...say next weekend?"

Daniel flashed a big grin and she suddenly noticed he had dimples how did I miss that? "I would really like that...could it be someplace other than here though?" He gestured to the Goth club behind her and she laughed "I could tell it's not really your thing...sure, call me this week and we'll figure something out." Climbing in her car, she felt herself grinning like a fool and had to remind herself to put it in drive. Daniel sat with his truck idling and watched her drive out of the parking lot and out of sight before he did the same.

Daniel got back home and finished the dishes, then let Kirby out back to do his business and walked about the house straightening up. He grabbed his clothes from last night off the bedroom floor and the three packs of condoms fell out of the pocket of his jeans. His mind rebelled at what he was seeing. How did I forget to slip one on! What if...He grabbed up the clothes and tossed them into the washer along with his comforter. Impatiently he sat and waited for Jason to get home. It wasn't until late afternoon when Jason staggered in smelling like strong perfume, his clothes askew and his gelled hair mussed. Daniel jumped up the minute Jason came through the door causing Kirby to start barking. Jason grabbed his head in both hands as the loud barks caused his head to start

pounding. Jason glared at the dog "KIRBY GO LAY DOWN!" Kirby whimpered and

trotted off to his pillow.

Jason gave Daniel his signature half grin, "How was your night stud?" Daniel

smiled, "It was...she is amazing, but I forgot...." Daniel through his hands in the air and

let them drop to the sides. "I forgot to use a condom." Jason snorted which then burst into

a full laugh. "Don't worry about it Danny, one time is not going to kill you or her, just

remember for next time before things go to your head." Jason staggered towards the

kitchen and called back over his shoulder "You my man are not the only one who got

lucky last night and if Hecate is anything like her sister....well then we both have earned

the right to sleep in today." Daniel heard water running and Jason emerged from the

kitchen drinking a tall glass of water. Jason slapped himself upside the head "Almost

forgot, here ya go." Jason handed him a slip of paper from his front pocket. When Daniel

unfolded the paper, he found a number scrawled on it in Jason's untidy scrawl.

Jason mumbled something as he walked back into the kitchen, when he came

back out Daniel watched him dry swallow a couple of aspirin. "That is Hecate and

Belladonna's home number, Hecate has a cell phone but since I am dating her sister I

don't have the number."   Daniel glanced up at him with an unbelieving smirk "So

you and Belladonna are officially 'dating' now?" Jason tossed a pillow at him and

collapsed on the couch, which Kirby took as a sign that it was safe to return to the living

room. Kirby got up on the couch next to Jason and started panting in his ear; Jason threw

an arm over Kirby and started rubbing his ears. "Yeah yeah laugh it up...I'm getting too

old and too tired to keep chasing women. Besides Courtney and I just click ya know?"

Daniel sat down on the other end of the couch, "You're 26 you are not too old, hell I am 3 years older than you are so what does that say about me?" Jason waved off the comment then quickly glanced over Kirby's head at Daniel "I KNOW you made her breakfast...is there anything left?"

Daniel gestured to kitchen "There are leftover waffles, berries and bacon in the fridge..." He had barely finished saying the word waffles before Jason was vaulting over the back of the couch and sliding into the kitchen like a kid half his age. Daniel heard the fridge door open and then Jason gave a groan of ecstasy "If only I were gay Danny, I would marry you for your cooking and have a headache every night." Danny laughed and went over to the phone.

Dialing the number from the paper Jason had given him and knowing that Jason was eagerly listening in, he almost hung up but the phone picked up after four rings and a tired voice answered. "Ummmm Hecate?" The voice on the other end laughed and answered in the negative. "Oh um sorry Court...umm Belladonna, is she...oh OK, well when she gets in could you...yeah that would be great thanks...yup you too." Jason smirked "You got it baaad Danny boy." Daniel stuck his tongue out at him and headed back to the bedroom to catch some much needed rest. Grabbing his pillow, he buried his face in it; it still smelled like her shampoo, feeling like an idiot he dropped off to sleep.

Daniel must have slept most of the day away because when Jason sat down on the edge of the bed to wake him up, the sky outside the window was dark. Jason shook his shoulder, the phone in his hand and his face looking extremely haggard. "Danny you got to wake up man...something has happened." Daniel sat up abruptly disturbing Kirby where he lay snoozing next to him on the bed. Shoving his hair out of his face and feeling like his head was packed with cotton he looked over at Jason "What are you talking about?" Jason shook his head "Courtney just called me...she just got a visit from the police...Hecate was in a car accident." Daniel shot out of bed and hit the switch near the door, the room was suddenly flooded with bright light. Turning to Jason, he grabbed the front of his shirt and pulled him up to stand in front of him. "Tell me this is one of your sick fucking jokes Jason!" Jason gently pried his hand loose from his shirt, "I really wish it was bro, the cops are on the way here to talk to us both." As if summoned by the mere mention of them, the doorbell rang.

Jason got up and left the room and Daniel heard him let the cops in. When Daniel walked into the living room, both cops turned towards him. Officer Bennet was tall and blonde like Daniel but had dark brown eyes and a burn scar on his left cheek. He immediately stuck out his hand and apologized for their need to speak with him. They were just "filling in some gaps in the investigation", his partner Officer Larken had red hair buzzed short and unlike his partner did not jump up to greet Daniel but remained seated and seemed to be hanging back and observing the room. Daniel sat on one end of the couch and Jason on the other, after finding out that Jason had been elsewhere all night they concentrated their questions on Daniel and had him walk them through the entire night with Hecate right up to the point where he watched her drive off. Officer Bennet kept glancing up at Daniel from the notebook he was jotting notes in. "So you guys did not have any alcohol after coming back here?" Daniel shook his head.

Officer Bennet looked down at his notes again then glanced at his partner. "Did you notice her having any car problems before she left, car not starting right away, slipping on the gravel...anything?" Daniel shook his head again "What happened exactly, is she going to be ok?" Officer Bennet looked sharply at Daniel. "Apparently no one told you and I am sure sorry to be the one to do so but...she lost control of her car on her way to work, her car rolled into Walden Pond near Essex." Daniel did not even realize he had stood up until Jason and Officer Bennet were at his side. Jason wrapped an arm around him to steady him "I am so sorry Danny, God I am so sorry." Daniel pulled away and stepped back until he felt the wall at his back. Over and over, he kept thinking this had to be a nightmare, she couldn't be dead.

Daniel slid down the wall, he never knew when the cops finally left, he barely noticed when Jason slid to the floor next to him and handed him a cold beer. "I called Angelo and let him know what happened, he said take as long as you need, and you can come back to work when you are ready." Daniel nodded feeling empty "What about Courtney?" Daniel's voice was hoarse as if all the screaming denials in his head had affected his throat. Jason took a swig of beer. "I am going to head over there in the morning, I may stay there for a few days....just to help her keep it together, unless...." Daniel shook his head "No go to her man, I'm just gonna take it a day at a time ya know?" Jason nodded and headed for his room. Daniel pushed himself up off the floor and poured the rest of the beer down the kitchen drain. He called Kirby and went back into his room and knew nothing more until morning.

When Daniel awoke the next morning, he immediately started trying to rationalize away the sharp aching emptiness he was feeling. Grow up Danny! You knew Hecate less than 48 hours, hardly long enough to fall in love or grieve her like a missing body part. Yes, the sex was amazing and yes it had been (until that night) nearly two years since he had dated let alone been intimate with anyone. Nevertheless, logically it should not have been possible for me to fall that hard and that fast for someone I barely knew. Daniel stretched out on his bed with these thoughts going round and round in his head. Suddenly another thought occurred to him Funny how emotions rarely follow logic isn't it? Daniel had to agree, if love made sense than it probably would not be love. What he had been feeling as he and Hecate had laid on the bed both fully sated and staring into each other's eyes had been closer to love then Daniel could ever remember feeling.

Obviously some part of Daniel (other than the obvious one)had connected with Hecate and now he felt like some integral part of him had been ripped loose leaving behind a gaping hole in his chest. The official report deemed the crash due to possible driver fatigue and no signs of foul play or tampering had been found. Jason showed up from time to time but mostly he spent all his time when not working with Courtney. Daniel got used to seeing Jason rush home to shower and change and then head back out so often, that it no longer startled him to hear the door open and close.   Occasionally Jason would call from Courtney's to check on him, but after awhile he just pretended not to be home and let the machine pick up. Finally, Daniel got tired of sleeping all day and staring blankly at the same four walls. With an almost physical wrench, he got up, showered and dressed in work clothes. He refreshed Kirby's food and water and headed to work. It was hard to say who was more surprised to see Daniel walk through the kitchen door, his boss Angelo or his co-workers. Angelo turned to Daniel as if he had seen a ghost, forgetting that Daniel spoke very little Italian he rattled off "Che cosa stai facendo qui?" Daniel waited knowing if he stared blankly for a second, Angelo would translate. "I told you to take as long as you needed." Daniel gave Angelo a tired smile. "You are a wonderful Boss, but I need to work or I will go stir crazy." Angelo nodded as if he understood perfectly. "E' bene il mio amico" then untying the apron from around his waist, he handed it to Daniel and made his way through his gawking employees to his office in the back and closed the door.

For most of the day Daniel was able to lose himself in the repetitive and familiar sensations of work, even the sounds of the kitchen chatter lulled him into a false sense of peace and he was able to forget and just be. He could almost believe he had managed to pull himself together until suddenly he saw a flash of dark hair with alabaster skin and then he would catch himself whipping his head around as if expecting the brunette to turn and be Hecate.

The funeral was three days away and Daniel spent every minute he could at work. The day of the funeral dawned bright and sunny with clear turquoise skies. Hecate was being buried under a beautiful Beech tree on top of a rolling hill in their family plot in the Cherry Hill Cemetery near Essex. Daniel stood watching as everyone came up and laid either a black or red rose on the casket and said a few words. The eulogy might have been beautiful and inspiring but he never heard a word of it so caught up in his own troubled thoughts. A brisk wind sprung up turning the sunny day cold, pulling his long coat closer about him and stuffing his hands in his pockets Daniel became lost in thought. Daniel found himself staring intently at the black and red roses stacked atop the gleaming wooden casket as if trying to decipher a hidden meaning. Daniel was pulled abruptly from his tumbling thoughts when Courtney suddenly wrapped surprisingly strong arms around him and caused him to grunt in surprise.

For someone so petite she sure had a strong grip. She held him silently for a moment then pulled his head down and kissed his cheek and just as suddenly released him and headed to the parking lot. Jason glanced at her then came over and hugged Daniel as well. "Hey we are going to grab something to eat and then heading back to her place, did you want to join us?" Daniel seriously considered it for a minute then shook his head. "I think I am going to stay a bit longer then head home." Jason nodded clearly torn between going after Courtney and staying to comfort Daniel. "Alright, well call if you need anything." Just like that, Jason was trotting after Courtney's retreating form.

Daniel went back to staring at the roses and the wooden casket as it was slowly lowered into the ground. The grounds keeper then left him alone with the open grave. Daniel was not sure how long he stood there lost in thought before he realized he was no longer alone.

The blonde that Hecate had gotten into a fight with and her dark haired companion were standing nearby, the blonde was dabbing a white handkerchief to red-rimmed eyes and sniffling ever so often. As soon as Daniel looked up and noticed them, the blonde hurried over as if to join him in their shared grief. She stopped just out of arms reach and spoke with a timid quaver in her voice "I don't know if you remember me, my name is Rue Bishop and this is my roommate Kate." She gestured to her dry-eyed companion standing looking at Daniel with an unreadable expression on her face. Daniel nodded cautiously "I remember you, you are the one Hecate got in an altercation with at the Goth club." Rue shook her head and dabbed her eyes again and sniffed. "Kendra never realized how broken I was when her brother Bryan broke my heart and left me....and then when I heard he had killed himself well I .....I nearly lost it myself." Daniel had not missed the fact that Rue had used Hecate's real name, the name she despised which is why she went by Hecate.

The words sounded right but the tone Rue was using to convey them was too rehearsed, the dabbing of the eyes (without evidence of tears) and the well-timed sniffling seemed like too perfectly timed to be genuine. Daniel glanced over Rue's shoulder at Kate; Kate gave no pretense of emotion but stared at Daniel as if waiting for an inevitable conclusion. Suddenly Rue laid a well-manicured hand on his bare wrist and his eyes were jerked back to her. Her long blood red nails contrasting with his tan forearm.

Suddenly his body was flooded with warmth and all his doubts vanished like magic. He was overwhelmed with the urge to comfort her and more than comfort. When did the top two buttons of her dress come loose? He was staring at the enticing glimpse of firm tanned flesh. As if no longer in control of his body he saw his hand raise to stroke across the upper swells of her well rounded breasts, two fingers dipping into the shadowy valley between and causing her eyes to flutter closed and her breath to catch in a delighted gasp. Daniel's mouth watered to taste the tawny flesh glimpsed between the edges of her undone bodice, her full parted lips.

Daniel shook his head and the feeling popped like a soap bubble. He stepped back apologizing and stumbled away from the open grave. Trying not to look like he was running away, he hurried towards the parking lot. He allowed himself a single glance back as he reached his car and saw Rue standing where he had left her with Kate whispering in her ear. Rue's eyes blazed with fury and her fists were clenched in anger, the heat of that anger burned into him even from halfway across the parking lot and helped speed him on his way. Daniel hurried home and headed for the shower, he felt shaky as if coming down with or recovering from a bad flu. His stomach was roiling with hot bitter gall, he let the hot water run down his face. Pressing his forehead against the tile wall, the images and feelings that had come to life when Rue touched him came flooding back. The fierce waves of desire and lust, two more minutes and he would have torn the clothes from her body and taken her like an animal atop Hecate's open grave.

Daniel suddenly lurched from the shower and nearly didn't make it to the toilet before his stomach violently emptied itself. Crawling back into the shower, he curled on the shower floor and let the hot pounding spray rinse him clean. Finally feeling if not better at least less shaky, he pulled a robe on and went to the kitchen to heat up one of Jason's cans of stew and fed half of it to Kirby in a bowl on the floor.

Daniel's dreams that night were anything but restful. In his dream he awoke to the feel of a warm female body pressed against his back, rolling over he pressed his face into the curve of her neck and inhaled spicy incense like scent. Gently he ran his rough hands down her soft skin and heard small moans of pleasure. Tracing down her arm to her hand and entwining his fingers with hers, he felt long nails. The nails were smooth and filed like acrylic, scooting backwards off the bed he stood and flipped on the bedside lamp. There laying nude on his bed features flushed with desire was Rue, her golden hair tousled. Yelling denial, Daniel woke when he fell off his bed tangled up in his blankets and looking around quickly saw that he was alone and it was morning. Kirby crawled to the edge of the bed and looked down at him and whimpered. Daniel scratched Kirby's ears and assured him he was alright and got ready for work. The next few nights were pretty much the same; he went to sleep in his room alone or with Kirby nearby and awoke in his dream getting ready to make love to a woman who always turned out to be Rue. The funniest thing (funny weird not funny ha ha) was the look of anger on the dream Rue's face right before he woke himself up each time. Daniel started to wonder if he was losing it, the only time he was safe from Rue was when he was sitting at home awake. Rue and her ever-present companion Kate showed up at his work, they shopped at all the same food stores, gas stations, every time he turned around they were there.

Daniel started looking around whenever he left the house and couldn't make himself stop even though he knew he looked paranoid. So far, he been able to keep her from touching him, that all ended the day he went for more condiments in the pantry at work and the door shut behind him. He quickly spun to the door to check it and heard a noise behind him in the pantry; suddenly he was spun around and pressed against the door. Rue's lips were on his, his brain shut down as he had lust surge through him making him instantly hard. Rue reached down and ripped the front of his jeans open, his hard cock springing into her hand. Daniel heard a guttural groan rip from his throat as she closed her warm hand around him. Acting on instinct alone, he shoved her back against the wall and shoved her skirt above her hips. With a sharp tug, he ripped her panties off her and pressed his throbbing cock to her. Rue was making eager whimpering noises as if she was dying to have him buried deep inside her.

Suddenly the door was thrown open and the spell was once again broken as his co-worker George came in looking for Parmesan cheese and stopped in shock. Daniel backed away from Rue his stomach churning, with only a seconds warning he shoved past George and ran to the employee bathroom where he promptly lost everything he had eaten in the last three days. Daniel knelt next to the toilet dry heaving, his hair sweat plastered to his head and once again feeling like he had been hit with a very virulent flu bug. Worse as he knelt, there feeling sick and feverish was the look on Rue's face as George had interrupted them just in time, the look that could not have been described as anything but murderous.

Ten minutes later George knocked at the bathroom door to check on Daniel. Wiping his face with a towel, he dropped the towel in the garbage and opened to the door to George's apologetic face. "Damn Danny, I didn't know you and your girl were..." Danny grabbed George up in an extremely uncomfortable not to mention unmanly hug "She's not my girl and thank you so very much for interrupting us when you did George." George raised an eyebrow "um you're welcome?" George took a good look at Daniel's haggard appearance. "Danny no offense but, you look like shit." Daniel attempted a smile that came out more like a grimace "Well at least then I look exactly like I feel." Daniel tried to hug George again but George stepped just out of reach. "I don't know what's wrong with me George, every time I she touches me, I lose control of myself and want to tear her clothes off and have sex with her no matter where we are." George smiled as if he thought Daniel was joking "Yeah it's that way with me and my wife too." Catching a glimpse of Daniel's frightened face, George lost his smile. "George cocked his head "Does this happen every time she touches you, I mean just her or other women too?" Daniel shook his head, "No it only happens with her, and only when she touches me, she's not even my....and we have never..."

Knowing he was making no sense, Daniel shook his head and gave a helpless gesture. "George pursed his lips in thought "What about memory loss, loss of control, shaking?" Daniel started to answer then closed his mouth and thought back to the times Rue had touched him. "No, there is no memory loss but definitely loss of control but I start shaking and vomiting afterward." George nodded and started rubbing the back of his neck, a clear sign that he was about to say something he wished he did not have to. "Well there are two things that fit what you are telling me, and one is being bound by a witch..."

Daniel gave him a skeptical look. "Hey now, do you know what is to the east of us? My

folks used to live near that blood soaked godforsaken town." Daniel knew George's

family believed in Witches and black magic and moved away from Salem to get away

from the 'bad air'. "The other and more likely alternative is GHB or rohypnol." Once

again, George had startled him "How do you know about the effects of a date rape drug

George?" George made a placating gesture with his hands "It's not what you think, my

dad is the head of ER over at St. Claire's in Salem and he has seen all kinds of things

come through there especially at night or on certain holidays." The thought that he was

being drugged by some sex-crazed woman might have some guys feeling flattered that

the woman would go through so much trouble, but it left Daniel feeling very scared.

How do you fight something when you never know in what direction it would

come from?

CHAPTER TWO

Rue's sharp shriek of rage was enough to make Kate cover her ears. Rue paced the knickknack-cluttered room and screamed out her defiance and rage at the fact that Daniel had slipped through her fingers once again leaving her unsated. This room like all others in this creepy colonial mansion was filled with a mixture of heirlooms inherited from generations of dead witch ancestors and gifts from Rue's now deceased fae lover and mentor. A large black tourmaline glittered darkly in the place of pride on the mantle. The stone seemed almost to be enjoying Rue's rage.

Kate jerked in surprise as Rue grabbed up a blue veined Bast statuette and launched it at a gilded mirror hanging on the wall sending thousands of glass shards in every direction. "WHY?!?!" Rue pounded her fists against her thighs as she paced, "I have used the doll, and the oil, why are my bindings not working?!?" Kate knew it was a rhetorical question and kept silent. Reaching to the side, Kate slipped a polished black ivory globe from its hand shaped cradle and began rolling it from one hand to the other while she listened to Rue throw a temper tantrum and hid a smirk. Finally, she decided to interrupt "Maybe you are wasting your time on this guy, maybe it's time to find someone else." Rue froze in place and turned to stare at Kate her eyes blazing in anger. "Daniel Warwick will be mine!" Kate rolled her eyes "He is JUST one man Rue, you are beautiful and powerful enough to get anyone else MAN or WOMAN, so what is so special about some Bethesda Pizza Chef?" Rue tossed her long hair angrily over her shoulder and resumed pacing. A dreamy look settled over Rue's face "He makes me FEEL, his lips soft on mine." Rue ran a long nail lightly over her full bottom lip. "His hands touching me, making me ACHE to be filled." Kate watched unable to tear her gaze from Rue as she slid her graceful hands down her body and cupped her own breasts, the dipped her hands lower and pressed her hand firmly between her legs. Rue collapsed onto the floral patterned Fainting Couch monstrosity that had been in Rue's family for generations. Kate sat up and looked over where Rue reclined "That still does not explain why HIM, you can find any guy to 'fill you' if all you're after is the almighty PENIS". Rue smirked as she looked over at Kate "poor poor Katie darling, you just do not understand, he was HERS, and I will take EVERYTHING from HER." Kate tossed the globe back into its hand shaped holder. "What more can you take from her, she is DEAD for Goddess sake and by YOUR actions!" Rue laughed a girlish giggle and stood up her hands over her mouth to hide her delighted smile. "Maybe you are right; I am expending too much energy on this man and tiring myself out." Kate started to agree, glad Rue had come to her senses.

Rue spun in place her skirt flaring around her hips "I'll go refresh my strength and start again tomorrow." Kate dropped her head into her hands as Rue danced off to her room to get dressed for 'hunting'. It was amazing how quickly Rue's mood could change, then again she was planning on charming some poor unknown into going to a hotel room and having sex with her so she could vamp his essence and then probably kill him for the extra energy gained with the taking of someone's life. Kate had seen this game played too often to be surprised or horrified. Rue stepped out of the room and posed in the doorway She wore a snug green and gold bustier top with a long sleek skirt that slit to mid thigh on the left and gave an enticing glimpse of a silk clad thigh complete with black lace garter. Rue had strapped on a pair of high heels that laced up her calves with black ribbons. Kate felt her jaw drop, Rue's eye shadow matched her top and brought out the hints of green in her eyes, her hair hung in long springy gold curls and her ruby red lipstick all combined to make Kate feel the urge to drop to her knees in front of Rue and worship her. Kate knew that gesture would not be appreciated, not anymore anyway. Kate grabbed her coat and keys and prepared to play chauffeur for the night.

It took three hours and several bars and pool halls to find what Rue was looking for as once again they hunted Salem's underbelly. The 'mark' was named James Armand and he was 'not a nice guy'. James was a freelance enforcer that hired himself out to the local loan sharks when a debt was defaulted. James was a very attractive Haitian man with long tidy dreadlocks and a sexy accent that drove the ladies into his arms in droves. Tonight James was reclining with a young waitress wearing enough makeup for three women and was whispering something in her ear that made her laugh. Kate remained outside as Rue went into '8balls'. Rue looked about until she spotted James and slowly made her way past, she never looked at him, but the minute she was parallel to him she whispered his name on an exhale and his attention was drawn to her like a magnet. Rue walked around the pool hall looking at the cues and felt covered tables. If anyone thought it odd, a woman like her would be in a dingy pool hall it was nothing to what they thought as they saw James rapidly approaching her. The whispered conversation between them could not be overheard over the background noise of a blaring TV and several high stakes games going on. As if James had said something incredibly sweet, Rue laughed and touched her hand to his cheek. If James had been able to see what Rue was doing, he would have seen sharp red lines flare up and lash out like tentacles from Rue's hand and spear through his chest and wrap around his brain and finally around his cock. As if he was a puppet and Rue the master, James stood straighter and followed her to the door. The waitress started to go after him and then seeing how that would look gave the room a haughty look and flipped James off before heading back to the bar. Anyone who saw that exchange would say without a doubt that James approached Rue and not the other way around. Kate had called ahead and reserved three rooms under three different names at the Dew Drop Inn. James and Rue sat in the back seat where Rue could keep touching him and strengthening the bindings around him. Kate drove half distracted as she felt brief flares of power from the back seat and knew Rue was amping up James desire as she ran nails up and down his thighs and unbuttoned his shirt to press her palms on his bare chest. The vibes were becoming so strong in the car that Kate felt herself starting to respond and was grateful when they finally arrived and she could step out into the cool night air and clear her head. Kate went to the office and brought back the keys, and then she went to the trunk and pulled out black linens and a scarred wooden box that contained everything else they needed for the energy transfer. It took Kate a mere ten minutes to get the first room ready. When she came out to let Rue know, Rue was rubbing her body against James and making purring noises that were causing James to shake like an addict in need of a fix.

Kate stayed outside in the car as Rue took James into the room. Grabbing a magazine from under the seat, she settled in for a long wait. Inside the room Rue looked around to make sure that everything was ready, a faintly glowing chunk of black tourmaline sat on the small table. Rue smiled, most black tourmaline only absorbed negative energy but this stone had been re keyed to capture passionate energy derived from sex as well as fear and that brief flare of energy as a soul passed beyond the veil. The stone also allowed her to drink from it, passing what it absorbed back to Rue and strengthening her inherent power. Perhaps tonight if James was as skilled a lover as she had been lead to believe, passion would be enough and there would be no need to kill him.

James stood staring at her, his eyes glazed with desire and his body fairly vibrating with need. Rue ordered him to remove his shoes and socks and place them by the door; she did this as a test of her bindings. The bindings were always weak at first and especially if you were not familiar with the 'subject'. Next Rue walked around him and trailed her hands across his shoulders. She stopped in front of him and smiled up at him "Do you like my top James?" James eyes followed her finger as it traces the top edge of the bustier. Swallowing hard he nodded and his body jerked as she crooked her finger and his already firm cock became even harder. "Do you want to take it off me James?" She had barely finished the sentence when he reached out with his strong black hands and tore the bodice down the center and exposed her rose tipped breasts to his hungry gaze. A brief frown crossed her brow as she checked her bindings again but then she laughed and decided to go with it. Reaching up, James cupped her breasts and rolled her nipples in his smooth palms. Rue hissed in pleasure and arched her back as he took first the left and then the right into his mouth, his teeth plucking at the sensitive tips. Rue clenched her fists in his dreadlocks then gave a gasp of surprise as he suddenly shoved her back onto the bed and stood over her. With a twist of her wrist, she tightened her bindings and decided it was time to tell James the rules. "You will please me and you will finish deep inside me so I can steal your essence James, if you do well tonight I swear you will live to leave this place though you will have no memory of me." She sat up and trailed a hand down James bare chest. "If I am not pleased..." Her eyes went cold and dangerous "then you will not leave this room alive."

James eyes showed a shadow of fear but he could no more disobey her then he could refuse to respond with her bonds tightening around him. James knelt at the end of the bed and trailed his hand up one silk clad leg. He untied the ribbons and removed her shoes, Rue had a moment of warning as a flare of violence flashed and James had grabbed the slit of her skirt and torn it wide open. He pulled the remnants of the garment from beneath her and dropped it to the floor. Rue was clad only in a black thong, garter belt and silk stockings now.

With firm pressure, he placed a hand on her stomach and laid her back on the bed. Rue's breath hitched as his warm breath fanned across her parted thighs. She gasped as she felt his tongue slip under and lift the thong and then felt his teeth take hold and with a sharp twist of his head, he tore the thong from her with his teeth. Rue chuckled and reminded herself she would have to teach Daniel that trick once he was hers. Rue's thoughts were on Daniel as James drove two thick fingers deep inside her, thrusting over and over, as his thumb made delicious circles against her clitoris. Rue cried out in ecstasy. James grunted as he let her come again and again. Then grabbing her shoulders he pulled her up to sit on the end of the bed. With quick motions he divested himself of his slacks and briefs and then threaded, his fingers deep into her hair and pulled her face towards his waiting cock. Rue hesitated then decided she would oblige and opened her mouth. James groaned as he thrust into her mouth again and again, her tongue making spirals around the throbbing head. He tensed as he felt himself getting close and a sudden hand on his stomach stopped him cold. Rue's cold eyes were back as she withdrew him from her mouth. "I said James that you would finish deep within me and you will obey." To Rue's eyes the bindings once again flared red and tightened around him, if the bonds had been physical, they would have been cutting deep into his flesh now. Yet somehow he managed to bend them ever so slightly even as he obeyed her, this was something to think on later. Again, the brief flare warning of violence and Rue was flipped facedown onto the bed, she felt James arm come around her middle and lift her to her hands and knees and with no more warning than that, he thrust deep inside her. His cock while impressive was less than what she had expected from a black man. Still, she enjoyed his hard thrusts and just as she was about to finish....he was done and collapsed on top of her on the bed. Rue lay beneath him fuming and working herself into a rage until with red filled vision she shoved him off her onto his back.

Standing over him shaking with anger, she sneered at him "I said if you pleased me, I would allow you to live James!" Rue stomped to the door and opened it, holding her hand out, she waited while Kate handed her a leather bound journal and a black dagger with a triangular blade. Opening the journal to the appropriate page, Rue began reading and watched as the 'cords' wrapped mummy like around him until only his frightened eyes showed. Rue closed the book and handed it without looking to Kate who stepped up to take and then retreated again into a self-drawn protective circle. With one last angry toss of her head, Rue plunged the dagger seven times into James chest. Her hair started whipping around her as if she were caught in the middle of a vortex. Kate opened a space in her circle and Rue stepped into it as the Black Tourmaline stone flared to life. Kate replaced the breach and both watched as red energies hovered over James cooling body and his aura faded to nothing. The energy was then sucked into the vortex and funneled into the Black Tourmaline. Only after sufficient time had passed did Rue and Kate step out of the circle and start packing things up.

Kate went about picking up the torn clothing and muttering under her breath at the waste. Only after every identifiable trace of a woman had been removed from the room did they move everything including the car to the other end of the hotel where their other two rooms were located.

Rue went into her room and cradled the tourmaline between her bare breasts and spoke the power word that sent the stolen power rushing into her. She felt exhilarated and more than a little euphoric as she climbed beneath the satin sheets Kate had remade her bed with. Sleep was quick in finding her as she snuggled down and let out a contented sigh.

Next-door Kate was far from ready for bed, her mind seemed intent on rehashing painful memories. Kate remembered how it had been before, when she and Rue had been lovers and Rue had looked at her with more than just pity and irritation. That was before Bryan....before Angelique. Angelique was the one that had taught Rue all about 'vamping' and the energy gained from death and fear, although Angelique would never dream of 'vamping' any but the most passionate energies. Angelique had been tall and statuesque with long auburn hair and deepest green eyes and she seemed to have several lifetimes' worth of knowledge. Angelique a self proclaimed 'Mistress of the Dark Energies' had taken Rue under her wing and into her bed and taught Rue how to harness her 'inherent powers' to gain what she wanted out of life. It sure had worked for Angelique, who had money to burn and adoring followers wherever she went. Kate had been set aside in favor of the great lady of wisdom and found herself constantly trailing behind waiting for a scrap of attention like a forgotten dog.

After many years of traveling with Angelique, Rue and Kate had managed to purchase a large colonial style two story on the outskirts of Salem. The main attraction of the house for Rue had been the fact that it had once belonged to Bridget Bishop who happened to be one of Rue's descendants and had been hanged as a witch during the witch trials of 1642. Rue then spent the next five years filling it with a motley assortment of Victorian and colonial furniture and every Egyptian and esoteric knickknack she could find.

They never spoke about Angelique or "that day" and in fact, it was a forbidden subject. Rue had fallen hard for her mentor but over time, Angelique's ardor for her protege had cooled and Angelique's eyes had started to wander. They had been staying at Angelique's quaint Tudor style cottage near the Pere Lachaise Cemetery where Angelique frequently went to collect old bones and special herbs that grew most potent in the presence of corpses (or so she claimed). Rue had been out collecting herbs and Kate had been outside reading in the garden (she and Angelique had never gotten along), Rue had come home with a hand picked bouquet for Angelique and had been surprised by what she had found in the bedroom they shared. Angelique had brought home a drifter and was sprawled on her back with the drifter rutting atop her when the door to the bedroom had been thrown open and Rue had frozen in shock at the sight before her. Kate never learned how it was that Rue had over powered Angelique and the drifter both; she had merely helped clean up the aftermath. Rue had taken the granite replica of Cleopatra's Needle that had stood on the bedside table and beaten both of them until neither was recognizable as human.

When Kate ran in she saw Rue on her knees in the gore weeping, strangely enough Kate's first impression had not been horror but relief. With Angelique gone, Rue would obviously return Kate's affections again and they could be happy together. Kate helped clean up and dispose of "the mess" and neither spoke of the incident although Kate suspected the incident had unhinged Rue. Once the room was scrubbed clean, Kate lead Rue to the bathroom and cleaned her like a child and then led her to the bed and

spent three days comforting her. Rue allowed Kate to comfort her and even responded in

kind and it was almost like old times, but when the three days were up Rue once again

pushed Kate away and turned to researching Angelique's power collecting spells and

trying them out on those who would not be missed.

Eventually they returned to their home in Salem and Rue had met Bryan.

Bryan was the head contractor/landscaper for Colonial Renovations. Rue had decided

the backyard needed a half-acre hedge maze; a three tiered fountain and paved "walking

paths" winding through the garden. Bryan and his crew had gotten started on Monday and

by Wednesday; Rue had decided the muscular red haired contractor was hers for the

taking. The fact that Bryan was engaged to be married and flattered by the attention but

not interested did not deter Rue from her pursuit of him. Bryan was to be Rue's first real

attempt with the red silk doll that Angelique had sworn by as the best way to bind a man

or woman to you. Unfortunately, Angelique's life had tragically ended before giving Rue

more than the basic concept on how to use the doll and the accompanying "Sex oil" that

combined was alleged to give you absolute control over your "victim". The doll needed

to have hair, or other material components from the one you were attempting to ensnare

and the oil was fast acting and needed to be applied to bare flesh as often as possible to

get the drug into the "victim's" blood. Angelique HAD warned Rue not to be heavy

handed when using this spell but had not elaborated on that warning. Rue started taking

bottles of water out to the crew while they worked and found reasons each time to touch

Bryan's arm or hand. By Saturday, there should have been some sign of the spell taking

hold but Bryan continued to shrug off any and all effects. Bryan's company operated out of Boston and due to the length of time needed for such a large project, had put all ten of the crew up at the local Cozy Rest Inn.

Rue took advantage of that fact on Sunday night after a fruitless day of throwing herself at Bryan and showed up with the black tourmaline that Angelique had re keyed to act as an energy conduit at the door to Bryan's hotel room. Bryan looked surprised and irritated to see her when he opened the door and saw who it was. Seeing his reaction Rue broke into crocodile tears and claimed she needed to speak to him in regards to one of his crew. Bryan hung up the phone with his fiancee and let her in the room. Rue hit him between the eyes with a prepared spell that left him paralyzed. Reaching into her pocket, Rue removed the silk doll and placed it beside the tourmaline on the table. She carefully pricked Bryan's thumb and added a few drops of blood to the spell inscribed doll before releasing his paralysis. Rue had no warning about what would happen if she added blood to the doll while leaving it keyed to maximum lust. She felt a bright flare of violent energy and then Bryan and grabbed her and thrown her to the floor and violently took her like an enraged animal. Rue managed to kick free of him and locked herself in the bathroom while Bryan roared and tried to break the door down. Shaking yet trying to regain her composure, Rue re-keyed the doll. Rue made sure that the weaves to control each part of the body were exceptionally strong, completely forgetting about Angelique's warning in her haste to adjust the spell before Bryan broke through the bathroom door. She released the spell and the silence was deafening as Bryan stopped beating on the door.

Cautiously Rue opened the battered door; Bryan was standing like a zombie before the door with a blank expression on his face. When Rue had added strength to the woven strands that controlled his mind, she had been overzealous and had broken his mind. Bryan would obey any command given but only what she commanded and only when commanded to do it. Rue quickly lost interest with Bryan, the spark she had been attracted to in him was now gone. After a week of "playing with him", she cut loose the bonds and set him free, but even with his freedom he never fully recovered.

Bryan ended his engagement with Susan and spent every waking moment following Rue and telling everyone how wonderful she was whether they asked or not. Finally, Rue confronted him and let him know how pathetic and disgusting she found him and never wanted to see him again. Bryan went home and slit his wrists, bleeding out in his bathtub and being found two days later by his sister when she came by to check on him. Rue used the door more and more often after that and with much better results for she decided to never again use blood on the doll, the results were too unpredictable. The more people Rue "ensnared", the more Kate feared Rue would never "Come back" to her and the deeper into depression Kate fell. Kate felt the pressure building to do something drastic to reclaim Rue's affection.

After Daniel's discussion with George, he started carrying a Tazer with him and telling himself that should Rue come close to him he would make sure she did not make contact. Like magic she disappeared, the dreams stopped and he no longer spotted her and Kate lurking wherever he went. Far from making him feel better, this made him more paranoid as if she were just waiting for the right time to pounce. When several months had gone by without a sighting, he started to relax but kept the Tazer close just in case. Life almost seemed to go back to normal, or as normal as it could anyways. Daniel was even able to produce a genuine smile and a hearty congratulation when Jason announced he was heading over to Courtney's to propose to her. With a spring in his step, Jason took off

yelling a promise to call Daniel to confirm Courtney's answer even though neither had

any doubt what that answer would be. When Daniel did not hear from Jason that night, he

shrugged it off and assumed Jason had forgotten in the excitement of the moment. When

Courtney called the next morning as Daniel was headed to work and asked him if he

knew why Jason had never showed up last night, Daniel felt his stomach tighten with

cold dread. All the way to work, Daniel tried to convince himself that this had

NOTHING to do with Rue.

When two more days went by without either of them hearing from Jason,

Courtney came over and they called the police together. The same two officers were

dispatched to handle the call and neither Officer Bennett nor Officer Larken looked

thrilled to be coming back so soon. No accidents had been reported between their house

and Courtney's and no Jason did not have a habit of going off and not telling anyone. The

police seemed to focus all their attention on Daniel and directed all the questions at him

as if Courtney were not even in the room. By the tone of their questions, Daniel got the

impression that they were sure he was to blame for Jason's disappearance. When

Courtney and Daniel had answered all the questions the police could come up with,

Daniel walked them to the door. Officer Bennett seemed eager to get going but his

heretofore silent partner stopped just outside the door to pose one last question to Daniel.

"Would you say there is any known history of mental illness or irrational aggression in

your family?" Daniel looked surprised at the question but answered in the negative to

which Officer Larken grunted and went to have an unheard conversation with his partner

before they got in the car and left.

Courtney stayed for dinner but the conversation was stilted and she left immediately after they had finished. Daniel wondered later if he should have told the cops about Rue, then again based on Larken's questions about a history of mental illness.... Daniel knew Jason would never (despite the cop's assurances that it happened all the time) up and take off without telling anyone. The cops were sure that Jason had just "gotten cold feet" and gone off to have some alone time. Another week had passed with no sign of Jason and even Courtney had stopped calling to see if he had heard from Jason. Daniel was sitting at the table making a shopping list when he noticed Kirby staring at the front door. A loud rumbling growl erupted from Kirby followed by ferocious barking. Daniel got up and grabbed his Taser from his coat pocket and went to the door. He put his ear to the door and hearing nothing opened it cautiously. The front porch was empty and behind him Kirby had stopped barking and growling and was now pressing against his legs. Looking down he noticed something white sitting on the mat. Crouching down he lifted what turned out to be a folded sheet of lined paper with something heavy wrapped inside it. As he unfolded the paper, something metal hit the porch. Daniel stood staring down at Jason's "serenity" collector's edition key chain. There were no keys attached to the ring, just the key chain. Tearing his eyes away, he looked at the note The note was written in an untidy scrawl on a torn sheet of lined paper and stated: **She is getting stronger, leave before she hurts you too.**

There was no signature but there was no doubt in Daniel's mind that the note referred to Rue. Officers Bennett and Larken were just as thrilled to be dispatched to the house this time as they had the previous times. This time before they left, Larken's question to Daniel was asking whether there was a history of people coming to bad ends around Daniel and again he answered in the negative, which earned him a grunt before Larken joined his partner at the car and they drove off. The cops had taken the keychain and the note and Daniel's fingerprints since he had handled both. Taking a deep breath, Daniel called Courtney to tell her what had happened and listened with his heart in his throat as she wept on the phone. When she had calmed a bit, he suggested she go visit some relatives for a while and get out of town just until everything blows over. Courtney agreed and promised to let him know how to get a hold of her "just in case".

Rue felt like she was on cloud nine, she was not only able to siphon off all of Jason's passion energy into her conduit stone, and she was also able to get a decent amount of his death energy as well. On top of the energy she was able to replenish, she was also able to get a lot of useful information from Jason while she had him ensnared. She had even surprised herself at how good she had gotten at siphoning off only small amounts of energy at a time, which enabled her to milk Jason's demise over the span of nearly a week. The energy she had gained from Jason, she would use to strengthen the spells she had woven around Daniel. Rue found herself giggling as she pictured the look on Daniel's face as he finally realized just how helpless he was in the face of her power.

Courtney called Daniel a couple days later to let him know she was staying with her aunt in Providence Rhode Island and would probably be there for the next few months or until she was sure that coming back was safe. Daniel went to work that day extremely tense, he even started asking George to go and fetch supplies from the pantry for him. For the next few weeks, Daniel kept within the sight of George and the other employees but only George knew the reason for it. George had no problem with playing bodyguard and was more than happy to check out the pantry and bathroom before Daniel went in, he also walked Daniel out to his car after work every night. Daniel laughed at one point and mentioned that he felt like the president with his secret service. That very night George went out and bought a pair of government looking shades and a black blazer that he would toss over his clothes and practice looking intimidating. Every time Daniel came out and saw George with his shoulders back and his hands clasped in front of him looking like some paramilitary nut, he could not help but laugh.

It had been just another day at work Angelo's had been a busy but pleasant mix of raucous teens and couples spending "date night" at the only decent Italian place in Bethesda. George once again had made a big production of guarding Daniel as he walked him to his car. Daniel was laughing so hard it actually started to feel like old times again, like the past few months had never happened. The good feeling disappeared as he pulled up to the house and saw Kirby in the front yard, the front door wide open. Daniel approached the house cautiously and gave the dark front porch a wide berth as he made his way towards Kirby. Kneeling down he reached for Kirby and jerked his arm back in surprise as Kirby made a whining mad dash around the side of the house. Daniel stood up and headed in the direction Kirby had gone, as he rounded the side of the house he saw something sprawled in the grass. Kirby was dancing around and whining near whatever was there. Daniel could barely make the object out in the dim light from the distant street lamp.

When he got closer, he could see that the object was a body laying face down in the grass. Slowly he pulled the Tazer from his pocket and grasped the shoulder to quickly toss the person onto their back. Daniel fell back in shock and horror as he found himself staring into the wide-open eyes of ....Jason! Kirby stretched out in the grass next to Jason and whined. Daniel jumped up and slipped and slid as he ran towards the open front door forgetting his previous hesitation at running into a dark house. Grabbing the phone from the wall, he nearly tore it loose in his haste to call 911. Daniel was nearly incoherent as he babbled at the operator, his voice shrill and cracking. The dispatch operator got the gist of what he was saying and reassured him there were officers en route.

Once again, officers Bennett and Larken were dispatched to question Daniel; although this time, they seemed to be less inclined to look skeptical at his answers. After the coroner had picked up the body and the forensics people had roped off the yard, the officers asked him to accompany them back to the station where they could ask him some routine questions. Daniel thought nothing of it and followed them to the station where they immediately hustled him into an interrogation room and spent the next three hours having him go over every second of his life starting with the day he first went to Pariah's. Daniel decided to tell the cops about Rue and Kate following him around, George's theory about the drugs and the way he felt sick and drugged out whenever she touched his skin. For obvious reasons he refrained from mentioning the dreams or the almost sex in the pantry at work. The cops stared at him for a moment then made noncommittal noises and stated they would "look into it". Daniel was released but told "not to leave town" by Officer Bennett who sounded like he was quoting an old black and white movie. Daniel's brain was going 90 miles a minute as he drove back to the house. The side of the house was still taped off and there were still cops coming the yard and neighborhood and questioning neighbors.

Daniel had locked Kirby up before he left to go to the station; he let Kirby out and proceeded to make dinner for both of them. Spaghetti with real meatballs and homemade sauce for him and a can of 'Mighty Mutt' Beef stew for Kirby. By the time, dinner had been finished and dishes cleaned up, the cops had left. The yellow tape still blocked off most of the yard and looked like tacky Halloween decorations. Kirby wandered out of the kitchen and Daniel went and sat on the couch once again feeling like his world was falling apart. Kirby suddenly shoved his shaggy head into Daniels lap, Daniel absently scratched Kirby's ears and suddenly realized Kirby had deposited something wet in his lap. Pushing Kirby back, he expected to see one of his nasty old tennis balls. Instead of a ratty old ball, Daniel saw a drool saturated scrap of what appeared to be expensive floral patterned satin. Lifting the torn fabric up to the light he saw a brown stain along the hem, the scrap looked to have been torn from a larger garment.

Daniel had grown tired of calling the cops and waiting for them to show up and ask the same questions in different ways like they were trying to trip him up. Loading Kirby up in the truck, he decides to take the fabric and drop it off at the police station. Daniel left Kirby in the truck when he arrived and took the fabric, which he had stuck inside a Ziploc baggie, into the police station. Daniel stood talking to the desk sergeant when suddenly the door to an interrogation room popped open and Officer Bennet came out...followed by Rue bishop. Rue laughed at something the officer had said and placed her hand atop his like an old friend, maybe it was Daniel's imagination but it seemed that the officer's smile widened as he gestured for her to precede him to the door. As Rue passed by Daniel, she dropped her eyes to the floor and looked up at him from under her lashes, a devilish smile on her face. Daniel watched them go out the door. When Officer

Bennett came back inside he only noticed Daniel because Daniel stepped into his path.

Officer Bennett's dreamy smile turned instantly to an irritated frown "Something else I

can help you with Mr. Warwick?" Daniel holds up the Ziploc baggie in front of the

officer's face "Kirby apparently attacked someone at my house, possibly whoever was

dropping off Jason's body in my yard. I believe this came from that person."

Officer Bennet looked it over again and shrugged, "We'll see what the lab

boys can make of this." Stepping around Daniel, the officer headed towards the back

hallway, leaving Daniel to walk himself out. As soon as Daniel walked out, he saw Kirby

facing the other side of the truck and barking and growling fiercely. Slowly Daniel

moved around to the other side and saw Rue standing there smiling at him. Without

planning what he was doing, he whipped his Taser out and hit her square between the

eyes and dropped her like a stone. Rue lay on the ground twitching and gasping. A pool

of urine spread around Rue as she lost bladder control. Suddenly realizing what he had

done and how this would look, Daniel jumped in the truck and peeled out. Daniel glanced

once in his rear view mirror as he sped off and saw Kate charge out of a newer model

sedan that he had not noticed and get rue to her feet.

Rue and Kate went back to the house and Rue got cleaned up and changed and

starting going over in her mind everything, she had tried with Daniel and the effects of it,

kind of like a mental checklist. Much as she hated to admit it, it was time for Rue and

Kate to return to Angelique's cottage library in Italy. Angelique had been using binding

spells for far longer than Rue ever had and unlike Rue, Angelique had used those spells

to gain power, wealth, and an enviable esoteric library. Although Angelique had several houses and cottages around the world, the most extensive of her libraries however were located in France, Italy and Romania. There was no way that Rue was returning to France unless there was nowhere else she could get the info she was seeking. She would try Italy first and Romania if needed but she got the heebie-jeebies last time she was in Romania. The people of Romania were primitive and scary, and neither her nor Kate spoke Romanian so she would need a translator to follow them around which might cause unnecessary questions. Unless she thought of a reason to be researching spells from the locals, she would think on that. Maybe she could say that she is a writer, or even better that she is a college professor of esoteric studies. Rue liked the idea of being thought of as a professor. Rue looked over at Kate who was sitting reading with a sullen expression on her face. I am going to have to make a decision real soon on whether keeping Kate around is going to be useful or a drag, her moods and jealousy are really starting to get to me. Deciding she would start compiling the pros and cons of keeping Kate around later, she motioned Kate over and stuck her leg out. Taking that as a cue to check the bandage, Kate started removing the blood spotted bandage and took a look at Rue's calf. Daniel's dog has surprised them and Rue had gotten bit by the stupid animal. Jason had stated the Dog 'Kirby' was peaceful and lazy, obviously that only applied if the dog was familiar and friendly with you.

Daniel started wondering if it was past time to relocate, he could just pull up stakes and find a new place to start over. He really did not feel safe here anymore and now that he had found Jason's body in the yard, it was obvious that Rue knew where he lived. That settled it, tomorrow he was going to let Angelo know he was going to be leaving, he would make something up as to why. Feeling better after having made his decision, he called it an early night. As he climbed into bed he sighed, his mind played the what if game...what if he had never met Hecate, what if he had never gone to the club, what if he never let Jason talk him into sharing in his interests.

Rue was pouring over the books that she and Kate had absconded with from Angelique's library in her chateau in Paris the night they fled. These were nowhere near all the books that had been in the library but then again they would not have been able to make off with the whole library. Rue had become obsessed with discovering the reason behind Daniel's resistance to her spells. Rue suddenly stopped on a likely paragraph, once again, it took twice as long to read the passage because of the fact that the book itself was hundreds of years old and the author judging by the spelling and grammar was barely literate. "theree kinds of kreechurs ar nown to bee stronger in shaking off majik: wiches, Majik borned kreechurs (dragyns and such), Fae or Fae blud." Rue had always believed that things like dragons and unicorns and Fae were myths and children's stories. The author obviously believed these things to be real or else why write about them, and if a master of the magical arts believed in something then there had to be a basis for those beliefs. Rue looked up and stared at the wall as she thought about what she had read and let it sink in. Clearly, Daniel was not a witch; she did not believe he was anything that could be considered Magic born, which only left Fae or Fae blood. Rue ordered Kate to do a search on Daniel Warwick and find out where he was born and his family etc. Kate gave her a scathing look but complied.

An hour later Kate had found that Daniel had been born in Willow Grove Pennsylvania, his birth certificate had listed Arlene Warwick as his mother and father was listed as Unknown. Another hour of researching old newspaper archives revealed that Willow Grove was a hotbed of unexplained phenomena and there was a small nearly missed article about a woman during a geological surveying trip she was doing. She claims to not have seen her attacker and had hit her head during the attack. The woman who had been attacked near a famous pagan ceremonial site was named Arlene Warwick. To Rue's mind this banished any doubts whatsoever about whether or not Daniel had Fae blood, it also explained why her spells which had worked on everyone else were weakened when cast at Daniel. Knowing that Daniel was not completely human only enhanced her attraction for him, it did however mean more research to see how to work around his blood's aversion to binding spells. Yet another hour dragged by as Rue struggled through translating the ancient tome, what she found was sketchy "The Fae are as eels, so shood yor spells bee, cast not on thar flesh, but on the ayr. Mayk a hedj rownd the Fae." Rue looked up at the wall and once again processed what she had read. "So the reason my spells are not affecting him the way they should is because his blood is fighting my magic." Upon further research she found that Fae could however be controlled by use of enchanted objects (most commonly rings and jewelry).

Rue giggled and clapped her hands like a little girl. Deciding not to wait, she took out a silver cuff bracelet and started layering it with obedience spells and other "special" spells she had perfected over the years. When the spells for the bracelet were done, she placed it in a small black velvet valise and pulled out eight smooth river stones the size of walnuts. On the stones, she layered containment and fencing spells, she planned on placing these around the house itself so that they would act like an invisible hedge that would keep Daniel from leaving the house unless she wanted him to. Giggling again as she hatched a plan, she jogged into her room and slipped into a black leather miniskirt that laced up the sides and a tight black leather vest that accentuated her full breasts better than a push up bra. Grabbing the tourmaline, she put it in the velvet bag with the bracelet and the river stones and stepped out of the bedroom. Kate looked up and arched an eyebrow at her outfit. "We are going vamping again?" Rue giggled and beamed at her, "We are going to finish this." Turning on her heel, she headed out the door. With a sigh of frustration, Kate realized if she wanted more answers, she was going to have to follow.

On the way to Daniel's, Rue explained what she had found out and what she had planned to Kate. The minute that they came to a stop behind Daniel's truck, Rue handed the eight stones to Kate to set up around the house. Then while Kate left to place the stones, rue got a hard black case from the floor of the car, she opened the case to reveal a large black tranquilizer gun such as is used at zoos. The tranquilizer gun had only three darts but they were preloaded with a high enough dosage to drop a charging elephant. Kate came from around the side of the house which still had the tattered remnants of the yellow police tape and gave Rue a thumbs up. Rue stared hard at the house and let her eyes unfocus for a second and the crisscrossing gray lines sprung into view looking like nothing more than a chain link fence. Blinking the sight away, she approached the front door and stood Kate in plain view of the door while stepping to the side and whispering a spell of opening. Rue smiled as the lock clicked and remaining out of sight, she threw the door open and a second later a blur of fur darted past her with a savage growl. She raised the gun and fired two darts into the dog's side dropping him less than a foot from Kate who stood cowering. Heading into the house, she gestured for Kate to dispose of the dog and shut the door quietly behind her. Rue wanted to dance at how close she was to victory. With a sudden inspiration, she stopped at the hall mirror and concentrated on building a picture of Kendra in her mind, releasing the will and the words necessary to complete the spell, she opened her eyes. In the mirror stood Kendra and until she dispelled the illusion she would look and sound just like the very woman she loathed.

Rue stepped into the dark bedroom; she could hear Daniel's breathing from the bed. She whispered his name and suddenly the lamp was on and Daniel was instantly awake and sitting up in bed. Daniel sat in bed wearing only a pair of white drawstring pants and stared at Hecate who was standing just inside the door to his room and biting her lip as she gazed at his bare chest. "I thought you were dead, am I dreaming?" Hecate laughed "I am dead, but sometimes if the dead want something very very badly......." Daniel slid out of bed and approached her cautiously hope and fear warring in his expression. Hope that she were really here and fear that he would wake up alone again. He reached out and his hand met warm flesh as he touched her arm. "God you're really here, what is it you want?" Hecate looked up at him with deep soulful eyes and in a voice cracking with emotion ,"I really need you to make love to me Daniel, give me one more night in your arms...please?" Hecate's voice seemed to break at the word please and the remains of Daniel's doubts fled. Grabbing her shoulders, he pulled her towards him and captured her lips in a passionate kiss filled with longing and desire. His hands slipped down to unbutton her vest, she was wearing nothing beneath it and they both groaned as her full breasts tumbled into his waiting hands. He rolled her nipples between his rough fingers as his tongue plundered the depths of her mouth. He heard her whimpering as she pressed more firmly against him.

The sound rang a bell in the back of his head but he was too distracted to take note. Hecate shrugged the vest down her arms and ran hands through his hair. Pulling back, he trailed his mouth down her body, he stopped at each erect nipple to take it briefly between his lips and tease it harder with his tongue and teeth. Hecate was panting and moaning now as she gripped his hair. Kneeling in front of her, he undid the laces on the left side of her skirt and let it fall. Next, he lifted her knees one at a time and slipped her boots off and tossed them behind him. She was left standing there in a filmy pair of black panties. Taking her hand, he led it to the straining erection pulling the front of his pants tight. "I have missed you very much." Hecate's eyes went wide at the size of him and she rubbed her palm up and down his cock making him groan. It was her turn to kneel in front of him and slowly peel his pants down past his throbbing cock, which jerked towards her face as she uncovered it. Hecate chuckled and parted her lips taking him deep into her mouth, Daniel hissed with pleasure and gripped her braids in his fists whispering "God yes!" In and out, she slid his cock while bringing a hand up to gently cup his sack. Daniel's breathing was labored and he groaned at how skilled her mouth was. Feeling like he was going to explode, he reached down and gently tugged her up onto her feet. Again, he captured her lips in a passionate kiss and walked her backwards to the bed. Laying her on the edge of the bed, he removed the filmy panties and bracing her knees on his chest slowly pushed his cock deep inside her. Hecate cried out with a loud "Yes!" and began pumping her hips against him.

Taking the cue that she did not want slow and gentle tonight he began thrusting hard and fast into her as she gasped and moaned. "Yes Daniel Fuck me harder!" Another bell went off in the back of his head and the distraction lasted a little longer

Hecate hates the word 'FUCK' being used in reference to sex. The distraction was not enough to hold his attention before getting shoved away by the heat of the moment. Daniel continued to thrust inside her, his fingers biting into her hips until with loud cries the both exploded together in a combined orgasm. Hecate laughed breathily as he slid up onto the bed and pulled her head onto his sweaty chest. "I knew you would be a fantastic lover." The bell in the back of his head was much louder this time and his eyes popped open. Daniel felt Hecate slide something onto his wrist; he lifted his wrist to see a silver cuff bracelet glittering on his wrist.

Just as Daniel was about to ask her about her comment, the bedroom door opened Kate walked in with a bored look on her face. Daniel rolled off the bed and grabbed the Taser on the bedside table, when he turned to look at Hecate, her features blurred like a camera going out of focus and then it was Rue laying naked on his bed and laughing at him. Daniel lunged for her and was brought up short; she pointed a finger at him and in a cold commanding voice told him how things were going to be from now on. "You will fuck me anytime I want it no matter how often and you will NEVER harm Kate or I and you will be my obedient fucktoy until I choose to release you." Daniel dropped the now useless Taser onto the floor and glared at her. "You cannot FORCE me to have sex with you Rue..." His voice faltered as he felt a buzzing in his cock and looked down to see that it was once again rock hard. Rue giggled again, "I think you will find I can do anything I want with you, and I do believe I want you to FUCK me again immediately!" Like an outsider watching someone else control his body, he watched himself climb back on the bed and start screwing Rue. Kate gave a disgusted groan and exited the bedroom with a slam of the door. Kate silently wept into her hands as she sat on the couch and listened to

Rue giving Daniel orders on how to please her. Kate's emotions warred between self-pity and anger. Now rue would have her "fucktoy" and once again, Kate would just be kept around to clean up the messes. Life was not fair and Kate was beginning to wonder why she bothered to stick around on the thin fragile hope that one day Rue would love her again.

The next week passed much the same way, whenever Rue was not ordering Daniel to cook elaborate gourmet meals(the ingredients of which Kate had to shop for) she was in the bedroom with him. Daniel began to lose weight, he barely ate, barely slept and only showered when commanded to do so. Rue had added another layer to the Bracelet's command weaves, Daniel could not tell anyone about the bracelet, or the spells binding him, nor the situation. Once rue Had added that compulsion, she allowed him to return to work, Kate of course had to drop him off and pick him up. Kate could tell that Rue was getting restless and losing interest as Daniel continued to sit and stare morosely at blank walls and take interest in nothing at all. Rue suddenly announced that she and Kate would be returning home but dropping by daily to "play" and ,make sure that he had enough food and supplies and of course Kate would continue to drive him to and from work. Shortly after she had announced they would be leaving, they were packing what little they had brought with them and left.

Daniel felt as if a stone had been lifted from his chest. He actually felt safe enough to sleep. When he woke up, he reached for Kirby and remembered....Rue had taunted him with what she had done to Kirby. Kirby had been tranq'd but quite alive when Rue had finished with Daniel and gone out and slit Kirby's throat. Kirby's life's blood had drained out into the front lawn and not a soul had seen it.

Daniel's stomach clenched as he tried to stifle the agony that welled up in him at the thought of poor Kirby bleeding out, hurting and scared in the front yard. Remembering that Rue and Kate had gone home, he let the sobs out and cried until he felt hollow. Rue and Kate showed up together about every three days, only Kate showed up every day and that was just to take him to work and when his shift was over she would be waiting impatiently in his truck in the parking lot. Months passed with nightmarish regularity, cooking, screwing, working, screwing, cooking, and sleeping only after they had left. He found out the hard way that he could not harm himself either, one night when Rue had worn a filmy black negligee and demanded he tear it from her body and "fuck her" but had not invoked the compulsion that would force him to obey her words. He had grabbed a serrated knife from the dish drainer and tried to plunge it into his own chest instead. He found himself on the floor wracked with pain, all his muscles spasming like he was being electrocuted. On top of it now Rue was pissed and throwing his breakables against walls in a rage and cussing at him for making her use the compulsion instead of him complying out of desire for her. When she had finally exhausted her rage and the floor lay littered with glass, she climbed onto the bed and gave him the same command as before but invoked the compulsion this time smiling as he tried to fight it and ended up tearing her clothes off and screwing her anyways.

Kate knew she was not being fair to Daniel when she turned her hate filled gaze on Daniel, but hating Rue would have been counter productive to getting her back. Besides, he was a man and Rue was only doing what thousands of men throughout history had done. Even that rationalization fell flat as she realized she truly was starting to feel sorry for Daniel. Daniel actually started to feel excited as Rue described the trip to Italy that she was planning for Kate and herself and best of all she was leaving him here. She would be gone for a month but left an account at the local grocer to deliver the same staples every three days and he had only to call in any additions the night before for it to be included in the order. Daniel would need to call his work and make an excuse that would clear him from work for an indeterminate time. Since Angelo thought of Daniel as a son, this would not be an issue.

Daniel spent the entire day after they left testing his boundaries even though it meant a lot of pain and blacking out. He could not find a single gap in the "fence". For four days, he got up and tested his boundaries and kept checking to see if the fence was weakening since Rue and Kate had left, but it did not appear that distance was a factor in the strength of the magic. That night when Daniel went to bed, he felt genuinely lonely without hearing Kirby snoring on the other side of the bed. Daniel woke to a crack of thunder so loud it made him jump, he got up and looked out the window. The rain lashed at the glass and the wind made the trees bend almost parallel to the ground, every so often, the sky lit up like daylight with the brightness of the lightning or he could see streaks of lightning like white skeletal fingers caressing the dark night sky. Daniel shivered and closed the drapes and climbed back under his blankets thankful he was not out in that and glanced at the ceiling as he heard the roof creak.

CHAPTER THREE

Lauren Mayhew needed a vacation more than she needed air right now. When Trevor had broken off the engagement she had been devastated, when she found out that it was because he was screwing her sister Shannon on the side, she was pissed! Lauren was a professional nanny through a high priced service called Mary Poppins Domestics. She was between families right now, which made it a perfect time to get away from home and go on an extended vacation that she had promised herself years ago before she had met Trevor.

Lauren had a yearning to see some of those quaint new England towns that still had horses and buggies going up the street and non-GMO vegetables that did not cost an arm and a leg an ounce. Lauren was happy to escape Atlanta Georgia and head north along the coast. Buzzing along the freeway in her cute little powder blue Sunbeam Tiger Convertible, three suitcases in the back and the wind fanning her long red hair out behind her, she felt empowered! She stopped at a motel 6 just after dark and ordered a pizza.

Sitting on the end of the bed eating pizza and painting her nails, she decided to check her voice mails. She had three messages. The first was from Trevor "Babe we need to talk, look I am sorry about what happened but there was no reason for you to take off like this, maybe we can make this work, I just...really need to talk to you, I know I screwed up but just call me OK? I love you babes." Lauren rolled her eyes as she deleted the voice mail. Yeah like I am going to go running back into your arms over a voice mail apology for lets see what was it again.... oh yeah...SCREWING MY SISTER!,

The next message was from her sister Shannon. "Grow the Fuck up Lauren, you were always such a fucking goody two shoes that it's no wonder he wanted a woman who would suck his cock instead of a virgin who thinks cookies and milk can solve the world's problems. Drag your lame ass back here before mom has a heart attack over her favorite daughter going missing!" Lauren deleted that message as well thinking no apology just insults; yup that's my darling foul-mouthed sister. The final message was from her mother "Lauren sweetheart it's mom, you know that Shannon is sorry and that there is nothing in the world that can keep two sisters from making up and setting aside grievances and you girls are too sweet to stay angry, come home and we'll have a nice cup of tea and talk about it."

Freud would have a field day with my family, with the final voice-mail deleted, she grabbed the remote and found a mindless thriller to watch while she ate her pizza and commended herself on making the right decision on leaving. Maybe if she found the right place, she would never go back again. Putting the now empty pizza box on the small table near the door, she climbed under the blankets and fell into a dreamless sleep.

Lauren woke feeling fully rested and refreshed although she did have a strange dream, the details had faded but it was something about an evil witch and a spell and a prince trapped in a tower. Obviously, she had spent way too many nights memorizing fairy tales for the amusement of the children she cared for. Lauren grabbed her belongings stopped at the office to check out before heading to her car out front. As she approached her car, she noticed a little old woman with long white hair wearing what appeared to be a tattered brown bathrobe and staring intently at Lauren's car. As Lauren got closer to the car, the woman suddenly spun and gave her a sharp look, which melted into a gap-toothed grin when she saw Lauren. The pervasive scent of Water Lilies seemed to becoming from the little old woman who wore upon closer inspection not a bathrobe at all, but more of a monk's robe or one of those scratchy wool robes that the witches in Hamlet had been clad in. As soon as that thought crossed her mind, she realized the woman looked EXACTLY like what she would expect a Macbeth Witch to look like if she had stepped into the real world. If she starts talking like she came from one of those Celtic European countries, I am going to be seriously freaked out. "A fine conveyance tha do be having lass to be sure." Lauren's mind was suddenly screaming Macbeth witch! Macbeth Witch! Lauren tried not to look like she was hurrying as she scooted past the woman and quickly unlocked the car, lowered the top and tossed her bags and herself into the car. Lauren looked up into the fathomless dark eyes and heard herself babbling "Thank you very much it was a gift to me when I landed the job with the nanny service." Lauren gasped, she had no idea why she had revealed that to the woman and closed her mouth with a snap to prevent anything else from slipping out. The old woman cackled merrily which confirmed absolutely in Lauren's mind that the woman was indeed a Witch from any number of Shakespeare's plays. "Tha do be what is needed I think lass and this one'll get tha there quicker now" the old woman patted the hood of the car as one might pat a favorite horse or beloved dog.

Lauren shook her head in confusion at the woman's words. The old woman shuffled closer until she was standing just outside the driver's door, the smell of Water Lilies so overwhelming that it brought tears to Lauren's eyes. Lauren tried not to flinch away when a leathery hand patted her shoulder "Tha hear old Mab now...There it goes round and round but arrogance looks neither to sky nor ground. A virgin lass of golden heart shall the curtain force to part" The old woman grabbed Lauren's wrist with a strength that belied her age and frail appearance, a silver chain reminiscent of something found at Tiffanys now circled her wrist. "A pass I give thee lass, enter freely her spell but to leave, he must be with." Lauren nodded stupidly hoping she could get out of here before the old woman's sisters showed up and started chanting over a cauldron.

The woman started to shuffle off then spun faster than a woman of her age should be able to and called again to her "Tha do tell him 'you fool you fool, back to the beginning is the rule'!" Then with a harsh cackle, she finally shuffled off and around the side of the motel and out of sight. Lauren stared at the spot where the old woman had disappeared *Did she just quote Fezzik from the princess Bride?*

Lauren let out a deep sigh and started her car, the car gave an animal like growl that she had never heard before and shivered all over as if in eagerness to get going. The annoying ticking sound she had been hearing from her engine had vanished, in fact all the complaints she had been having with her car were suddenly gone and the slow moving vehicles in the fast lane suddenly decided to change lanes as soon as she appeared in the rear view mirror. Shortly after she passed the exit for Charlotte North Carolina her stomach lurched, she looked about and saw nothing to indicate anything wrong and there were no warning lights lit on the dash. No more roadside burritos for me! Suddenly the sky was black with clouds a she was hit with what felt like a waterfall hovering above her. Lauren swerved on the suddenly slick road and pulled off to the side of the road. She sat staring in shock as at the sign that had been briefly illuminated by a bright streak of lightning. BOSTON-35MILES.

Lauren was unaware of the water collecting in her car or the fact that she was now soaked to the skin. There is no way that I could have made it from Charlotte NC to Boston MA in less than 10 minutes, it just was not possible. A sudden peal of thunder made her jump and jolted her back into action; she quickly got out of the car and fought to put the top back up. Once the top was back up, she turned the heater and wipers on full and waited a few minutes chafing her hands in front of the heater to regain feeling. Leaning close to the windshield and trying to see through the sheets of rain obscuring her vision, she pulled out onto the road. Shortly after passing the exit to Boston, she felt another lurch in her stomach and although she could hardly make out the road, she knew something was different. Another brief flash of lightning lit up a white town sign that read "Welcome to Bethesda" Lauren leaned closer to the windshield as the storm got worse but even the wipers only gave a half second of clarity before the rain obscured everything again.

Lauren was never really sure what happened that night, whether the car had hydroplaned or her grip on the wheel had slipped or maybe she had started to doze. Whatever the reason, one minute she had nearly had her face pressed to the windshield to try to see the road and the next she glimpsed a tree right before she had a head on collision with it. Her head hit the steering wheel at the same time that her seat belt jerked her backwards, causing pain in her head, neck and shoulders. The car engine was still running but the smell of burning plastic or maybe rubber was filling the car and she quickly shut off the engine.

The sound of the rain was almost deafening on the fabric roof, in fact the roof was starting to bow under the weight of the water. Lauren's arms and legs felt shaky and something kept running into her eyes, she swiped her hand to brush whatever it was out of her eyes and found her hand red with blood. Pressing a wet towel onto her forehead and hoping it was clean; she used her belt to tie the towel onto her head and pushed against the door. At first the door seemed to be stuck but with several more firm shoves against the door it popped open with a screech of protesting metal. Lauren's whole body was shaking with cold and pain as she lurched in the direction of the distant lights she had been heading towards.

It seemed like hours before she noticed she was passing buildings instead of trees, everything was closed for the night. Lauren had stopped feeling her body a while ago although she was shaking so hard from the cold now that she had to grit her teeth to not be sick. Up ahead on the right she noticed a light on, it looked like a living room lamp, she lurched faster thinking they might have a phone she could use and maybe she could get warm and dry. As she stumbled past a white picket fence, she suddenly felt lightheaded and barely managed to catch herself on the door frame before she could fall. Pounding on the door, she tried to yell hello but her voice was a squeak. She pounded again and heard someone coming to the door, after a long moment a bare chested guy stood in the doorway with an extremely confused look on his face. Lauren heard the man calling to her as if from far away "Lady, Lady wake up I can't come out and get you, you need to get closer to the door...please if you can hear me crawl towards the door...please lady I can't reach you!" *Why can't you reach me? Step outside the door....*Lauren's thoughts were very muzzy but somehow she managed to pull herself closer to the door before she passed out.

Lauren knew she had to be dead, no food on earth could smell that good, as she moved to sit up pain shot through her head. Ok not dead but sure want to be right now. The smell of food got closer and suddenly someone was messing with the towel on her head. Lauren opened one eye blearily and looked up at the bare chested blonde man who had answered the door earlier. The man was checking her head and dabbing blood with a square of gauze. On the bedside table next to her was a plate of what smelled like scrambled eggs and ham, her stomach growled and he smiled and noticed she was awake. "Hi there, my name is Daniel and I'm sorry I did not get your name before you collapsed." Lauren smiled and managed after several tries and a sip of water to mumble her name. Daniel covered her head back up with not a towel but an actual bandage and then pulled the blankets tighter around her to ward off a chill. It was at that moment Lauren realized she was laying in a big comfy bed .....moreover, she was naked. With a yelp she tried to jump away from him and nearly passed out from the pain in her head. Daniel placed a hand on her shoulder to push her back down again "I really wouldn't do that again if I were you, you hit your head pretty hard, you don't need stitches from what I can tell but head injuries are nothing to play with." Lauren swallowed hard and tried to force her eyes to stare him down "Why ....am ....I....naked?" Daniel stood up from the side of the bed and walked about ten feet away from the bed before answering; obviously he knew she would feel more comfortable with him further away. "You were soaking wet and shivering, I undressed you, checked for any injuries and put you in the bed....that is it nothing else." Lauren thanked him and abruptly passed out again.

Daniel sighed as she passed out again and cleaned up the bloody bandages he had removed from her, thankfully the bleeding seemed to have stopped and he hoped she would not need a doctor because after she had managed to crawl into the house, he realized that she was now as stuck in this house as he was. He went back into the living room and climbed into the makeshift bed he had made on the couch, obviously he couldn't share the bed with her so that left sleeping in Jason's old bed or the couch. Which is why he had chosen the couch, and it was close enough for him to hear if she called out or needed anything. Sometime around three AM or so Daniel heard someone calling him out of his deep sleep "Mr. blonde guy? Please can you hear me....I really need help going to the bathroom." Daniel woke looked confused for a moment then remembered Lauren the redhead who had collapsed on his porch.

Pushing the blankets aside he stumbled half-awake to the bedroom and saw Lauren sitting up with the blankets clutched to her chest. Daniel grabbed an oversize t-shirt from his drawer and helped her into it much to her embarrassment. When he was sure she was completely covered, he pushed the blankets back and turned her towards the edge of the bed. With an arm under her shoulder, he helped her stumble to the bathroom and sit down on the toilet. Daniel stepped just outside the door and left it opened a crack as he leaned against the wall. A few minutes later he heard her clearing her throat to get his attention. Walking in, he saw her standing a little steadier but still holding onto the sink. He let her walk in front of him keeping his arms out to catch her if she wobbled but she managed to get back in bed unaided. He placed the plate of food on her lap and waited while she devoured the food making happy noises of enjoyment as she finished every crumb. He took the empty plate and after her assurance that she would not need him again, he took the dish to the kitchen and quickly washed it before going back to his nest on the couch.

Daniel must have slept hard after that because the next time he woke it was to the sound of someone opening and closing kitchen cabinets. Groaning he got up and walked into the kitchen, Lauren was scowling as she looked around the kitchen with her hands on her hips and her hair standing up in stiff spikes around the bandage. Trying not to laugh as the image of an upset rooster springs to mind "What exactly are you looking for?" Lauren jumps apparently she was not aware he had walked into the kitchen. "Jesus jellybeans make some noise when you creep up on someone." Daniel wiped the smile off his face and repeated the question. "I was looking for a fondue pot, I have a hankering for some melted cheese on toast points and I found all kinds of awesome gadgets but no fondue pot." Daniel smirked and stepped past her to the pantry which looking at the disorder had been rifled and reaching up to the top shelf slid his hand along it until he felt what he was looking for and pulled the fondue pot down and turned to hand it to her. Lauren thanks him for finding the fondue pot for her and silently admires the view as he heads to the bedroom to get dressed. As Daniel was pulling clothes on for work, he knew he was going to have to tell her about the boundary spell. He waited until she had finished her breakfast before joining her at the table and folding his hands in front of him. "We need to talk Lauren, how much do you know about magic?" Lauren gave him a skeptical look "Like David Copperfield and quarters behind your ears magic?"

Daniel slowly shook his head "Like witches and sorcery and objects that can contain and control people." Lauren started looking uneasy "Are you about to tell me you are a Satanist or something?" She stood up and put her back to the wall, the width of the table between them. Daniel shook his head again and ran a hand through his head in agitation "I am going to tell you a story and at the end of it I am going to prove the things I told you are the truth." Over the next hour Daniel told Lauren everything starting from the first day at Pariah's and ending with them sitting at the table with him explaining everything. Lauren had not spoken the whole time and had in fact looked as if she were listening intently to everything he was saying, when he finished she stood and took a deep breath " you said when you were done with the story you would be able to prove you were telling the truth." Daniel stood up and went to the front door but did not go out it; instead he stepped back and gestured for her to go out the door. Lauren peered through the door as if expecting to see something that would stop her, when she didn't see anything she stepped through and hit the porch convulsing as she was wracked with what felt like a million volts of electricity shooting through her, vaguely she was aware of Daniel pulling her back in through the doorway. It was several minutes before she was able to slow her breathing and open her eyes. Lauren swallowed hard and tried several times to speak, on the third try she succeeded "So I am trapped here?"

Daniel nodded looking anything but happy about the fact "Looks that way, at least until I can find a way to break through or counteract the barriers." Daniels comment stirred something in Lauren's brain but not enough for her to be able to remember it, her brain was still buzzing from the barrier's effects. Daniel helped her up and walked her to the couch. The day went by slowly with Lauren drifting in and out of consciousness as her body healed. Daniel in deference to her preference for healthy meals, cobbled together a dinner salad with a side of homemade garlic bread and mandarin oranges.

The phone started ringing as they were finishing up the dinner dishes, the both stared at it like a poisonous viper that had suddenly appeared in the room. Daniel walked over to the phone and put his finger to his lip to remind Lauren to not make any noises and answered the phone. Judging by the look on his face he was listening to "the witch" talk, he listened without speaking and then with a gasp his eyes flew wide and he doubled over and nearly dropped the phone. Clenching his teeth he brought the phone back to his ear "Please stop rue, I will be ready for you when you get here." Hanging up he slowly stood and adjusted the front of his jeans in embarrassment. Lauren stood at the sink staring wide-eyed at him "Did she just...?" Daniel nodded and slapped a hand on the underside of the silver cuff circling his left wrist. Lauren dried her hands and came forward to look at the cuff; it was old and tarnished but clearly silver.

Lauren took the cuff in her hands to examine it closer, just as Rue invoked the spell to resume tormenting Daniel. Daniel sucked in a breath as his cock sprang to life, he had a mere second to register the sudden flare of desire in Lauren's eyes and mumble an 'aw hell' before she was on him. With one hand she unsnapped his jeans and had her hand slipped inside and wrapped a tight fist around his throbbing cock, her other hand grabbing the back of his neck to pull him in for a passionate kiss. Daniel was panting against her lips as she began to stroke his cock, her tongue plundering his mouth and just like that the surge was gone. Lauren jerked away from him and ran for the bathroom her stomach clenching in reaction to the magic, Daniel ran to the second bathroom with just as much haste and for much the same reason. Lauren could hear Daniel's retching above the sound of her own as both of them were violently sick in their respective commodes.

When Lauren was sure her stomach had nothing left to purge, she washed her face and mouth out and emerged from the bathroom and a moment later saw Daniel do the same. "I am so sorry Daniel, I didn't mean to...I would never....I am a v... a virgin." Daniel nodded "I know the magic controls my sex drive and forces me to respond physically, she can also add commands which I am then forced to obey. You must have been affected simply by being in contact with the cuff when the spell was invoked." Lauren still stared at him as if afraid she might suddenly attack him again, Daniel smiled at her to reassure her and suddenly heard a car door slam. Panicking he grabbed her arm and rushed her to the attic stairs and barely gave her time to clear them before he slammed the hatch closed again and rushed back into the living room just as Rue and Kate came through the door.

Rue was wearing a sleeveless blouse that was cut to the waist and left the inner curves of her breasts bare. Her skirt looked barely wider than a belt and combined with the stiletto heels she was teetering on, she looked like a high priced prostitute. Knowing what kind of reaction that comparison would cause, he wisely kept his mouth shut. Kate went to the kitchen to scrounge up some food and Rue stepped past him into the bedroom, Daniel sighed and followed her knowing she was going to want to screw him before she ate. Rue kicked her heels off and tossed him an enigmatic smile "did you miss me lover?" Like a rash on my ass, like an STD ... the responses that ran through his head were better left unsaid. Rue stood and slowly slipped off her blouse, letting it hit the floor followed by the skirt and showing off an overpriced negligee. Spinning in place she laughs "what do you think of my lingerie darling?" Daniel cocked his head as if seriously considering the question "I think if you are going to force me to screw you, you should do it already because that is going to be the only way you are going to get sex from me and this pretend relationship shit is getting boring." Rue's face went a mottled red and walking up to him she hauled back and slapped him hard enough to cut his lip with her rings. "YOU WANT IT, YOU GOT IT ASSHOLE!" With a wrench she pulled open his pants and smiled as the compulsion forced him to have an erection, jerking his jeans down she commanded him to remove all his clothes, then she went to the closet and opened it wide to reveal shopping bags. Rue rummaged through the bags and came up with a riding crop, "I went shopping with you in mind sweetheart, now kneel before your goddess!"

Daniel gritted his teeth as he was forced to obey, Rue laughed and brought the crop whistling down onto his shoulders. Daniel hissed at the burning pain the crop left him with, "Just get this over with Rue!" The crop descended five more times each stroke following a bellowed word "YOU *smack* DON'T *smack* GIVE *smack* ME *smack* ORDERS!" *smack* Daniel closed his eyes and refused to respond to the blows. He heard the bed creak as Rue climbed onto it, her ass in the air as she positioned herself on her hands and knees "Now lover, FUCK ME like a good little SLAVE!" She smiled as the compulsion pulled him to his feet and no matter how he tried to fight it, he still found him pumping his cock into rue amid her cries of ecstasy and constant orders. The small triumph Daniel could take away from these 'sessions' was that she could order him to screw her, she could force him to have an erection but she could no longer compel him to cum in her and give her his 'essence'. Rue got dressed and left the bedroom to go eat whatever Kate had scrounged for them; Daniel curled up on the bed and tried to will his heart to stop. Not surprisingly, it kept beating and he was once again driven deep into a black depression.

Lauren could hear every word of their exchange as if she were standing in the room with them thanks to the vents in the attic floor. She felt herself shaking with rage at how "the witch" was treating Daniel, when Rue began hitting him with the crop she felt herself wincing in sympathetic pain at how loud the sound of the leather was when it connected with flesh. Lauren started pacing trying to talk herself out of doing something stupid. The turn of conversation convinced her to sit next to the vent and listen. "Why me Rue? What makes you so dead set on having a leash on me, what did I ever do to you?" Daniel knew he sounded like he was whining but couldn't seem to help it. Rue smiled as she clasped her hands in front of her and turned her back on Daniel. "Well there has been a long time rivalry between Kendra and I and the fact that you are half-Fae is always a plus." Rue spun around to see what affect her words were having on him and found him laughing. "Two things wrong with that Rue, one (he holds up one finger) Hecate never claimed me because we only had sex once and two (holds up a second finger), a Fae is an elf and other than Orlando blooms depiction of Legolas there has never been an elf with my build. And that is going under the insane premise that elves actually exist." Daniel started laughing again and was cut short as Rue backhanded him across the mouth and once again split his lip. Rue bared her teeth at him in a snarl of rage "They DO exist and YOUR FATHER was FAE!" Daniel stood slowly, all mirth gone from his face as he reached up and wiped blood from his lips with the back of his hand "You are basing this on the fact that my mother was raped and never saw the face of her attacker?" His tone was disbelief as he stared at her as if she were insane. Rue clenched her fists and stomped her foot "There are other signs as well!" Taking a deep breath and smoothing back her hair, she once again regained her composure "Since you have so greatly vexed me you will make it up to me for the next .....three hours with orgasms."

Rue might have been ordering him to make her some tea so cold was her demand. Settling herself on to the bed, Rue spread her knees and the compulsion took over his body. Daniel dropped to his knees and closed his eyes as the spell brought his face level with her open thighs, for the next three hours he had no choice but to follow Rue's every command.

Lauren tamped a pillow down over the vent to block out the sounds of what Daniel was doing to Rue and to block out Rue's snide insults and instructions on how to please her better. Y Lauren's way of thinking, what Rue was doing to Daniel (although she was not sure how she was doing it) was akin to rape. Rue was forcing Daniel to respond to her and follow her every sexual whim. Lauren was almost curious enough to wonder if worked with every action or just carnal ones. Lauren was disgusted at Rue's treatment of Daniel and her cavalier attitude at what should be an act of love and desire and not superiority and self-gratification. The only good thing that had come from her listening at the vent was that the earlier conversation had reminded her of something important, the 'Macbeth Witch' back at the motel had mentioned a free pass to enter her spell but to leave he would must be with. Could she have been talking about the barriers? What am I thinking how an old homeless woman would know what's going on hundreds of miles away in Bethesda Massachusetts is beyond me. Shortly after dark, Rue and Kate left to go back to their own home and Daniel called to her and gave her the all clear. Lauren was struck once again with a wave of remorse as she looked at Daniel's haggard expression and the scratches and red slap marks on his face and neck. Obviously Rue enjoyed being able to hurt and humiliate Daniel even knowing he can do absolutely nothing to refuse her while under her spell.

Daniel gestured her to follow him to the kitchen and started loading up a plate with the marinated chicken breast, fettuccine alfredo and steamed veggies that he had made for Rue and Kate's dinner. Lauren's mouth watered at the smell of it, she had been hiding in the attic all day and not had a chance to eat until now. Feeling like a pig she wolfed down the first plate and went back for seconds, I gotta hand it to him he CAN cook! It was only when she was halfway through her second plate that she realized he was not eating. "Did you eat earlier with ...them?" Daniel shook his head staring at the wood grain of the table with distant eyes. "I'm really not hungry right now" Lauren felt like a complete idiot, she had heard what Rue had commanded him to do before she had covered the vent; he was probably feeling sick to his stomach. Lauren reached out and laid her hand atop his "I am so very sorry that this is happening to you, I may not know much about you but I do not believe anyone deserves what she is putting you through." Daniel gave her a brief smile of gratitude before announcing he was going to go take a shower and just like that he got up and left her to finish her meal alone and went into the bathroom. Lauren heard the water start in the bathroom and suddenly the food tasted like ash in her mouth who knows how long he has been imprisoned by this Rue person, someone has to help him.....maybe the Shakespeare Witch WAS talking about the barriers... Daniel finished his shower and stared at his pale reflection in the fogged mirror. He didn't know how much longer he could go through this, his whole world and everything he knew to be real and true had been turned upside down and now an innocent woman was trapped in this nightmare along with him.

Lauren decided there had to be a reason she was able to get through the barrier the first time and not since. Since Daniel had been too busy with caring for her to openly question what had happened, maybe it was time to tell him about the strange old woman and the riddled message. Daniel emerged from the bathroom in a pair of sweats and a worn out T shirt and Lauren took his hand and led him to the couch. With the surety that any moment he would decide she was insane, Lauren explained about the 'Shakespeare Witch' and her Fezzik message to the mysterious 'him'.

Daniel listened and did not interrupt, when she had finished he spoke aloud though the question was not directed at her "what does she mean go back to the beginning...the beginning of what?" Testing a theory, Lauren went to the door and opened it, nothing had changed outside, the world looked saner then she felt at the moment. Reaching her hand towards the street outside, Lauren was hit with the same wracking pain she had felt before and quickly dropped her hand. It took a few moments to organize her thoughts. Reaching her other hand towards Daniel she gestured for him to join her at the door. Not sure where this was headed, he stood and took her hand. With a deep breath Lauren extended her hand out the door again and flinched in surprise as her hand passed the same point she had been stopped at before with none of the pain. The message given by the witch when the bracelet appeared now fell into place. Lauren could enter alone but to leave, Daniel had to be with her.

Smiling Lauren explained the message and watched as Daniel's eyes lit with comprehension. "we gotta get out of here so we can get a head start before she comes back." Heading quickly into the bedroom and she hears the dresser drawers squeak. Peeking her head in to check on him she found him stuffing a duffel with clothes, towels, and some toiletries. His next stop was the kitchen where he dropped cans of spam and pop tarts, bags of dried fruit and things they could eat on the go into the bag along with bottled water.

Lauren watched his preparations with trepidation. A thought occurred to Daniel, "You came by car right? Where did you leave it?" Lauren had to think about that, the accident had happened so quickly and she really had not been paying much attention when she stumbled from the wreck. She shook her head in confusion "there was a white sign that said 'welcome to Bethesda'". Daniel cocked his head in thought, "was there a big white church across the street or just woods on either side?" Lauren thought about it, she did not remember a church but the storm had been so bad that she had barely been able to see the road let alone anything around her. "I remember a lot of woods; it took a long while to get to where buildings were." Daniel nodded and pointed off to the south, "You came in there; your car is about two miles from here if we avoid the road and cut through the woods." Closing the door solidly, Daniel took Lauren's hand and led her into the woods down the road. Daniel felt the sudden urge to laugh and cheer at his freedom, but he knew as long as he was where Rue could reach him, he would never be truly free.Clutching Lauren's hand he led her deeper into the woods and hopefully in the direction of her car.

The woods were dark and the wind that whistled through the trees was chilly, Lauren and Daniel shivered as they slipped through the dark woods. Neither spoke, so wrapped up in their own inner thoughts and the need to put as much distance as possible between them and Rue. Daniel kept moving and tried not to sigh in irritation at the increasing number of times that Lauren tripped and fell behind him. The moonlight filtering through the canopy made the deer path they were following dim and uncertain. Daniel knew it was unfair to rush her through the dark woods at night and expect her to keep up but he felt a rising sense of urgency. Maybe his urgency was akin to a long confined prisoner who suddenly finds himself free or maybe some small voice was warning him that time was rapidly growing short. Whatever the reason for his haste, he still had to bite back a curse as Lauren stumbled and hit the ground with a huff of expelled air. Daniel helped her up and called a rest; Lauren breathlessly thanked him and dropped down onto a nearby log breathing hard. "How much further do you think it is to the road?" Daniel shrugged and rubbed his arms wishing he had thought to bring a jacket.

Turning back to Lauren he checked her bandage again but her head wound was healing nicely "Probably another half mile or so." The two of them sat in silence for another ten minutes before Lauren felt ready to get going again. The rest seemed to do Lauren a world of good because her stumbles were fewer and far between, the sense of rising urgency Daniel was feeling however had increased. Thankfully the came through a wall of brush and found themselves looking down on the road and just up the road they could make out her car still kissing the tree.

Carefully they made their way down the bluff until their feet hit asphalt. Daniel looked the car over and had to admit it was pretty bad. Lauren pulled the top back and pulled her musty smelling bags from the backseat, almost everything had gotten wet and dried again leaving a mildewed smell behind. Daniel looked into the crunched engine bay and determined there was no way to save this car, crouching down he saw a puddle of something beneath the car. Extending his hand, he touched the puddle with one hand and found it congealed, pulling his hand back into the light he could swear it was dried blood on his fingertip. That is impossible, cars don't bleed! Standing up again he brushed his hands off on his pants legs and looked over to where Lauren was sorting through her bags and checking to see what could be salvaged. Daniel heard a faint vibration in the air like the sound of an approaching vehicle; Daniel grabbed Lauren around the waist and hauled her quickly into the bushes. Just as they crouched down, a pair of headlights lit the road and her poor mangled car. A silver SUV pulled up and stopped even with the wreckage, Daniel could not see much of the driver but the silhouette was enough to tell him it was not Rue. Before he could think better of it, he found himself jumping out of the bushes and waving and calling to get the driver's attention before he could drive away. For just a second it looked as if the SUV had shivered in surprise at Daniel's sudden appearance. I am going insane, cars do not shiver and they do not bleed! Daniel approached the dark passenger side window cautiously and flinched when the cab was suddenly lit up by the interior light, the driver was a leathery older man with bright blue eyes and crooked teeth. The man had a kind look about him despite the state of his dental hygiene and Daniel was suddenly overwhelmed with the urge to trust him. "Looks like ye had a bit o a tuss up with yon tree thar me lad." Daniel nodded trying not to think how similar this man, must sound to the 'Shakespeare Witch' that Lauren had met in Virginia. Daniel tried to think of what to tell the man...obviously they could not to tell him the truth. "My sister and I were heading to ...Willow's Grove when we got caught up in a bad storm and ..." He gestures to where the car sat. The man nodded in understanding "name tis Hunter and ye be?" Daniel introduced himself, gestured for Lauren to join them, and introduced her as well. If Lauren was surprised at being introduced as his sister, she hid it well. Hunter's eyes narrowed at them "ye realize ye were going in the wrong direction for Willow's Grove..."

Daniel forced a laugh to cover the Lauren's gasp as she heard Hunter's accent. "Guess we got turned around in the storm, it WAS a pretty bad storm." Hunter nodded in agreement and gestured for them to climb in. Lauren grabbed her bags, tossed them into the backseat, and climbed in next to them, leaving Daniel to take shotgun next to Hunter. Daniel and Hunter kept up a steady dialog and Lauren felt herself getting drowsy until she felt herself nodding and finally leaned against the door and started snoring.

Hunter looked over the seat at Lauren's sleeping face and then nodded as if he had expected that very thing and turned in his seat to face Daniel leaving the car to drive itself. Daniel felt his mouth go dry, Hunter fixed him with those bright blue eyes and suddenly Daniel no longer had the urge to panic or be nervous, in fact, he was very very calm. "Now ye listen here Daniel Warwick, ye have caught the eye of a witch and not just any witch but one that was taught by a Fae afore she did away with her." Hunter shook his head and sighed, "We were ne'er proliferate at the best of times but less so now, still once ye go down that path thar is no way back." Daniel wanted to nod but his body seemed completely frozen, he should have been panicking at his sudden paralysis.

Hunter narrowed a blue eye at him as if searching for something then nodded to him "I'll let ye go now but none o' that screaming and fighting nonsense deal?" Daniel suddenly found the ability to nod and pressed himself firmly against the passenger door. The car continued to drive in a straight line even though Hunter's hands were nowhere near the steering wheel. Daniel glanced out the windshield then back at Hunter, hunter chuckled and pulled a lit pipe out of his pocket and the faint smell of cherry tobacco wafted toward Daniel. "Ye're wondering how the car is driving when clearly thar is no hand at the wheel yes?" Daniel nodded again and felt completely lost as if he had stepped out his door only to find a rabbit in a waistcoat running past with a pocket watch. "Oh lad ye'll see a lot stranger bits than that afore this quest is over I'll wager...but the short of it is that some o' us can breathe life into that which does not nor ever has had it." Daniel thought about that one for a minute before asking his next question "I thought Fae had a problem with iron and steel, an aversion to it or something." Hunter touched the side of his nose and grinned, "Ye're a smart one I'll give ye that, but that only applies to certain tribes o' the Fae." Daniel started to ask but Hunter waved him to silence "Just as thar are many types of humans, so thar be many types of Fae." Daniel finally smiled different tribes with different strengths and weaknesses made perfect sense, the world was starting to stop spinning for him.

One minute Daniel was sure he was starting to get a grasp on things and Hunter's next words knocked, his feet back out from under him. "Now take yer Da for example, he was an Eldritch Seelie and had no issue with iron or steel, couldn't have in his line of work." Daniel felt short of breath as if someone had punched him in the Solar Plexus, "my father was a Fae?" Hunter laughed, a thick plume of cherry scented smoke suddenly erupting from his gaping mouth "calling yer Da a Fae is akin to calling a Dragon a lizard lad...yer Da was an Eldritch Seelie or what ye might call an Elven Knight." Daniel felt his jaw drop even further and a burning began in his chest until he reminded himself to breathe. "That can't be, my mother was raped and never saw the face of her attacker....knights are always good in stories...they don't rape...do they?" Hunter gave him a stern look from eyes that only a moment ago had been bright blue but now resembled polished steel "knights are titled and treat lessers like trash to walk on and use as they please, what of yer own history and that of the knights Templar during the Crusades?" Daniel flushed as memories of the atrocities committed by the infamous church knights. Hunter ignored Daniel's look of chagrin and continued "yer own history gives lie to the 'stories', knights are no better or worse than the ones that have not the title and fancy steed."

Daniel swallowed hard "so my father...." Hunter tapped a gnarled finger roughly into Daniel's chest "I knew yer father and knew him well which is more than most could say, Aelon Dryearghym is a good seed and never have done what ye've been told." Hunter shook his head again, "I suggest ye ask yer mum again what happened that night and watch her eyes when ye do, the eyes cannot lie though the tongue might." Hunter sat back and let Daniel absorb everything he had been told. Daniel's head suddenly jerked and he stared at Hunter in sudden understanding "you said my father IS a good seed not WAS a good seed, so he is still alive?" hunter shrugged "Been out o' hill for a bit, he was alive when last I saw him, though that was before ye were born lad." Daniel drummed his fingers and stared out into the dark night as he thought about what else he wanted to know. "So this witch that is after me, how does she figure into all this?" Hunter grinned and touched the side of his nose again as if Daniel had scored another point. Hunter puffed on his pipe again for a moment or two before answering, "This Rue lass was mentored by a Fae what had gone wrong, taken the magic and twisted it for personal gain." Hunter snorted a puff of smoke out his nostrils "now that might do for the dark court but not for one of the Queen's court." Hunter sat up straight with a look of outrage and contempt on his face "Angelique left the hill to swan around in yer world and take many a human lover lass and lad alike." Daniel rolled his neck and shoulders and shuddered at what type of person might have mentored Rue and taught her to be the way she was.

Hunter laughed, "Yer not the on'y one had that reaction to Angelique, beautiful as the dawn but born to the wrong court and as selfish and vain as possible, worse she hated bowing to rules and then one day she was just gone." Daniel started to ask then closed his mouth and waited, finally when the silence had stretched a bit Hunter chuckled. "Ye learn fast Danny boy, there is not a Fae born that doesn't like the sound of their own voice...alright I'll tell ye." Puffing on his pipe again for a minute, "We do not know precisely how Angelique met her end, only who twas that ended it and the power that should have come back to us ne'er returned." Daniel knew Hunter thought he was being wise by being silent but in truth he was still trying to make sense of everything, he had been told. Hunter had started speaking again but Daniel interrupted "But why me? She can't know about my father, not for certain." Hunter shrugged again as if it made no difference and maybe to Rue it did not. "Who's to say what she does or does no know, but she has chosen ye and by the looks of things there will be no swaying her until she gets what she wants of ye." Daniel started to speak when he suddenly broke into a jaw-cracking yawn. Hunter chuckled and turned back to the steering wheel "Ye go ahead and rest lad, we'll talk more when yer up for it." Daniel settled back in the seat and leaned his head against the glass and fell asleep with the dark world passing by outside. Daniel woke to the sound of a woman's laughter. He picked his head up and with bleary eyes noticed, they were parked at a rest stop. Turning his head, he looked out the passenger window and saw Lauren and hunter laughing and sharing a bucket of chicken at a nearby picnic table. With a yawn, he climbed out of the car and headed over in time to see Lauren cover mouth and exclaim, "You didn't!" Hunter laughed and slapped the table "I sure as hell did, when he came through the door my wrinkled ass went out the window and slid down the snow covered hill faster than an Olympic bobsled!" Lauren was laughing so hard now that tears were running down her cheeks, "How...How did you get home?" Hunter took a bite of chicken and answered around it "Well I sure as hell didn't grab a cab; the naked man has no pockets." Daniel chuckled at the last remark as he slid onto the bench next to Lauren "So since you know my father, you also know that Lauren is not my sister." Hunter nods "Knew that the minute I recognized ye lad."

Lauren slid a plate of chicken and biscuits over to him and he suddenly realized he was famished. Hunter stretched out a hand and laid a finger on the cuff on Daniel's wrist and Daniel instinctively jerked his arm away looking nervous. Hunter shook his head at Daniel's reaction "Do no be worrying about the spell affecting me lad, I'm of sterner stuff." Taking a deep breath Daniel slid his arm back into Hunter's hands and watched as he turned it from side to side and traced the engravings. "I'll give her this lad; she made this to stay on ye." Daniel found his appetite suddenly gone as the vision of a future as a controlled sex slave for the rest of his life flashed before his eyes. Hunter chuckled as he dropped Daniel's wrist "There be some who would be flattered at a woman wanting them enough to hunt them down and en-spell them." Hunter lost his smile as he looked up at Daniel's face. "I'm sorry lad this be no laughing matter, tis no funny to have no choice but to obey." The happy mood was gone and they silently cleaned up the meal and got back into the car to get back on the road.

Rue had changed into a short and slinky flame colored dress with matching stiletto heels prior to heading back over to Daniel's house. The moment Kate parked behind Daniel's truck, Rue knew something was different. The house looked the same but it was lacking an energy that had always been there before. The house almost felt empty but the barriers were still up so he could not have escaped. Walking towards the door, she saw two objects laying in the front yard, bending down she plucked an old dusty shoe out of the grass. Turning the shoe over in her hands, she suddenly looked up at the house and could just see the slat covered vent that presumably led to an attic and was far large enough for someone to crawl through. A sick feeling twisted her stomach and she hurried to the front door and throwing it open, yelling Daniel's name she ran through the empty house. Kate came through the front door a look of confusion on her face, Rue turned and ran into the hallway looking for the drop down ladder for the attic. Yanking the cord hanging from the ceiling, she barely stepped back in time to avoid the ladder as it unfolded at her feet. Rue and Kate hurried up the stairs, the attic looked no different then her own did with less stuff crammed into it of course. She had expected to find him hiding but was stunned by his absence, he could not have gotten out by himself, someone had to help him. Rue shrieked and tore at her own hair in anger "damn you Daniel Warwick!!!"

Kate turned away to hide her smirk and spotted the footprints in the dust collecting on the floor of the attic not one set but two! Kate knelt on the floor and examined the prints closer. "You may want to look at this Rue sweetheart." Rue's ranting cut off abruptly as if someone had pulled a plug and her head joined Kate's as she looked at the prints "Someone definitely helped him escape?" Kate stepped back and scratched absently at her arms "You made the barriers to keep things from leaving but not to prevent anyone from coming into the house, but if they came in they too would be trapped unless it was you or I, which means they had to have been here during our last visit." Rue thought back to her last visit, Daniel HAD seemed a little off, she looked around the attic but there was nothing to indicate anyone had been here except the lack of dust on this side of the attic, which implied it had been a woman. "Lets go home, we have to pack, we are going to Moldova, Angelique's biggest library is there and we are going to need it if we are going to find him." Kate shuddered but followed Rue as she swept regally out of the dusty attic and headed back downstairs.

Rue and Kate headed back to their house where they spent the next four hours making phone calls and packing for an extended trip. Ok Kate did all the packing and Rue did all the phone calls and when they were done there was a pile of bags in front of the door, a limo on the way to pick them up and take them to the airport and an executive suite at the Holiday Hampton waiting for them. The jet would not be ready until tomorrow morning. Kate was glad she would not be the one lugging the bags this time and gave a sigh of relief that they were going to an expensive hotel and presumably, she could get in on the pampering as well this time. The limo showed up sooner than expected but since Kate had already packed everything, the chauffeur was able to start lugging bags out to the trunk immediately. Rue strolled to the limo with her head and shoulders back looking like a queen descending to her royal carriage. Kate followed behind feeling like a servant, things will be different once she tires of Daniel and kills him off just like all the rest, then we can be together again...maybe I should speed up Daniel's demise and our reunion... Kate's smile was almost frightening as she slid into the back of the limo with Rue.

CHAPTER FOUR

The atmosphere in the car was tense as they got going again. Daniel tried to break the ice "So what was that story you were telling Lauren at the rest stop?" Lauren snorted and started laughing again from the back seat and Hunter ducked his head a bit in embarrassment "One o' many tales of misspent lust with married women." hunter laughed and Daniel felt himself smiling at the thought of Hunter diving out windows as husbands showed up unexpectedly. "Didn't you ever think of hooking up with women who were NOT already attached?" Hunter gave him an incredulous look "Where would be the fun in that lad?" That got all three of them laughing and lightened the mood considerably. "So where are we going exactly Hunter?" Hunter waved his hand at the windshield "Headin to Willow's grove as ye requested Daniel and tis a good place to go too, there's a gate there that we can visit and see if tis still operational." Lauren leaned between the seats to join the conversation 'You mean a gate like....a portal or something?" Daniel jerks his head to look at Lauren in disbelief then joins her in staring at Hunter. Hunter cleared his throat, "Well ye need to talk to ye mum first and get straight what happened tween her and yer Da. Then it might be wise for us to get further away from Rue and her spells until we can find a way to break the spell and to top it off we can speak to those that created the magic that binds ye to her." Daniel had to admit that did make a lot of sense and he really did want to hear from his mother what happened with his father whether his father was the good seed Hunter thought he was or the rapist his mother had let him believe in for so long. Lauren perhaps sensing this was a private conversation between Hunter and Daniel now sat back and pulled her Ipod out of one of her bags and put her ear buds in, turning the music up and giving the guys a measure of privacy.

Hunter glanced over the seat and was reassured that Lauren was no longer listening, "Have ye thought of..." Indicates Lauren with a jerk of his head "What are ye gonna do with her, ye can't keep draggin her around with ye, she's free now though I doubt she realizes it, Rue will probably not chase her down if she parts from ye." Daniel glanced into the backseat "I really had not given it much thought; I was just trying to get us both away from Rue....guess I better talk to her soon and find out what she wants to do." Hunter started to give some advice then closed his mouth and let it be. When they stopped for bathroom breaks at the next rest stop, Daniel asked Lauren to go for a walk with him. Lauren was nervous as she walked beside Daniel, she knew it was irrational and was probably a rebound emotion in response to finding out about Trevor and Shannon but she felt attracted to Daniel. Daniel saw her glance at him and flush and wondered just what was going through her mind right now, she seemed like a sweet girl but...not really the type he usually found himself with, he was usually more taken by girls like Hecate. Thinking of Hecate caused him to flinch at the memory of everything that had happened lately. "Lauren I just wanted to ....thank you, if you had not figured out the limitations on the barrier we would still be stuck in that house and..." Lauren turned to him and seemed to be listening intently. "I mean, you do realize that you are free now and Rue probably doesn't even know you exist...you could go anywhere, you probably have people waiting and worrying about you." Lauren's thoughts flashed to Trevor, her mom and yes even Shannon but no, she really did not want to contact them right now, and Daniel needed her whether he knew it or not and maybe, he is what she needed too.

"I don't have anyone that is going to miss me for awhile and I would rather see this whole thing through to the end first, besides you can never have enough friends' right?" Daniel started to answer in the negative, to tell her to go while she still could but something in him caused him to smile and he took her hand and led her back towards Hunter.

Rue sighed as the masseuse pressed another tension knot free and started working back down her back again, beside her Kate was making equally appreciative noises as tension flowed from them both. "We need to do this more often Kate, I feel so much more relaxed..." she hissed as a stubborn knot suddenly released under her masseuses expert hands. Kate's masseuse was a woman and by the smiles flitting back and forth between them, Kate was probably going to be indisposed for a while. Rue rolled her eyes and turned away from Kate's flirting and concentrated on what she was going to need to reclaim her slave....she smiled as that thought drifted through her mind like a caress. Recapturing her sex slave...and making him worship her for as long as she chose. When her hour was up Rue wrapped her sheet more tightly about her and went into the dressing room to put her clothes back on and leaving Kate talking in hushed tones to the female masseuse. Rue got dressed and when she walked through the massage room Kate and her masseuse were nowhere to be found. Rue was not sure when Kate came in that night but she was in the second bed when Rue woke up. Rue again called for a limo to take them to the airport and they were able to take Angelique's jet. It took ten hours to fly from Salem to Bacau Moldova. The airport was noisy and crowded with people; Rue went to the visitor's center and hired an interpreter to follow them around for the next four days.

The interpreter was a short balding man by the name of Dan who made a great public exclamation of happiness that American Esoteric Professor Rue Bishop would honor him by securing his services while she traveled in his beautiful country. Rue took the homage in stride as if she was used to such treatment. While driving to Varsa Estate (formerly Angelique's Romanian home, they passed a field with several old wooden travel wagons in a half-circle. The wagons apparently belonged to a clan of gypsies and a crowd had already gathered and were clapping and laughing as the gypsies danced and performed various entertainments for their adoring visitors. Feeling the sudden need for entertainment Rue told the driver to pull over and Rue, Kate and Dan crossed the field to join the crowd. Several of the younger Gypsy women wore the expected bright colored peasant blouses and skirts. The older women wore drab earth colors and sat draped in dark shawls near the fire or talked quietly to visitors who had wandered away from the crowd to seek them out. The men were mostly older with a younger men scattered about and all of them playing a variety of instruments. As Rue watched the women dance, a young man of about 15 years suddenly cart wheeled over to her and ended in a theatrical bow before her. Dan stepped forward and listened to what the young man was saying to her and then turned to translate to her "His name is Artur and he is asking if it hurt when you fell to earth Professor." Dan rolled his eyes to show how he felt about the teen's attempt at flirtation. "Rue turned to the young man and smiled beatifically at him "Thank you very much for the compliment, how is it a young man of your age is so proficient at flattery?" Dan smirked as he translated her words to Artur. Artur smiled and lowered his voice, leaning in towards Rue; Dan's response was immediately loud and scathing. Rue gave Dan a startled look "My heavens what did he say?" Dan continued to glare at Artur who had pasted a mocking smile on his face as he waited for Dan to translate his words to Rue. "Nothing fit for your ears Professor; he is an impudent child with no manners!" Rue chuckled and touched Dan's arm to regain his attention "I would like to judge for myself if I might...please tell me what he said." Dan sighed "He said that his people are born knowing the art of love and he is especially adept at it." Rue turned her smile back on Artur "I am enjoying our conversation Artur; I would like very much to invite your family to share my evening meal at my estate." Dan translated to Artur and for a moment Artur looked uncertain then spoke rapidly to Dan and ran off to a nearby wagon where an attractive long-haired man sat watching them. Strange that she did not notice him there before. Artur spoke to the man and gestured at Rue and her entourage, the man stood and placed the piece of wood he had been whittling on the wagon step and stuck his knife into his belt before approaching Rue. The man approached them and stepped close to Rue, Dan started to speak to him in his own language and the man held up his hand while keeping his eyes on Rue. In heavily accented English he spoke to her, long dark hair falling forward over one eye until he tucked it behind an ear. "Artur says you have invited the family to dine with you at your estate is this so?" Rue nodded and felt herself reacting to the dark gaze, she felt flushed. "It is so...and you are?" The man flashed a very white smile and took her hand into his placing soft lips against the back "I am Alexi and I am the Rom Barra of this family." Dan translated Rom Barra loosely meant the leader. Alexi nodded in thanks to Dan and let rue know that his family gratefully accepted her invitation. Dropping her hand, Alexi turned and walked towards the crowd and thanked them all for coming as he signaled an end to the festivities. Rue noticed Artur making his way through the crowd with a scarred wooden bowl and where the bowl passed, coins and paper money dropped into it as if into a church collection plate.

The Gypsies promised to arrive at her estate no later than sunset and Rue and her entourage departed. The estate came with a crew of twenty highly trained servants, which was a skeleton crew for an estate as large as Varsa. As soon as Rue had Dan relay her instructions to the staff in regards to her dinner guests, the staff went into a frenzy of activity with out being told what to do. The gypsies arrived right on time and parked their wagons or 'Vardo' in the circular courtyard, the horses were unhitched and put into pasture while their owners dined. Dinner consisted of several courses of food that Rue could barely recognize but which the gypsies looked upon with great admiration. Vegetable stews, fish with their eyes still staring at the diners, round pastries filled with cheese and potatoes and spicy lamb kabobs. Dessert was more pastries and fruit served with a sour cream that left an odd taste in Rue's mouth. The gypsies all seemed to be enjoying themselves thoroughly; Alexi even sat next to Rue and whispered admiration of her great beauty and grace into her ear. A sudden thought occurred to Rue and she leaned over to whisper an invitation to stay the night into Alexi's ear. Alexi beamed but then loudly proclaimed that he could not possibly sleep in such opulence while his family slept in drafty Vardos. Rue taking the hint extended her invitation to the entire family and watched the staff depart to prepare rooms. Her invitation was met with toasts and cheers from the rest of the clan. Across the table Alexi's brother Gregori was whispering in similar fashion into Kate's ear with less success than his brother. Kate was discreetly rolling her eyes at Gregori's continued attention. Alexi laughed at Gregori's less than victorious seduction of Kate and caused his brother's face to turn a dark red. Rue leaned close to Kate and had a tense and whispered conversation and suddenly Kate responded warmly to Gregori, playing with his curly hair and squeezing his thigh under the table. Both brothers toasted across the table as they threw their arms possessively around the women at their sides.

When dinner had been cleared away, several of the gypsies went to stable the horses for the night and bring in anything that might be needed from the wagons. Some of the elders stated that the estate had a bad feel to it and chose to sleep in the wagons instead of in a room. Alexi cut himself off from the Tuica (also known as Romanian white Lightning) after dinner and switched to tea instead. When Rue questioned him about it, Alexi gave her a rakish grin and respond that he did not want to be too drunk to enjoy tonight. Gregori by contrast kept drinking glass after glass of the strong drink and became more and more aggressive in his heavy handed pawing of Kate. Finally, Alexi stood up and ordered Gregori to go for a walk and clear his head before he dishonored his family. At first Rue thought, Gregori was going to start a fight, but then amazingly enough he laughed and walked out to cool down. Kate thanked him and announced she was going to follow the others and go to bed. Alexi rose from his seat and bowed at the waist before wishing Kate a pleasant night. Rue watched Kate ascend the stairs then faked a yawn and announced with a grin that she was quite ready to go to bed herself. Alexi offered his arm as he escorted her upstairs to the master bedroom. Rue had forgotten Angelique's love for brocade fabrics; the master bedroom was completely decorated in blue brocade fabrics in various shades. The furniture was of heavy dark colored wood in an older medieval style, Rue gestured for Alexi to make himself at home and she went into the adjoining bathroom to 'freshen up'.

Rue smiled at her reflection as she slipped out of her traveling gown and slipped into a red silk merry widow with garters and thigh high silk stockings. Stepping out of the bathroom, she noticed that Alexi had lit the scented candles displayed in flower shaped crystal bowls around the room. The scent coming off the candles was...different as if something had been added to the flames. Alexi recaptured her attention as he shifted his weight, he stood in the middle of the room wearing the same tight black leather pants that had been distracting her at dinner but his white shirt was now unbuttoned to the waist. Rue felt slightly lightheaded and wondered if it was whatever Alexi had added to the candles having an effect on her, she smiled at the expanse of washboard abs and sexy bare chest revealed by his open shirt. Alexi once again bowed at the waist and gave her that rakish half grin as his long dark hair fell forward obscuring the right side of his face. Rue walked forward and ran his silky hair between her fingers as she tucked the hair behind his ear. "Alexi may I have a lock of your beautiful hair please?" Alexi looked confused for a moment then nodded and grabbing a wick trimmer from beside the bed, he clipped a lock of hair and placed the hair in her hand. Rue stood on tiptoe and kissed his nose then walked directly over to the window where four red silk dolls sat behind the lace curtains. Rue lifts up one of the red silk dolls from its resting places and tucks the lock of hair into the pouch sewn on the front and begins chanting the spell of compulsion and control.

Alexi hears her start chanting and his eyes go wide, slowly he turns and makes for the door, his hand touches the door just as the spell hits him in mid step and causes him to stumble to a halt. Rage flares in his eyes as he realizes he no longer has control over his body, against his will his body turns back towards Rue. Rue flashes a gloating smile and hugs herself in glee "now Alexi do not be angry, I could not take the chance that you might disappoint me, I do so hate to be disappointed...." Seeing the intense anger shining bright in his eyes she pouts and walks up to him, her fingers reaching up to caress his chest through the open shirt. "Now dear Alexi, I will make you the same promise that I made all the others...if you please me I'll let you live." Turning she goes over to where several of her bags and been placed carefully against the wall and pulls out the black tourmaline and positions it on the table next to the bed. Rue looks down into the candle and sees herbs burning next to the wick "What are the herbs Alexi?" Alex struggles not to answer then replies through gritted teeth "Special herbs grown by my people to enhance passion and physical sensations." Rue smiles at him as his body shakes with the effort to throw off whatever spell is holding him. "You are strong I'll give you that, but you will not escape the spell that is even now wrapping you tightly in its coils....you willingly gave me a lock of your hair and as a gypsy you should know better shouldn't you?" Rue giggles at the look of realization on Alexi's face. Rue sees the look in Alexi's eyes shift right before his body relaxes and he gives her a sexy smile "release me from the spell love and I swear I will give you more orgasms than any man has ever given you. On top of it I will swear that my people will not hunt you down and skin you alive for the insult of be-spelling a son of the Rom." Rue's eyes showed uncertainty for a moment and maybe even a trace of fear but her arrogance quickly won out. "You will not speak to me of threats again Alexi, you will undress yourself and then you will undress me and we will make love until I decide I am sated." Alexi smiled and approached her and taking her hand he lifts it to his lips and places them on the back of her hand "I'd rather die you fat hideous troll!" Rue gasped and stepped back in surprise then swung her hand and slapped Alexi enough to snap his head around. Rue started chanting again and suddenly Alexi was completely frozen in place. Rue gave him a mocking smile and shoved him backwards onto the bed. Alexi dropped backwards, as inflexible as a statue with his legs sticking straight out from the bed. Rue went to the large oak wardrobe with the runes carved around the edges and threw the doors open revealing a variety of mortar and pestles, dried herbs, knives, books and other unrecognizable objects. Rue took a dusty hide bound tome and a black stone dagger from the shelf and brought them over to the bed and laid them next to Alexi's prone form.

Rue flipped the book open and paged through it until she found the entry she was looking for and in an absent-minded fashion as she ripped Alexi's shirt open and traced lines in charcoal on his chest she informed him "remember you could have prevented this if you had just obeyed me Alexi." She finished the lines and slid off the bed and walked across the room to the window again and turned on the radio, flipping through stations until she found a local music station playing folk songs then smiling she returned to the bed and straddled Alexi's waist. "Poor poor Alexi, you will not scream or be able to make any noise at all but you will want to before I am through." Taking up the blade stone bladed dagger, Rue started carving the charcoal lines deep into Alexi's chest and she was right for many hours he wanted to cry out and fight at the pain.

Rue washed the blood off her hands and went to go check on Kate, as she stopped by the door she heard a muffled thumping and a whimper. Slowly she opened the door and peeked through the door and saw Gregori's naked backside as he thrust and cursed in Romani at what she assumed was Kate although she could not see her from this angle. Closing the door again she went back to her room and flipped through the tome again until she found another needed entry. Alexi was still unconscious which meant she had plenty of time to exact retribution on his brother before she had to deal with him. Taking what she needed from the cupboard, Rue returned to Kate's room and laughed at the look of surprise on Gregori's face as he jumped naked off the bed and pulled a blanket to cover his groin. Kate lay on the bed tied wrist and ankles, her head turned towards the window and her eyes shut tightly. Rue's eyes smoldered "You dare to defile what my servant?" Dropping her armload of ingredients she grabs a small alabaster angel from the bedside table and launches it at him, as luck would have it she caught him between the eyes and he dropped like a stone. Smiling to herself she walked over to stand above him and chanted the same paralyzing spell that his brother was currently held by and then untied Kate. Kate sat up, her eyes were red and swollen, and she looked with nervous eyes at where Gregori lay on the floor. Rue took a handkerchief from the bedside drawer and dabbed it in the filled washbasin. Gently she wiped the damp cloth across Kate's face and smoothed her hair from her face. "You and I are going to perform great magic tonight Kate my sweet and together we will punish this barbarian for his affront to your dignity." Kate stared with eyes suddenly filled with hope Kate pressed trembling lips to Rue's lips and felt Rue start to respond in kind before pulling away and slipping off the bed to collect the ingredients she had dropped. Propping the book open on the table, she dragged Gregori into the center of the room and stripped the rug out of the way. Carefully she drew the containment circle around Gregori's body and carved specific runes into his chest, not the ones his brother now wore for these were runes of summoning.

Kate watched Rue scampering about the room in her lingerie and adding runes here and there and running back to the old book propped on the table to check accuracy. Then grabbing Kate's had she brought her over to the circle and gave her the words to chant. Chanting together the room filled with a static electric feeling that caused the hair on their arms to stand on end. Then just as quickly a cold fog seemed to appear from nowhere, obscuring the floor and causing the temperature of the room to drop several degrees. Rue looked startled as her breath fogged before her, Gregori's body had gone blue with the cold within the circle, and suddenly his body bounced on the floor as if he were silently coughing though his eyes remained closed. Twice more the Gregori jumped before a trickle of blood appeared on his bare chest, the trickle became a river pooling on the floor and then a gaping hole appeared in his chest. A long, thin, ash colored hand reached up through the hole and was followed by a head and then a body. A short gray and black mottled creature with black eyes stood in the circle beside Gregori's corpse and looked out at Rue and Kate with a small smile on its lips. The creature was bald and completely hairless with small round ears and thin lips, it was humanoid in appearance but definitely not human. The eyes staring at Rue and Kate were large and round and completely black, they almost drew you in like pools of dark eternity, and Rue tore her eyes away from his." "Who is your master and whom do you serve creature?" The creature grinned at her revealing shark like teeth as it tested the boundaries then finding them adequate bowed to her and in a hiss replied "Thou art my master and thy whims I do serve." Rue laughed and clapped her hands, "It worked Kate, and we have a seeker to find Daniel!" Kate turned horrified eyes on Rue "No Rue, this is too far, send it back where it came from, do not go down this path....you summoned a fucking demon!" Rue made a face and rolled her eyes "Of course I summoned a demon, I never lose what is mine and now I will send it after Daniel." Turning back to the circle she traced runes in the air that glowed with a dark light, "You will find for me Daniel Warwick, he whom I have shared my body with and you will bring him to me unharmed....do you obey me in this?" The creature again tested the barriers before answering "This will I do for thee oh master, have I leave to begin?" Rue nodded and released the floating runes and watched

them be absorbed by the dark creature before it sunk through the floor and vanished with

the cold fog.

   The car ride was once again tense as they got back on the road headed to Willow's

Grove. Wanting to break the ice and more than a little curious about Hunter, Daniel

turned in his seat and asked "So how do you know my father Hunter?" Hunter cocked his

eyebrow at Lauren and Daniel shook his head "I don't care if she knows, she has stuck by

me this far." Hunter nodded before continuing "Aelon was a good seed even back when I

first met him, there are them who are noble of birth but not of spirit and treat lesser Fae as

pests unless they are needed. Aelon was never that type." Hunter waited for that to sink in

and watched Daniel's glance towards him become a little more cautious "So you would

be considered a 'lesser Fae'?" Hunter laughed and nodded "I be a ... 'Gremlin' is a close

enough term, though I am also a 'seeker of lost things' guess you could say." Daniel

turned to look back out the window and watched a sign for Willow's Grove 25 miles.

Soon he would be standing on his mom's front porch and asking her to relive something

he was never brave enough to ask her about growing up. Silently Daniel prayed that

Hunter was wrong about his father's character, better Hunter be wrong about what his

father was capable of than Daniel find out his mother had lied to him all these years and

allowed him to harbor hate in his heart for an innocent man. Lauren wisely kept silent in

the backseat and plugged into her Ipod and gave the guys what little privacy she could

give considering they were sharing a vehicle. Hunter argued they should go directly to

the gate and see how they could get the cuff off him. Daniel argued he wanted to go get this conversation with his mom over with. When Hunter started to argue again for going to the Gate first, Daniel held his hand up to interrupt. Daniel explained that going through the gate was going to put them Underhill. True Underhill was a big place but it was also the last place Hunter had seen Aelon, if Daniel is going to chance meeting his father he wanted to have all his facts straight first which meant speaking to his mom and getting the full story. Hunter started to argue, then bowed to Daniel's logic and drove across town to Daniel's mom's house. Hunter pulled up in front of a cute blue Tudor style house with white trim and a wraparound porch. The mailbox was an exact replica of the house itself in miniature; the yard was trimmed and geometrically laid out with raised flowerbeds containing seasonal flowers in full brightly colored bloom. Hunter and Lauren both stared at the house and silently wondered if Martha Stewart was going to walk out the front door. Daniel stared at the house for a second then asked them both to stay in the car while he went to talk to his mom. Hunter and Lauren both agreed enthusiastically, neither wanted to be witness to what would probably be an explosive situation. Daniel stepped out of the car and felt like he was dragging a huge weight behind him as he walked up the tiled walkway and stopped at the whitewashed front door. Daniel took a deep breath and raised the brass knocker to knock twice then wiped palms gone suddenly damp on the legs of his jeans.

Arlene was smiling brightly as she answered the door; she was half expecting it to be one of her neighbors stopping by unannounced. The minute she saw her son on the porch, she knew something was wrong and her smile lost some of its intensity. "Daniel sweetheart, I didn't even know you were in town." Daniel ducked his head in apology and couldn't help noticing his mom looked years younger with her professionally whitened teeth and her long blonde hair sheared off into a fashionable bob. "I really needed to talk to you mom, its kind of important, may I come in?" Arlene wrinkled her nose as she looked at her unkempt son and sighed as if his being here was a huge inconvenience, finally she nodded and stepped back to let him in "you just make sure you wipe your feet good, I just had the carpets shampooed." Daniel bit back a retort and wiped his feet over and over until she nodded that he had done a good enough job. Following his mother down the hall to the living room, he noticed she had once again changed the decor to reflect the change in local fashion. Gone were the colorful geodes she had once displayed on shelves along the wall, the wallpaper was now a brightly colored floral pattern that matched the curtains and upholstery fabric making you feel like you were standing in the middle of a garden in full bloom. "So Tom is not home right now?" Daniel had not seen his stepfather in years, not since he had left home anyway. Arlene waved her hand back at him "No he is at work, which is where you should be." Daniel watched his mom perch on the edge of the floral settee as if afraid to wrinkle her white linen pants and lavender sweater set. Daniel sat on the couch across from her feeling grungy in his pristine surroundings. It was almost as if the woman who had raised him, held him when he was sick and taught him his love of cooking had been disappeared and left behind this Stepford wife/Martha Stewart clone. Daniel sighed "Mom...I "Daniel was stopped mid-sentence by his mom's raised hand. "Stop right there...calling me mom was fine when you were a child, but we are both adults now and I insist you respect me as a person and call me Lena." Daniel's jaw dropped open in surprise "but your name is Arlene, not Lena." Daniel watched her pluck invisible lint from her linen pants and flick it to the floor as she avoided his eyes. "Arlene sounds so old fashioned and country and as I am neither, I prefer to be called Lena now and I insist if we are to converse that you call me by that name."

Again Daniel was left stunned and took a moment to resign himself to the fact that there was no trace of "mom" left and that Lena Warwick was the woman who had replaced the mother he had been looking forward to seeing again. Nodding in acknowledgment of her insistence that he call her 'Lena' he started again "Lena...I need to ask what happened the night of April 18th 1984?" Lena's eyes shot sparks at him as she turned a furious gaze on him "What right do you have to ask me about that night, I have put that night behind me and am no longer that girl!" Daniel threw himself to his feet "What right? I was conceived on that night by a union between you and Aelon Dryearghym, I am your SON!" Lena's face lost all color and a hand sneaked up to her throat at the sound of the name she had never thought to hear again in her lifetime. Trembling she wet lips gone suddenly dry and asked "H...How do you know that name?" Daniel shoved his hands in his pockets and tried to fight the rising anger in himself, the only way his mother would know that name was if she knew the name of her 'attacker'. Closing his eyes he counted to ten before looking up at the pale woman before him. "you lied to me all these years, you were never attacked, and you let me feel nothing but hate for the man who fathered me." Lena pushed herself to her feet and gracefully staggered to the side bar and poured herself a large brandy. "Do not call him a man, a man would not have left the woman who loved him alone and crying while carrying his child and never come back to check on them." Daniel sighed and looked at his feet "I need to know what happened that night m....Lena...please." Lena turned with her glass in her upraised hand as if posing for a picture as she thought about what to tell him, then with a sigh she returned to perching on the edge of the settee and waived him back to his seat as well. "It was a long time ago but, I still remember how excited I was when I found that small cave in the field where my company was excavating." She glanced up at Daniel then away again "we were looking for a rare form of Amorite crystal that had been discovered in the area." Lena took several deep drinks from her brandy before continuing "I was so excited about finding a cave where there should not have been one at all, I told no one about it and returned that very night to explore it on my own and that is where I met Aelon." Taking a deep breath and another drink she avoided looking at Daniel now as if she would lose her courage to continue if she looked at him. Aelon had been camping in the cave and I had surprised him when I broke through the north wall, he helped me find more of the Amorite crystals but really that was just an excuse for us to be together." Daniel barely breathed so caught up in the story he was afraid to move lest he break the spell. "Aelon was so very handsome and seemed to be just as taken with me as I was with him and then that night in April we finally...." She cleared her throat as if suddenly remembering who she was talking to and looked over to where Daniel was staring at her avidly "That was the night I was conceived, not by some faceless stranger that happened to attack and rape my mother but by a man you were in love with." Lena jumped to her feet and clenched her hand around the now empty glass "He is NOT a man, if he were any kind of decent man he would have STAYED, he would have defied his queen's orders to return and STAYED!" Lena's eyes got huge as if she had said to much and with trembling legs she sat back down, one hand pressed against her lips. Daniel nodded going pale as if all his worst fears had been confirmed, his mother had chosen to nurture hate in the heart of her son for the man who had conceived him because of the sting of rejection.

Daniel slowly walked toward the door feeling the weight of the world on his shoulders and wanting nothing more than to be out of this sham of a house and away from this selfish woman who had replaced the mother he loved. He heard her shriek behind him "Daniel it doesn't matter he was not even human for God's sake!" Daniel paused in the doorway and looked back at 'Lena' with her fashionable hair and clothes and surrounded by her fashionable furnishings "So what the hell does that make me then?" Turning he closed the door and walked back to the car as his world crumbled around him.

Chapter five

Daniel's heart felt like a stone in his chest as he walked back towards the car, the setting sun casting strange shadows across the tiled path as he avoided looking at the car and the faces of his friends. A noise slowly started registering, he glanced at the car and saw Hunter and Lauren mouthing words he could not hear and gesturing furiously for him to get in the car. Daniel came to a stop and gave them a confused look; Hunter rolled the window down and pointed at the sky yelling "I'd be getting in the car now if I were ye!" Daniel followed Hunter's finger and saw what looked like an emaciated man encased in a small black cloud with dead black eyes swooping towards him like a bird of prey. Daniel let out a yell and charged the last yard to the car and slid in just as Hunter threw the door open. Daniel quickly slammed the door closed behind him and the entire car rocked if something had hit it broadside. Hunter gunned the gas and sent the car peeling out spewing gravel and dirt into 'Lena's yard. Whatever it was stayed above them making diving runs at the car but every time it tried to catch hold of the call, Hunter would wrench the wheel left and right and throw it aloft again. Daniel and Lauren kept their faces pressed to their windows trying to keep the creature in sight and calling out directions "Its dropping on the right!" or "Here it comes on your side Hunter!" Hunter suddenly made a decision and spun the car 180 degrees heading back the way they had come. Daniel pulled his face away from the window and gave Hunter an incredulous look "are you nuts...we can't go back to my mom's there is no way she could handle this!" Hunter Snorted "I'll no be taking ye back there again lad, I'm leading this thing to the cavalry...if it wants ye, it can follow ye Underhill and take ye from my brethren." The turn off for the Gate was coming up fast and once again Hunter wrenched the wheel hard and left their stomachs behind as they drifted sideways onto the rutted dirt road and Daniel felt the car shake in protest before straightening out. The bouncing and jouncing the car was doing was doing nothing to improve their ability to keep the creature in sight as both he and Lauren kept hitting their heads on the glass with every rut they hit. Suddenly there was a screech of something dragging on the metal and Daniel realized the creature had finally managed to latch onto the roof. Hunter wrenched the car from side to side but was unable to shake the creature loose. Suddenly there was a squeal of metal and the wind in the car increased. Daniel's head jerked up and he noticed a fist sized hole through which he could see the sky had been torn in the roof. The creature's face suddenly pressed against the hole, dead black eyes boring into Daniel's. The black eyes drew him in and took hold of him in much the same way Rue's spells had. From far away he heard Hunter screaming at him to look away. Then the world seemed to explode, his vision going black yet he could still hear a shriek from the creature and the screech of tortured metal, Lauren and Hunter screaming....then nothing

Rue was not sure how she was going to explain the body to the servants; she stood at the door with a blade behind her back and pulled the braided rope that would summon servants from downstairs. It was not as she had expected, a maid that answered but Nikolai the estate's Majordomo. Angelique had introduced Nikolai as her Majordomo when they had first come here but Rue had gotten the impression they had been much more once. Nikolai placed his hand over his heart and bowed to her as she opened the door. "There has been an accident and I have need of a....things disposed of discreetly." Nikolai nodded and gestured for her to step back into the room, Rue slipped the knife further behind her back and tightened her grip on the handle as she stepped back to let him in. When Nikolai stepped into the room and saw the body he tsked and shook his head but did not seem surprised at all. "Mistress Angelique had many such 'accidents' when she first started her studies here, while she was in residence there were oft times I was called in the night to 'take care of things discreetly'." Rue stared at him and he flicked his fingers in her direction, "Have no fear this will be taken care of without his family even realizing what has happened." Rue gave him another incredulous look and Nikolai burst into laughter and placed his fingers on his lips as if to hide his mirth. "You must understand Mistress, many such as yourself have resided in these halls and we servants come from generations of those who served their masters and mistresses in all capacities Arcane and Esoteric as well." Rue looked doubtful "So you can really get rid of everything?" Nikolai nodded and bowed again to her deferentially "most assuredly Mistress." Nikolai stepped past her and pulled the rope again and two maids showed up as if by magic. Rue listened to him give instructions for their mistresses to be cleaned and gowned and brought refreshments and for the maids to have the room stripped and cleaned. The maids curtsied and quickly springing into action, Rue allowed herself to be cleaned and wrapped in a quilted robe before a roaring fire with a sense of bemusement. Beside her Kate had a bewildered expression on her face as if waiting to wake up from a dream. Rue looked over at Kate "If we do not want the Gypsies to question why Gregori ands Alexi will not be leaving with them, we must make it appear that you and I are enjoying their sexual prowess. Then we can have Nikolai inform them that the men will be following when they are finished with us." Rue laughed at that thought and took a few sips from her steaming cup of tea "That means of course that once the rooms have been cleaned we will need to stay closeted in our rooms until the Gypsies have been fed and have left. Rue sat staring into the flames as plans tumbled about in her head. Kate on the other hand found herself staring at Rue and wondering not for the first time and probably not for the last where the woman she loved had gone to.

A maid came in and stood within sight of Rue and curtsied, her eyes took in Kate's untouched refreshments and Rue's half-devoured plate and she sniffed as if slightly insulted that neither Mistress had finished what was brought to them. Rue was glad that the servants here all spoke and understood English, which brought another thought to mind. "Has my interpreter Dan come down yet?' The maid curtsied again before answering "I am afraid Mistress that the Gypsies have in some way offended Mr. Dan and he has left your employment and has asked that I would let you know that he did." Rue nodded to herself that was one complication that had fixed itself. "The man in my bedroom, is he awake yet?" The maid nodded and curtsied again, Rue smiled and patted Kate's hand as she rose "Do not forget to go straight to your room and stay out of sight Kate." Rue swept out of the room with the maid following and leaving Kate staring into the flames, her troubled thoughts tumbling about in her head. Rue returned to her room to find someone had sat Alexi up in a chair, obviously so he would not be in the way as they stripped and changed the bed linens. Alexi's eyes burned with hate as Rue entered the room; smiling at him she closed the door behind her and swayed seductively as she approached him. "If you had just done what you were told Alexi, you would not be in the situation you are in now." Rue pulled the edges of his shirt wide to admire her handiwork "This is a more permanent leash than what I gave Daniel, I may have to do the same thing to him once I get him back." Alexi had no idea who 'Daniel' was but if he had managed to slip the noose then maybe there was hope for Alexi to do so. Rue snapped her fingers in front of his eyes to recapture his drifting attention. "Clearly you have no idea how much power I hold over you Alexi, but you are about to find out that you are now my puppet." Rue giggled at her own joke.

Rue straddled his lap and caressed his face, his chest, traced the lines she had carved into him, she knew how very painful it was but the thought of his helplessness aroused her. Looking deep into his eyes she saw her own very slow and painful death if ever he got free of her. Invoking the compulsion, she felt him harden beneath her and laughed at the sudden look of comprehension on his face "That's right Alexi, I OWN you." Rue gave a creepy giggle and hugged herself "Daniel found out I could make him do whatever I want and so will you, and if you please me well enough I may make you the first of my harem." Rue paced in front of him touching her neck, sliding her hand down to her breasts, "I could have as many exotic lovers as I want, all of them completely obedient to my every whim and when they displease me I'll kill them and use their death energy to capture my next 'pet'." Alexi's mind screamed in horror at what she was describing, innocent men enslaved to her desire, not given the choice but forced to obey. He tuned back in to what Rue was saying "None of you will ever be able to leave me or hurt me or tell me I am not good enough..." A shadow crossed Rue's face as if she were remembering an unpleasant event. Then glancing at Alexi, the shadow cleared and she grinned at him "Go to the bed Alexi!" Alexi tried to fight the compulsion but as strong as his will was he was only able to slow his progress so he lurched towards the bed instead of simply walking to it. Rue looked impressed that he was even able to do that much. Rue laughed as he fought her every command but could not shrug off her spell even as she ordered him to undress himself and stand before her nude and aroused. Walking around him she marveled at the toned muscles and the 'size' of him "Yes I think it will be awhile before I tire of you my handsome Gypsy." Rue toyed with his long dark hair a moment before commanding him to lie back on the bed. Alexi lay on the bed and closed his eyes as Rue quickly disrobed and climbed atop him, The sound of Rue's laughter as she realized how much he hated his helplessness left a bitter taste in his mouth. Rue took his hands and brought them up to cup her breasts as she rode him. Alexi tried to clench his fists, wanting to cause her pain but his hands merely twitched and caused her to chuckle.

"I'll admit you have a lot of fire Alexi and it is going to be extremely pleasurable breaking you; you will learn that I always get what I want." If the hate in Alexi's eyes as he opened them had been physical, Rue would have been in exquisite agony right then. Alexi grit his teeth and once again closed his eyes and allowed Rue to use his body to pleasure herself. He silently released a sigh of relief as she finally climbed off him and allowed his body to relax. Alexi's body felt bruised as she finally allowed him to regain control of his body. Alexi learned quickly he was not able to touch a weapon and when his hands froze mere inches from Rue's throat he realized he could not harm her with bare hands either. Rue found his constant attempts to break her control amusing, even knowing that she was laughing at him, he refused to simply accept his enslavement and stop trying. When Kate finally showed up in the room he learned that his family had left believing that he and Gregori were still closeted away with Rue and Kate having sex.

Alexi stared at Kate until she looked in his direction and with a dangerous glint in his eyes spoke to her "Where is my brother Gregori?" Kate glanced at Rue with a guilty expression and Alexi knew what her answer would be. Rue turned and smiled at him "Really Alexi, why ask a question you already know the answer to...your brother was a stupid rutting brute and about as useful as a dog in heat." Alexi pulled himself to his feet and spat at Rue "You stupid, filthy whore, do you have any idea what evil you have brought upon your own head by slaying the Son of a Rom?" Rue jumped up and slapped Alexi across the face with all her strength. Alexi's head snapped back and once again her jeweled rings had cut his face. "You will not speak to me like that again Alexi or I will take your talented tongue from your mouth ...are we clear?" Alexi gave a short nod and slowly sat down in a nearby chair, his hands clenched on the thin wooden armrests. He continued to glare at Rue until Kate rolled her shoulders clearly uncomfortable with pretending he was not there. Kate Leaned forward to whisper to Rue "do we have to speak in front of him? He is glaring at us." Rue turned a cool look on Alexi "Alexi close your eyes." Alexi's eyes snapped shut and he clenched his jaw at how easily his body responded to her commands. Kate glanced at where Alexi sat, you could almost imagine he had fallen asleep if you ignored how stiffly he held himself. Turning back to Rue, "so the creature you summoned from the Gypsies' body ...Kate was interrupted by the sound of snapping wood. Both women's heads whipped towards Alexi who sat as before but the right chair arm was no longer attached to the seat. The chair now showed a clean break that separated it from the rest of the chair; Alexi lowered the arm to his lap. Kate gestured at the chair to Rue as if to say 'look what he did' then stood and headed for the door and gestured silently for rue to follow. Rue stood and smoothed her skirt and briefly thought about slapping Alexi again for the intrusion, then followed Kate out of the room. When they entered Kate's room Rue immediately noticed all the linens and rugs had been replaced and the room smelled like bleach and lavender.

Kate sat on the end of the bed looking frustrated "Why would you do that to him Rue...you had to know he was going to react negatively when he heard about his brother." Rue laughed "Kate you are thinking too much of him, you did the same Daniel Kate." Kate started to interrupt and Rue held her hand up "You need to think of them as pets...pets that need to be tamed and broken to my will." Kate stood up with a look of astonishment on her face "Rue you don't mean that, these men are people not pets." Rue smiled indulgently and explained as if to a slow child "Kate they ARE my pets, and there will be many more...I will have a harem of exotic pets." Rue was practically purring as she pictured all the lovers she would ensnare. "Perhaps I will even make a harem for you as well Kate, a room full of exotic lovelies all completely devoted to you Kate, wouldn't that be great?" Kate forced herself to smile and nod even as the bitter taste of bile filled her mouth at what she was hearing. Kate felt her stomach cramp as she finally realized that the Rue she had known and loved was gone and had been replaced by this monster who would enslave innocent men to satisfy her every carnal desire. Rue suggested they get dressed and head downstairs for breakfast. Kate waited until after Rue left, to strip out of the robe and get dressed. Maybe it was past time to start thinking about getting out of here, the thought brought tears to her eyes and made her want to crawl into bed and weep inconsolably. She knew she could not do that though, she had to keep pretending to be happy with the scraps Rue offered. The thought of being on her own again was painful; Rue had been her whole life. Kate had cleaned up Rue's messes, and comforted her after broken hearts and kept her secrets. There HAD to be a way to get HER Rue back, if magic made her this way, maybe magic could change her back. With her spark of hope restored, Kate skipped down to breakfast. The servants were just setting the food on the table plates of Garlic sausages sat next a green leafy vegetable she did not recognize, a huge tureen of some kind of corn based soup sat next to a plate of fried turnips with a creamy paprika sauce and for dessert there was fruit with a sour cream dipping sauce. Rue came down shortly after Kate and after looking at the food turned pale and put a hand on her stomach. Gesturing a servant over she whispered an order for broth and crackers and water. When she noticed Kate looking at her curiously she waved the concern away "Probably just overdoing it, or catching a bug."

The first thing Daniel was aware of was coolness on his forehead and hushed voices speaking in a musical flowing language he could not understand. His eyes were bandaged and he felt very achy all over as if recovering from being sick. The minute he became aware, the voices faltered and he felt something warm pressed against his lips and the musical words were spoken again but this time he got the feeling they were spoken to him. Reaching a hand up to the object pressing against his mouth, he realized it was a bowl or cup and opened his mouth. A salty soup was poured into his mouth and after he swallowed it he felt sleepy again...apparently the soup contained medicine because he fell back asleep almost immediately. The next time he 'awoke' his aches were gone but his body felt very heavy and tired as if he had been sleeping for a while. Daniel was aware that time had passed but had no way of knowing how much. He could hear birds and feel a breeze blowing across him, then the sound of slippered feet approaching the bed and again the bowl was pressed against his lips, when he drank he fell once again into a dreamless sleep. When he woke for what he thought was the third time he heard Hunter's voice close to his ear "Alright lad, ye need to be waking and returning to the land of the living." Daniel tried to open his eyes but the bandages prevented it. He opened his mouth to speak and his voice rasped as if from disuse..."Where...?" Hunter patted his hand "That creature was trying to take control of ye and nearly did, until I came up with the idea to ram the car into the Gate." Hunter laughed "On the down side that little maneuver got me into a mort of trouble." The musical language was spoken around him again although it lost some of its musical quality when spoken with Hunter's harsh voice. "We should be able to remove the bandages now; ye got a mite banged up in the accident." Daniel felt arms helping him sit up in the bed and then he could feel the bandages being unwrapped.

He was told to close his eyes by Hunter and he complied then waited until the bandages had been completely removed before slowly opening his eyes. The room looked like a loft in a cabin; the walls and floor were smooth wood in a reddish hue. The large windows showed the tops of trees, but nothing he recognized for one the leaves were silver colored. He turned towards the other person in the room and his jaw dropped. If beauty could have been collected like water and put into a single vessel, this would be the vessel. The woman was short and willowy with platinum blonde hair that reached past her hips and almond shaped eyes the color of a cloudless sky. She smiled and turned her head to speak to Hunter and Daniel was staring at some ears that tapered to a definite point. Hunter chuckled "That will be enough of that lad, ye stare any harder and Silaya is likely to burst into flames." Daniel quickly dropped his eyes to the floor and noticed forest scenes had been carved into the floor. Hunter spoke to Silaya again and Daniel realized that listening to Hunter speak in that beautiful language was akin to a lumberjack dancing the ballet, it somehow lost something hearing it in his voice. Daniel slowly got to his feet and Silaya and Hunter automatically moved to either side to bracket him in case he needed assistance. Daniel walked from one end of the room to the other until his legs stopped shaking. Silaya and Hunter paced beside him until he nodded he was sure he could continue on his own. Waving Hunter and Silaya's concerns aside, he kept pacing while he asked the questions crowding his mind. Hunter sat on the bed and waited for what he was sure would be quite a few questions from Daniel "Did Lauren...?" Hunter smiled "Naw she's right as rain, just kept in a different house is all, ye are in the bachelor house and she was taken to the maiden house ye see." Daniel shook his head in confusion "they segregate patients in this hospital?" Hunter laughed "Hardly a hospital lad." Hunter gestured to Silaya who inclined her head to Daniel "This here is Silaya, she is head of her healing order The Order of Belethai and they separate lads from lasses unless they are bonded, it's the rules of her order ye see." Daniel nodded to Silaya; he knew how inflexible rules could be at any establishment. "Sooo we are Underhill I take it?" Hunter nodded and explained "We are in a small outlying bit of the claimed lands, wait until you see a city proper, ye'll think you stepped into a fairy story what with the castles and steeds and such." Daniel was not sure if Hunter was pulling his leg so he remained silent. Silaya spoke in her musical language again and then inclined her head to Daniel and descended a set of stairs that Daniel had not noticed half hidden in the far corner.

Daniel turned towards Hunter with a startled expression "so Silaya is an honest to God elf?" Hunter slapped his hand across his eyes, "Lad you cannot run around calling people 'Elf', there are many types of Fae and quite a few that would take exception to being called 'Elf'." Daniel nodded and filed that away for future reference. "You mentioned getting in trouble for ramming the Gate, trouble from whom?" Hunter sighed "Ye sure do know how to ask the difficult ones don't ye?" Hunter stood and interrupted Daniel's pacing and lead him back to the bed to rest his legs before he overdid it. "All Fae are governed by a court, the Seelie Court what you might call Light Fae, and the Unseelie court, what you may call the Dark Fae." Daniel nodded to show he was following "We are in the domain of the Seelie Court, as such we fall under the rule of the Queen Sadronniel and her consort Lithaldoren. Daniel grabbed a pencil and pad from the bedside table and began writing the names down. Hunter continued after spelling the names for Daniel. "Had we been in the domain of the other side we would have fallen under the rule of the Unseelie King Melcindo'mien and his Queen Mo'readhiel.' hunter shuddered as if the very thought of being ruled by the Unseelie gave him the horrors. "So we got in trouble with the Queen for wrecking the Gate then?" Hunter waggled his hand as if to say kinda sorta. "She be not too happy that is true but we will have the chance to plea our case when we meet with her tomorrow, but there are other things we need to talk about first." Daniel's eyes met Hunter's and he saw Hunter flinch "What things are you talking about?" Hunter dropped his eyes to the floor and pointed to a mirror hanging in a carved wooden frame on the wall. Daniel stood and walked over to the mirror, the minute he looked at his reflection he knew something was wrong. Daniel's eyes had formerly been a bright blue, now they were steel gray as if the color had been leached from them and a thin black line circled his iris. Daniel stared in shock at his reflection, his eyes shifted to meet Hunter's in the mirror. "What happened to my eyes Hunter?!" turning from the mirror, Daniel saw Hunter spread his hands and shrug "we do not know why this happened, it MAY have something to do with the fact that the Daemon creature was somehow connected to ye when we hit the Gate. The Daemon followed us through the Gate but we lost it on this side." Daniel closed his eyes and tried not to think of that 'thing' being loose on this side of the Gate. "You said there are 'things' we need to talk about, what else is there need to know?" Hunter looked at him soberly. "yer father is here...Underhill, I saw him and he looks much the same, cept for a new battle scar or two." Daniel's eyes snapped open again and he ignored Hunter's flinch. "My father is here...has he...does he know?" Hunter was shaking his head "he knows nothing of yer presence here." Daniel's mind was awhirl; he was finally going to meet his father. Hunter walked to the floor to ceiling window and looked out, his eyes drifting over the scenes below. Daniel joined him and saw more of the willowy Fae going about their various tasks. The clearing was large and seemed to be ringed with more of the towering trees with the silver colored broad leaves. There were flashes of light where some of the Fae were enhancing the food plants, there were also some tending large and fat red-splotched cows in a paddock to his left. Off to his right he could see Lauren laughing and dancing with several pale haired Fae in bright colored dresses and wearing flower circlets on their heads. Lauren looked young and carefree and it occurred to him that he had never truly seen Lauren laugh in the entire time he had known her, short as that has been. Turning away from the window, Daniel headed down the stairs and past the feast set up on a king-sized table in what looked to be a huge common room with comfy chairs and low tables scattered about the room and headed out the front door.

Lauren was learning a new dance called a Festival Branle which required several dancers to face each other in a circle and step side to side before leaping and twirling in place as the circle went round and round. Lauren's fellow dancers were named Daisy, Rose, and Lily and they were Flora Sylphs. At first Lauren had thought they had been joking about their names and had laughed, their faces became very angry at that point and she immediately apologized and blamed her lapse in judgment on the recent accident. The Sylphs accepted that excuse and explained to her that as the name implied, Flora Sylphs were responsible for tending all the plants in this part of the claimed lands with the exception of the Royal Gardens. Lauren had smiled and asked since there were 'claimed lands' were there also 'unclaimed lands'? The look of fear and horror on their little faces made her immediately drop the question. The Sylphs were more than happy to go back to dancing with her, and then suddenly they stopped and stared past her. When Lauren turned and saw Hunter and Daniel making their way across the clearing towards her she started to smile in greeting, the smile froze as she stared at Daniel. Daniel's beautiful bright blue eyes had gone the color of dead ashes, a deep black line ringing the iris. Tearing her eyes from Daniel's new eyes, she looked at Hunter "What happened to his eyes...was this from the accident?" Hunter scowled "Why does everyone keep askin me these things, do I look like a healer?" Hunter shrugged as she continued to stare at him "we have no idea what caused it nor any way to reverse it neither." Lauren reached out to touch Daniel's face "I am so very sorry about this Daniel." Daniel stepped back out of her reach and forced a laugh "Looks that bad huh?" Lauren's mouth opened and closed as she tried to find words to comfort him but not be lying at the same time. Daniel waved it off and mumbled something about needing to go for a walk. Lauren started to follow and Hunter grabbed her shoulder in one rough hand "Leave him be lass, he needs to work things out on his own."

Daniel crossed the clearing and even though he knew it was probably not a good idea, he entered the woods and headed towards the sound of running water. He found himself on the banks of a wide, slow moving river and sat with his arms wrapped around his knees breathing in the calm and trying not to think too much on the blow to what little vanity he had. He had always been complimented on his eyes if nothing else and now his eyes made people flinch. He never heard the man come through the brush, but suddenly a Fae in gray green tunic and pants that seemed to blend with whatever he was standing in front of appeared on the other side of the river. The Fae had long Dark hair, so black it almost looked as if it had blue highlights. The eyes that met his across the water were a familiar shade of turquoise blue. A jagged red scar reached from the Fae's hairline down to nearly his chin, the scar came dangerously close to his left eye. Daniel slowly pushed himself to his feet and gave the Fae a friendly wave, the Fae smirked and raised his own hand in greeting. When the Fae man rose from his crouch, Daniel noticed he was much taller than the willowy Fae who lived in the clearing, in fact this guy might top his own 6'4" height by a good couple inches. The Fae was built more along the lines of Ryan Reynolds character in Blade than Daniel's own broad-chested farm boy build. The Fae looked into the river for a moment then began walking across the water just downriver of Daniel. Daniel stared with his mouth open as the Fae stepped lightly onto the shore. "Holy shit that was awesome!" The Fae laughed, not a girly tinkling bells laugh but an honest to goodness hearty laugh that he had not thought to hear from a Fae. Sticking his hand out he introduced himself "Hey there, my name is Daniel Warwick." The Fae inclined his head and clasped forearms with Daniel "my friends call me Hart." Daniel smirked and drew a heart in the air "as in the shape?" Hart shook his head and pointed back across the river and when Daniel turned he saw a tall thin stag lifting its head from drinking out of the river and with a graceful leap, it disappeared into the brush in the same silent manner as Hart had appeared. Daniel glanced back at Hart and smiled "Now I know why they call you that, you gotta teach me them mad ninja skills dude, and the walking across water...dang thought only Jesus the son of God knew that trick." Hart cocked his head for a moment then nodded, "I see, you are a follower of the white robed Christ." Waving Daniel over to the spot her had stepped ashore, Hart pointed down into the river. Daniel came over to see what he was pointing at and noticed a line of flat-topped stones spaced across the river. Daniel shook his head and laughed "Haven't you ever heard the phrase 'a magician never reveals his secrets'?" Hart bowed at the waist "but I am not a mage Sir Daniel." Daniel nodded "Fair enough, but you don't need to call me

Sir, I'm no knight, nor am I nobility, royalty or anything special." Hart nodded albeit a bit skeptically "those are not your natural eyes are they?" Daniel rubbed a hand across his face "Nope just picked them up a bit ago, look I am getting a bit hungry and I happen to know there is a feast back the way I came and I am sure they can afford one more mouth." Hart cocked an eyebrow at him "Why would you feed and befriend a complete stranger, in a land where you are the outsider?" Daniel shrugged "where I come from, hospitality is a sign of respect and you and I have no quarrel and I respect what I have seen of you...plus it never hurts to befriend someone with those mad ninja skills you seem to take for granted." Hart laughed that hearty human laugh again and nodded his agreement and gestured for Daniel to precede him.

The clearing was mostly empty when they came through the trees and as the approached the main business they heard the sounds of eating and light conversation, which came to an abrupt halt as Daniel and Hart, came through the door. Daniel smiled and held a hand up in greeting as Silaya stood up from her chair looking startled, because Hart was behind him, he never saw Hart slowly shake his head while staring into Silaya's eyes. Daniel did not see Hunter or Lauren at the table. Silaya after a moment of silence mentioned they had grabbed some food and gone off to their rooms to eat. Daniel nodded and introduced his companion Hart and Silaya gestured for them to join the other Fae at the table. Silaya seemed more than a little nervous as Hart and Daniel sat next to her. Daniel joined in the small talk, asking Hart about what it was like growing up as a Fae and compared his own childhood much to the delight of the other Fae. In fact it was as they were all laughing about Daniel's antics when he was four had been trying to perform BMX tricks on his second hand tricycle using a couple rocks and a piece of stolen plywood. The resulting crash that broke the bike and caused him to paint the road with his knees, that Hunter and Lauren reappeared. Hunter froze as he came in the front door with Lauren, his eyes glued to Hart who stood slowly to welcome them and introduce himself with his eyes never leaving Hunter's own. Hunter gave a cocky grin and welcomed Hart. The meal continued with small talk and banter and the rapid emptying of plates. Daniel made a mental note to speak to the cook and introduce him to Pizza. Hunter asked If Hart would like to join them in stretching their legs about the complex and after a brief hesitation he agreed. Everyone pitched in with the clearing of the dishes and then left for their individual tasks. Hunter led them towards the small spring fed pond that supplied the Order of Belethai's fish and freshwater crops. From what Daniel could see this place was set up like one of those hippie communes' from the 60's. Everyone helped with the chores, they grew their own food and made their own clothes and had little contact with the world beyond their borders. Hart placed his foot on a rock near the edge of the pool and looked down into the water, watching the colorful fish skimming the surface collecting bugs "I've come here with a message from the Court; the Queen has pushed your audience back three days." Hunter nodded, his eyes quickly glancing from Hart to Daniel and back again before looking down into the pool. "Will you be staying on with us during those three days; we could always use a skilled ranger to escort us to the Royal Court." Hart looked over at Daniel and cocked his eyebrow as if asking permission. Daniel looked around at all the faces turned to him as if he had somehow become the leader of this motley crew. "So you are a ranger...like a Fae version of Aragorn right?" Hart laughed which seemed to startle Hunter before he composed his features "You are lucky Daniel that I have spent some time in your world and can appreciate the references." Daniel found himself smirking "Nah I don't mind you sticking around and escorting us to the Court." Hart touched his chest and inclined his head.

CHAPTER SIX

Rue's life had ceased to be enjoyable; from the moment she woke until she climbed wearily into bed constant nausea was her ever-present companion. Kate had cloistered herself in the library and Alexi sat about smirking and enjoying her misery. When she wasn't retching, she was sipping broth and nibbling crackers and accusing the servants of trying to poison her. After a week had passed with no relief, Rue finally allowed Nikolai to summon a doctor and stayed beside her to translate. The doctor had her disrobe and lay on the bed, took her temperature, checked her blood pressure, looked in her eyes and ears and then gave her a gynecological exam. Finally he sent all but Nikolai from the room and taking his glasses off asked when her last 'courses' had occurred. Rue had to think about that, she had not really been paying much attention; it had to have been at least two months since her last period. Nikolai relayed the information to the doctor and the doctor nodded as if it had confirmed what he had already surmised. He then said the words Rue had been secretly dreading from the time she started getting sick, Nikolai turned to her with a bemused expression on his face and proclaimed that she was 'with child'. Kate had come in looking elated and had heard

Nikolai's words and lost her smile as if she had been slapped in the face. "Rue is with

child?" The doctor stood and said his goodbyes and was lead out by Nikolai as Kate

stumbled into the room shaking her head. "Who's child is it...I mean is it...? " Kate

gestured to Alexi who had followed her in the door as soon as he saw the doctor leave.

Rue was able to smile at the look of horror on Alexi's face at the thought of her carrying

his child. "no, its not Alexi's child...based on the timing I would say Daniel's child." Kate

shuddered would they never be free of that farm boy? Kate sits at the edge of the bed and

reaches for Rue's hand. Rue slides off the opposite side of the bed and pulls her quilted

robe on and belts it tight. "I need a shower and I need to think, then I'll decide what I

want to do." Rue quickly avoided Kate and Alexi and headed into the bathroom and

locked the door behind her. Kate slowly pulled her hand back and looked at Alexi who

was staring at her with raw pity and disgust. Kate flipped him off and left to go back to

the library. Alexi silently laughed at the way things were working out, for the last week

he had watched the woman he had come to hate suffer in misery. Now he found that she

would continue to suffer if she kept this child. He planned on finding a way to break this

spell by the time the child was born and somehow he would return this child to this

'Daniel', better this child be raised motherless than raised with the she-bitch who

conceived it. Alexi heard the shower running and pulled the cord beside the bed, when a

maid appeared; he ordered Garlic sausages, boiled cabbage, fried oysters. The maid

nodded and left and Alexi smiled, when Rue emerged from the shower she would be

surrounded with all the strong food odors and spend the rest of the day vomiting over

them.

Rue stepped out of the shower; the bathroom filled with steam and wrapped a towel around herself. Standing in front of the mirror, she wipes a clear spot with her hand and starts tallying up the pros and cons of all decisions. If she got rid of the child she could continue as she had been with a little more precautions taken. If she kept the child she would have a child with Fae blood to mold into her protege. There was also the possibility that carrying Daniel's child would cause him to return long enough for her to put a permanent leash on him. Rue giggled and decided she would keep the child and threw open the bathroom door to tell Kate the news and immediately gagged at the smell of oysters and garlic, the fried smell of sausages. Rue barely made it to the toilet in time as she vomited, she faintly heard Alexi laughing over the sound of her retches. Kate could barely make out the words on the page as tears blurred her vision. Silent tears made tracks down her cheeks as her stomach clenched in agony, Rue was going to keep the child she just knew it. Suddenly as if a small voice had whispered in her ear, she realized if she could not have Rue, maybe she could convince Rue to give up the child to her and she could raise the child as her own. Kate looked up at the brightly sun lit windows and imagined what it would feel like to be a mother. Birthday parties, holidays, PTA...okay maybe not going that far but a daughter or son of her own would make it easier for her to leave, she would never be alone again. Wiping the tears from her face she set her mind to convincing Rue to keep the child and gathered up her pages of 'research' notes and carefully stowed her book where Rue would be least likely to notice it and headed back to Rue's room.

Three days seemed to pass in no time Hart was up at dawn practicing with various weapons and tracking his namesake through ground cover so thick he had to be psychic to know where to find the prints. Daniel begged him to teach him 'those mad ninja skills' and although Hart warned him it would take far longer than three days to get to the same level as he was, Daniel agreed to a crash course. Little did he know the first day was going to consist of a lot of sitting or crouching and listening to water, wind, and the sound creatures made moving through the brush. After a few hours either his butt (if he was sitting) or his legs (if he was crouching) would fall asleep and he would have to stretch and start all over again. Hart was patient rather than upset at Daniel's lack of progress, the man honestly needed to be nominated for sainthood. Hunter and Lauren stayed silent and watched as Hart corrected Daniel's posture for what had to be the three hundredth time and instructed him once again to silence his mind and use his senses to 'feel' the woods, the wind, the earth beneath his feet, the sky above him. Daniel blew out a frustrated breath and tried to 'tune in' to nature. The itch starting on his right calf, he could smell Lauren's perfume, Hunter was scratching his head, Hart was the only blank spot beside him that had no sounds or smells distracting him. Lauren and Hunter got tired of watching him since nothing was happening. As Hunter and Lauren headed back to the maiden house he heard Lauren ask Hunter why he could not move silently like Hart. Just before they passed beyond his hearing, Daniel heard Hunter reply "I am not that kind of Fae."

Daniel finally gave up crouching and sat on the ground rubbing his aching ankles "I am never going to get this Hart, it's been three days and I am no better at 'hearing the world' as I was three days ago." Hart dropped into a cross-legged position opposite

Daniel in a single fluid movement that once again made Daniel feel like a bull in a china chop by comparison. "It occurs to me Daniel that I may have been going about this the wrong way, clearly we have very different builds and skills and I am trying to teach you the way I was taught." Daniel stopped rubbing his ankles and shrugged "What is wrong with that?" Hart cocked his head as if considering how best to explain his point. "In your world there are many types of fighters and body types, could you see a bodybuilder or a Sumo wrestler using martial arts?" Daniel tried to picture a Sumo wrestler attempting a karate kick and ended up laughing and shaking his head. "You have an incredible grasp of my world Hart and a Human's sense of humor I am realizing." Hart smiled and pulled a pipe from a pocket in his jacket. "I spent a very long time Daniel and enjoyed nearly every minute of it learning everything I could about your world and the cultures your world plays host to. Hart held an empty palm up and blew across it, kindling a small flame, which he then transferred to the bowl of the pipe. Daniel whistled "Nice trick...so why were you studying my world, if I lived in a perfect world like this I would never leave." Hart puffed on his pipe for a moment in thought "despite its appearances, this world is far from perfect Daniel...this world as you may have noticed is bound in tradition and rules." Daniel nodded and shifted into a more comfortable position as he listened. "Like many of your past cultures in your own world, ours has begun to stagnate. I was on a mission to learn about the cultures of your world and bring that knowledge back that we might model certain aspects of our world after yours." Daniel thinks about that for a moment "Ok I guess that does kind of make sense, but why did you bring up Sumo wrestlers and Karate?" Hart smiled and gestured between them "It occurs to me that my training of you is not working because you and I are two very different type of warriors, perhaps I need to rethink my training and come up with a strategy that will work far more effectively then my present curriculum." Daniel winced at the muscle soreness as he stood "so no more sitting and crouching for hours on end while my body parts fall asleep?" Hart laughs and stands "I promise, no more torturing your limbs until after I have come up with a training regime that will work for you." Walking side by side they returned to the bachelor house and by the smells coming from the open door, they were just in time for the evening meal.

The Queen had sent mounts for them to ride back to the Royal Court; the 'steeds' were tall delicate looking white horses. Daniel looked his horse over and knew he was going to look like an unwashed barbarian on this elegant creature. Daniel had never spent much time in the saddle before this and now he knew why John Wayne had walked bow legged after a day in the saddle. Every break they took he would dismount and groan at the burning ache in his thighs. Finally after what seemed like far too short a break, Hart started handing out cloth bundles of bread, meat and cheese and announced their next break would be at the Royal Court. Everyone remounted and Daniel thought he was going to die when his legs nearly failed him. Daniel caught his first sight of Ceneca (home to the Royal Court) as he came over the hill and it was everything hunter had said and more. The streets were cobbled just like Bethesda's had been, but here the lowliest of homes was far richer than anything you would find in Bethesda. The streets were scoured clean and there was not an automobile to be found anywhere. Carriages and litters and even assorted riding beasts seemed to be the preferred mode of transportation for those who chose not to walk. In the center of the city a magnificent castle rose above the rooftops with towers reaching like fingers to the sky. The castle gleamed, the sunlight reflecting of the white opalescent stones and even off the many windows. Inwardly Daniel thought this must have been what Disney had been going for with the Cinderella Castle in Orlando. Fae stopped and stared as Daniel and Lauren an Lauren passed by. The carriages and litters hurried to move aside and let them by. The streets were packed in the city proper but the crowds seemed to gradually thin out as they got closer to the center of the city. Two armored guards stood to either side of the enormous wooden doors that seemed to come standard on every castle Daniel had ever seen in movies or pictures. Hart dismounted and walked forward to the guards and introduced the small party, Daniel noticed he excluded himself from the introduction. The guards nodded and opened one of the doors for them and a pair of liveried servants rushed up to take the horses as they dismounted.

Hart stepped forward to Daniel as the horses were led away, "I cannot follow you in this way but I will meet you inside and I have no doubt we will have much to speak of when next we meet." Daniel nodded and took a deep steadying breath before clapping Hart on the shoulder "Thanks for all the help Hart, any other advice you can give me before I meet the Queen?" Hart thought about it for a moment "Remember to listen twice as much as you speak and treat everyone with the utmost respect." Daniel nodded and thanked Hart again for everything and watched as Hart put a hand to his chest in a formal bow and entered the castle through a smaller door. Daniel's hand was suddenly grabbed in Lauren's firm grip and he noticed she had done the same to Hunter. Walking three abreast they entered the door, all of them gawked at the vaulted ceilings and the expected portraits of past royalty lining the walls to either side. Plush blue carpeting covered the floor and the walls were made of blue veined marble. Lauren whispered "I feel like

Dorothy going to see the Wizard of Oz." Her grip on Daniel's hand tightened painfully and he heard Hunter make a grunt of pain on the other side of her as well. At the other end of the hall two normal sized doors were bracketed by armored guards identical to those outside. Once again they were stopped by the guards and this time it was Hunter who made the introductions. One of the guards opened the door and slipped through, he returned a moment later with a robed Fae carrying a globe topped staff in his hand. Daniel snorted in amusement at the sight of this Fae with his long white hair and arrogant expression as he looked them over. Clearly Disney had a lot more influence on these guys than Daniel had thought because this guy looked like a stereotypical wizard minus the pointy hat, or better yet a Royal Vizier. The robed Fae looked at Daniel suspiciously "Thou wilt come before the Queen and consort as supplicants and explain thyselves and thy presence in our fair kingdom to her majesty Queen Sadronniel and consort Lithaldoren in a moment, but first how are you called?" Daniel smirked as a hundred smart-ass remarks pushed came to mind and judging by the smirk on Lauren's face she had come up with a few herself. Daniel had just opened his mouth to let one emerge when he glanced at Hunter and saw the warning look he was shooting him. "I am Daniel Warwick and this is Lauren..." Daniel looked at Lauren completely at a loss, he had just realized he did not know Lauren's full name. Lauren smiled "I am Lauren Campbell...and this is ...Hunter, our friend and traveling companion." Hunter looked surprised at being branded a friend then quickly recovered and nodded to the robed Fae. The Fae nodded and swept back through the doors and after an echoing thump of his staff announced them to what appeared to be a huge assembly of various creatures...none of them human. The robed Fae gestured for them to advance up the aisle formed between the two groups of creatures and approach the tall crystalline thrones at the far end.

As they made their way across the now silent room, Daniel glanced to the left and right and could vaguely recognize certain species believed to be myths in his world. Shaggy legged Satyrs whispered to equine-bodied Centaurs, Fauns and Fae gaped at them or nudged formidable looking Minotaurs who grunted and looked down on the strange trio. When they arrived at the dais, Daniel was momentarily blinded by the sunlight from the high windows and gleaming off the carved wooden thrones. Shifting to his left to avoid the direct rays of sun, he noticed a stark contrast between Queen and consort. Queen Sadronniel was clothed in a white silk gown that clung to her form yet retained its elegance and dignity with a high collar. Her platinum blonde tresses had been braided and secured to look like a cushion for her crown. Consort Lithaldoren by comparison looked as if he had only just pulled himself from bed. His long blonde hair was attractively mussed, his shirt left open to mid chest, snug leather pants and knee high boots completed the picture. Where Queen Sadronniel sat stiffly and regally on her throne, her consort lounged in his, one leg hooked over the armrest as he swirled the wine in his goblet and contrived to look petulant and bored. To either side of the crystal thrones stood fully armored knights, their visors closed. Unlike the previous knights they had passed, these knights armor had silver runes carved into it and they both stood several inches taller than Daniel. Daniel also noticed that while the Queen's guard appeared male, the consort's knight was definitely female if the breastplate was anything to judge by. The Queen started to speak and was abruptly interrupted by her consort who sat up abruptly as if suddenly noticing their presence. "Humans are not generally tolerated in Underhill and here you stand after having damaged one of our sacred Gates and bringing your summoned Daemon here to set loose on our people...all I might add which might be considered a declaration of WAR!" Consort Lithaldoren sipped from his goblet, a smug smile twisting his lips "What have you to say for yourselves?" Hunter looked in confusion from the Queen to the consort; the Queen was also staring at her consort in consternation. Stiffly she stood from her throne and raised her voice to the guards. "Guards clear the chamber now!" A moment of stunned silence followed then quickly the guards entered the assembly and started herding the onlookers towards the doors, closing them and turning to face the dais.

Queen Sadronniel turned towards the second throne and clasped her hands in front of her as if confronting a misbehaving child. "You once again overstep yourself Lithaldoren; you are consort and not King. You are present at my wish and now I wish for you to return to the royal apartments and wait for me there." Consort Lithaldoren stood and angrily tossed the goblet to the floor the metallic clanging echoing in the now empty chamber. "I am not your servant to be ordered to go hither and yon Sadronniel!" Queen Sadronniel lifted one arched brow "If you were a servant I would have you beaten for your presumption, as you are my consort you may retire to our royal apartments and we will speak when I am done here." Consort Lithaldoren stepped back as if slapped and then with a Elven curse grabbed the arm of his female guardsman and stomped off through the door behind the thrones. The fact that he had taken his female guardsman with him had not gone unnoticed. Queen Sadronniel stared at the door for a moment then turned and resumed her seat on the throne, a hand rubbing her temple for a moment. "While consort Lithaldoren was presumptuous to speak before me, he was correct in stating that your actions thus far speak less than favorably on your behalf." With a bow in the Queen's direction Daniel told the whole story as he knew it from the moment he had first caught Rue's attention, eventually Hunter took up the tale as they got to the accident at the Gate. The Queen sat back; her brow furrowed "you have given me much to think on, I ask that you give me three days to make a decision. I also ask that you allow me to have you housed here at the palace until I make my decision." Daniel was struck with a sudden thought. "Your majesty, would it be alright If I requested a specific person to act as a guide while I am here, I really don't want to make any serious faux pas while in your kingdom." Queen Sadronniel smiled "A wise request Daniel Warwick, whom would you request?" Daniel scratched absently at the back of his neck "well there was this guy named Hart, he was a ranger or something like that and he was very helpful as an escort here." The Queen looked uncertain at first then smiled and looked to the knight on her left "I think that could be arranged, but he will have to speak for himself...Aelon have you anything to say?"

The knight to her left steps forward and removes his helmet and Daniel is left staring at Hart's face in confusion. Hart's face was grim as he faced Daniel "I spoke no untruth to you Daniel, my friends call me Hart. My proper name is Aelon Dryearghym." Daniel stepped back and stared in shock at his father "Did you know who I was when you met me?" Daniel watched his father nod "I knew, there are only a few Fae who can sense one of their own blood, I am one of the few." Daniel looked over at where Lauren and Hunter stood listening. Lauren's look of shock mirrored his own but Hunter's face showed only guilt. "You said you knew my father Hunter, so then you knew recognized Hart as my father the whole time." It was not a question but Hunter nodded anyway. "Ye needed time to get to know him as Hart before ye knew him as yer father, 'sides it was his plan first I only went along with it 'cause it made sense." Hart stepped forward with a placating hand "I understand this is confusing Daniel, you may still refer to me as Hart and I pray that this does not cause you to retract your request to have me aid you, I would be honored if you would allow me the opportunity to get to know you Daniel." Daniel wanted to lash out...but what good would it really do. Finally he nodded and turned to Queen Sadronniel who had been sitting silently through the exchange. "You have made the request and so I grant it, I ask you again to not leave the palace grounds while I test the validity of your story." Three heads nodded and she gestured that they were dismissed. Hart led them through the same doors the Consort had left through and two guards followed behind them.

Rue started to be annoyed at Nikolai's insistence that she keep drinking mint tea whenever the nausea became too much for her. Nikolai had let Rue know that this was a cure that the women of his country had been employing for generations. Alexi had been forbidden from eating in the room and had been told in no uncertain terms that he was to eat only in the dining room. When Alexi had suggested she might be happier if he was given his own room she slapped him and burst into enraged tears. "You just want nothing more to do with me admit it!" Alexi smiled and bowed at the waist "I freely admit I would rather throw myself from the tallest tower then ever have to see your ever widening ass again dearest Rue." Rue shrieked in rage and grabbed the fire tongs and with a flick of her wrist, once again locked down his muscles so that he was helpless against her rage as she beat him with the iron tongs, mercifully he passed out. Alexi was not sure how much time had passed when he awoke to someone washing the blood off his face. He was in a room he did not recognize and a mad sat on the edge of the narrow bed and sponged the blood from his face and neck. "Where have I been moved to?" The maid gave him a scolding look as she stood and looked down at him "You have been moved to the servant's wing and might I add that you are lucky she did not kill you for your insolence." Alexi started laughing and quickly stopped as pain shot through what his ribs, looking down at the bandages he could only assume she had cracked or broken a couple of them. "You don't get it, I WANTED her to KILL me, I am her slave so long as I am alive!" Alexi spat the words at the stunned maid who quickly gathered her things and left, the door slamming shut behind her and the distinct click of the lock letting him know he was locked in. Alexi hobbled to the window and could see edge of the barn and a small lake behind and beyond that nothing but mist shrouded forests and mountains. Alexi knew that soon his family would come looking for him and Gregori again. The Rom were not stupid and if she tried the same story on them again, they would camp outside until their men folk emerged. Rue seemed to have the same thought as he was brought down to the dining room later for dinner and overheard her discussing travel plans with Kate and Nikolai. Kate seemed surprised as the 'discussion' became less of a discussion and more an announcement of Rue's intentions. When dinner had been cleared away Kate excused herself to the library and Alexi could hear her ordering several crates to be brought to the library so she could begin packing the books she did not want to leave behind.

It took nearly a week for everything to be made ready for travel and Alexi made a final attempt to appeal to Rue's humanity, if there was any. Alexi approached Rue as she reclined in her study sipping her nightly cup of mint tea. "Rue let us be honest with each other now yes?" Rue smiled as she noticed the bruises across Alexi's face and the noticed he held an arm protectively across his ribs, which meant they were still bandaged. "What are you talking about Alexi dearest?" Alexi tightened his jaw at the sound of the endearment and silently counted to ten before answering. "You and I both know I will never meekly submit to enslavement, why waste your formidable magic on such as I when you could easily capture one more tractable and compel them to serve you in whatever capacity you choose." Rue nodded and took another sip of tea as if she were agreeing that she could find no fault in his logic. "It is true that while your virility is entertaining, your attitude is wearisome." Again she sipped her tea as if drawing out her answer and knowing that Alexi was beginning to get impatient. "But I choose to keep you so this discussion is over." As if he hoping to catch her by surprise he suddenly lunged at her, his fist stopping a mere foot from the top of her head as if he had hit a wall. Baring his teeth in a silent snarl he leaned into the strike willing his fist closer, but he may as well have been pushing against a brick wall. Finally in frustration he cursed her in Romanian and spat at her feet before taking a seat in a chair across the room to rethink his strategy. Rue finished her tea and laughed at Alexi as if his constant attempts to wrest control from her were merely entertainments.

The next morning they all climbed into vans and rode to the local airstrip were the jet awaited them. The plane ride back to the states was a horrific experience for Alexi who had never flown before. Alexi spent most of the flight in the bathroom being ill; he now knew firsthand what he had put Rue through with the smell of his meals. Kate had called ahead and a Limo was waiting for them when they landed. Alexi was pale and shaky and Rue was suffering from her daily bout of Nausea but as soon as they were safely ensconced in the back of the Limousine, Rue's nausea seemed to ease and she was once again smiling and commenting on how great it was to be home. The moment they got back inside the house Rue gave the order for Kate to make up a guest room for Alexi. She also warned Kate not to unpack since they would only be here for a few days before leaving again. Kate seemed surprised at this announcement; usually Rue discussed her plans with Kate before she announced them. "Where are we going from here?" Rue waved off Kate's questions "I have to see what progress my Seeker has made on tracking down Daniel and then I will make my decision where we are going next." Kate nodded and backed out of the room to set up one of the guest rooms for Alexi who was looking like a beaten dog. Alexi sat quietly in the chair in the corner of the guest room and watched Kate make the bed up with fresh linens. Kate glanced at him before leaving and surmised he looked like a man waiting to wait from an awful nightmare. Kate shrugged and left Alexi alone and went to her own room to unpack some of the books she had not wanted to leave behind. Kate lost herself in her research and note taking as she continued to seek the answer to the question of how to return Rue to her former self. Kate looked up from her book only when the light had become bad enough that she could no longer read the handwritten words. Looking over at the red digital numbers on her bedside clock, she noticed several hours had passed. Emerging from her room, she went back into the living room and found Rue staring into a large and ornate hand mirror with black glass. When Kate peeked over Rue's shoulder she saw the black-eyed creature she had watched tear itself from Gregori's body. Kate could only hear Rue's response to the creature but not the creature itself. It was kind of like hearing one side of a phone conversation. Apparently everything had not gone as planned and the Seeker had missed its opportunity to grab Daniel and was now trapped somewhere. Rue insisted the creature get back on Daniel's trail and grab him at the next opportunity. Kate was not sure what exactly the creature told Rue but Rue quickly jotted an address down and mumbled something about a damaged gate that they should be able to follow Daniel through. When Rue closed the conversation with the creature, she turned to Kate. "Daniel has managed to get himself Underhill but since he damaged the Gate we may be able to follow him." Kate shook her head in confusion "What are you talking about Gates and Underhill...Daniel is underground?" Rue gave her a long-suffering sigh and started speaking slowly as if to a particularly thick-witted child. "Underhill is the Fae realm, you know where elves and fairies and leprechauns come from?" Kate stared at Rue as if Rue had completely gone around the bend. "You do realize that elves and fairies and unicorns are all myths, they do not actually exist.... Rue shook her head and turned away from her "Go be a good girl and fetch us something to eat." Kate got up and went into the kitchen to throw together a salad and some sliced fruit.

Kate brought the food out to the dining room table and encouraged Alexi to come eat. Rue was no longer in the living room, but her bedroom door was closed. Kate knocked on the bedroom door and Rue immediately opened the door with a beaming smile. "Dear sweet Kate, please come in we need to talk." Kate felt a quiver of trepidation in her stomach and couldn't help noticing there was a seductive sway to Rue's hips as she went to the end of the bed and sat facing Kate. Rue was acting the way Kate remembered from before but Kate had not had a chance to invoke any of the spells she had been gathering components for yet. Rue patted the bed next to her and smiled at her again.

"Please sit Kate, I fear I have not been the best friend to you in quite awhile and I..." Kate sat quickly and took Rue's hand between her own, her heart in her eyes as she heard the words she had so badly dreamed of hearing Rue say to her. Rue looked deeply into Kate's eyes and took her hand from between Kate's. "Sweet Kate can you ever forgive me for neglecting you so unfairly?" Before Kate could Reply rue's soft lips were pressed against her own, Rue's hands caressing her neck. Kate felt a soft fabric brush against her throat and suddenly rue pulled back with a smile "you do still love me don't you Kate?" Kate nodded barely breathing "I never stopped loving you Rue, not even when..." Kate stopped mid sentence as Rue stood from the bed and began laughing at her. "You are so weak and pathetic Kate, too stupid to see the inevitable conclusion that I do not NEED you anymore, except maybe to clean up messes." Kate stood and raised her hands to her throat where she could feel a lace choker and some round ornament clasped around her neck. "You will be ever so much more useful now Kate." Kate hurried to the mirror and saw a wide black lace collar with a large polished moonstone pinned to the front of it. The necklace would have been a beautiful gift if Kate had not already realized that Rue had just leashed Kate in much the same way she had done to Daniel. Turning to Rue with tears in her eyes she whispered "How could you do this to me Rue...to ME!" Rue laughed and headed to the dining room. "Get over yourself; it was obvious from your increasingly jealous and erratic behavior that I was going to have to bind you to keep you around." Alexi had nearly finished his meal when the two women appeared from the room. "Just think Kate now you and Alexi will have so much more in common." Alexi looked from Rue's gloating face to Kate's distraught one and noticed the way Kate was clawing at the antique lace choker around her throat and started laughing. Standing from the table he headed to his room passing just close enough to Kate to whisper "How does it feel bitch?" Alexi closed the door to his room still laughing.

The royal apartments were a polar opposite from the rest of the palace with its red and gold wallpaper and plush scarlet carpeting. Daniel and Hart were led to a suite of rooms to the left while Hunter and Lauren were led to a suite of rooms to the right. Since Hart was assigned as Daniel's guide, he was housed with Daniel. At first it was hard interacting with Hart knowing that Hart was actually his father Aelon. The Queen had not summoned them to join her for dinner so they were fed in their rooms. Daniel decided to break the ice over dinner, "So Hart can you tell me a little about what happened...you know with my mother?" A shadow of longing and sadness seemed to briefly pass over Hart's face. "Your mother and I met by happenstance, I was hunting when she broke through the wall of the cave I was camped in and discovered my camp." Hart reached for a goblet of wine that had been set in front of him and took a deep drink before continuing. "I was captivated by your mother the moment we met, she was looking for a type of crystal that was of little to no value to my kind and I was more than happy to provide it for her but really that was just an excuse for us to spend more time together." So far everything Hart was saying aligned with what his mother had told him, so Daniel had no reason to think he was being less than honest. "The night I found out about you we had a terrible storm, I was packing my camp up...the Queen had summoned me back." Hart sat forward and took another drink of his wine before he placed the goblet back on the table. "We were under attack from the Unseelie court and she was recalling her

Eldritch for the battle." Daniel leaned forward his hands clasped loosely. "Your mother and I were so happy when we learned she was carrying you, she knew what I was and about my position in court." Hart stood and started pacing, scrubbing his face in an all too human gesture of frustration. "Your mother and I had harsh words that night, she demanded that if I loved her the way I claimed I did I would abandon my people when they needed me most and stay with her." Hart turned towards Daniel a plea for understanding in his eyes "I knew if I defied my Queen the penalty was death, but if I went and fought then there was a good chance I could return for you and your mother."

Daniel nodded he knew that the decision for any man to leave the woman he loved and his unborn child was never a decision made lightly. "I swore to your mother that I would return for her and for you, she slapped my face and spit on me ...I understood she was distraught and did not mean her actions." Hart shook his head "She told me if I left I could stay gone...that when you were old enough she would tell you she was raped by a heartless monster." Hart sat down and dropped his head into his hands "I came back when you were three years old, she wouldn't let me near you and reiterated that she intended to tell you when you were old enough to understand that she was raped." Daniel felt his heart go cold at the picture Hart was painting, if he had not heard similar words from his mother just a few days ago, he would never have believed his mother capable of the things Hart was claiming. "I had given her knowledge of how to protect herself from Fae while I was gone; she threatened to use it to make you and her disappear to us if I ever tried to come near either of you again." Daniel grabbed his goblet with two shaking hands and drank half of it down in a single gulp. "I agreed to stay away from you; I figured at least if I knew where you were I could verify you were happy and healthy from time to time. I went to see you two more times once when you were five and once when you were seven, then I retreated Underhill and never went to see you again. Hart sighed "The pain of seeing you and never being able to know you was too much." Daniel wondered if Hart realized that this was the exact type of reunion conversation every fatherless boy in the world dreamed of having with the father they never got to know. Daniel never made the conscious decision to do so but one minute he was thinking how much he had dreamed of having this conversation with his father and the next he was walking over to Hart and pulling him up into a very unmanly hug. "I forgive you Hart...Dad...I know you did not willingly abandon me." Hart wrapped an arm around him briefly then stepped back slightly embarrassed. "That means more to me than you know Daniel, this is a place where words have power and forgiveness like love is a very powerful emotion here." Daniel chuckled "Where I come from men celebrate things like this over a beer, don't suppose that is likely though right?" Hart looked thoughtful for a moment then went to the door and had a hushed conversation with the guard outside. A moment later the guard handed Hart two clear glass bottles of an amber liquid. Hart brought the bottles over and handed one to Daniel without explanation. Daniel cracked it open and took a deep swig then started coughing as it burned its way down into his chest. Hart laughed after taking his own deep drink and suffering no ill affects. "Siobhan fire ale, best Underhill has to offer...has a bit of a kick though." Daniel resisted the urge to flip Hart off as he took another drink, this one went down a lot smoother, either that or he had no living nerves left in his throat.

CHAPTER SEVEN

Since they had not unpacked, it did not take long to load the car up with what Rue deemed "essentials". Rue briefly considered leaving 'Mopey' and 'Weepy' behind but in her condition she would probably need all the help she could get. She only needed to be within hearing range of Daniel for her to invoke the obedience command for the cuff. The only effect she could command from a distance was the physical response and while it was amusing to mess with Daniel, it did her little good this far away from him. Rue got Alexi and Kate loaded into the car and since she had the address, she decided to drive. Alexi was silent but smiled triumphantly whenever his eyes alit on Kate's new collar. Kate was also silent ...when she was not weeping and clawing at the collar as if it were choking her. Rue started to wonder if it was even worth the hassle to keep Kate around, she was three times as difficult to deal with now as she had been before Rue bound her. It would take two days to reach the damaged Gate. The first night, the stopped at a cozy wayside inn and got only a single room with two full-size beds. Rue invoked Alexi's 'leash' and laughed as Kate quickly scurried into the bathroom to avoid having to see or hear Alexi and Rue. The minute Rue had finished with him Alexi got up and shoved Kate out of the bathroom as he showered until every bit of hot water had been used up and his skin was red and raw from the rigorous scrubbing. Coming out of the bathroom with a towel around his hips, he made a bed on the floor rather than share a bed with either of the women.

The next day as they got everything once again loaded into the car, Kate started her daily pleading with Rue to release her. Alexi mostly ignored them as he made a makeshift bed in the backseat, he was exhausted owing to the fact that he had not slept very well on the hard floor. Looking over the top of the car at Kate's raised voice, he noticed Rue was once again ignoring Kate's whining and pleading. Alexi ducked his head briefly back into the car to tuck his bag more securely behind the passenger seat and heard the loud unmistakable sound of flesh striking flesh. Jerking back out of the car he looked at the women and saw Kate holding the side of her face in shock and Rue glaring at her. "Do not presume to grab my arm Kate, you do not have my permission to touch me not now and not ever!" Rue got behind the wheel and Kate stood there for a moment longer then slid into the passenger seat. Alexi got into the backseat and closed the door and they got going, somehow seeing Kate get what had been doled out to him should have been satisfying ...but it wasn't, it felt wrong somehow. The next night they got two rooms and Kate was sent to the second room and fenced in to keep her there. Alexi was once again compelled to perform and then spent the following two hours using all the hot water and again chose to sleep on the hard floor. The next morning Kate was the first to hop into the car and remained silent as the other two loaded the car up, her jaw clenched and a bruise already forming on her cheekbone. By the time they turned onto the dirt road that would lead to the damaged Gate, Alexi could cut the tension in the car with a knife.

The dirt road ended in a wide-open field surrounded by tall trees, there was a wrecked SUV sitting squarely between two trees that grew in the exact middle of the field. Rue parked near the wrecked car and got out to examine it. The front of the car was folded as if it had hit a wall but the two trees were to either side of the car and showed no signs of impact on their trunks. Rue made her way alongside the car and extended her hand past the end of it and felt a shiver of cold as her hand momentarily vanished. Pulling her hand back, she watched in amazement as her hand re emerged unscathed. Rue gave a high-pitched giggle and danced in a circle as if unable to contain her glee. Turning back towards the car she gestured for the others to join her. Alexi hopped out of the car immediately with his bag, Kate hung back with a stubborn look on her face. Rue rolled her eyes and walked over to Kate "stop acting like a child Kate, we have to go through the Gate so we can find Daniel." Kate crossed her arms over her chest and glowered at Rue "If you want me to go in there then you are going to have to drag me, I have no intention of helping you with anything ever again Rue!" Alexi knew this was not going to end well and edged closer, he could not see Rue's face but he could tell by the sudden tension in her shoulders that she was getting angry. Rue laughed at Kate's sullen expression and quick as a snake Rue's hand shot out and backhanded Kate across the face, Kate tripped over her own feet as she stumbled backwards and went down on her back.

Rue brushed past Alexi as she went back to the car and Alexi quickly went to Kate's side and knelt next to her in the dirt "you have to get up Kate and learn to pick your battles..." Alexi looked up as Rue approached and saw the knife in her hand and the fury blazing in her eyes. "If you won't help me then I have no more use for you Sweet Kate!" Rue lunged at Kate's prone form just as Alexi shoved his shoulder between Kate and the blade and gasped as he felt the blade enter his back and the tip slide out his chest just below the collarbone. Rue cursed and ripped the blade free, blood droplets landing in the grass nearby. Alexi braced himself on shaking arms over Kate and looked at Rue over his shoulder "Kate has been loyal to you thus far Rue, she can still be useful...if you feel the need to take your anger out on someone then do so to me and not her." Rue gave a cry of frustration and ordered Kate to patch him up, then turned and stomped back to the Gate. Kate shoved him back and went and got the first aid kit from the car. Kneeling next to him she roughly opened his shirt and bandaged his shoulder, wrapping the bandages around his chest to hold them in place. "You are an idiot, why would you do for me what I sure as hell would not do for you?" Alexi shrugged his good shoulder "Guess that just makes me a better person than you...surprised?" Standing he swung his bag over his good shoulder and joined Rue at the Gate. Kate slowly closed up the first aid kit and stuck it in her bag and joined the other two.

Passing through the gate was like stepping through an ice-cold waterfall, the woods on the other side were dark and a ground fog hovered around the base of the trees making the footing unsure. Rue stumbled a few steps before pulling the flashlight from her bag and lighting up the path before them. Kate noticed Alexi looking around them with great interest and would occasionally turn and stare into the woods as if he had caught sight of something but whenever Kate looked, there was nothing there but woods. Finally Rue called a halt, below them nestled into a small valley was what appeared to be a small farming community consisting of one main building and several outbuildings and outlying fields. Slowly they made their way down into the valley and angled over to the closest of the outbuildings, which turned out to be a fully stocked tool shed. Rue peeked inside and then had them all file in and locked the door from the inside. Rue took some chalk from her bag and began to draw a diagram that Kate remembered all too well. The last time Kate had seen Rue draw that diagram it had Gregori's body in the middle of it. Instead of placing a body in the center, Rue placed the hand mirror with the black glass. Waving Alexi and Kate against the wall, she began placing and lighting the candles and chanting the same words she had chanted the first time she had used this diagram. It took long enough for anything to happen that Alexi had begun to examine the tools on the wall as if evaluating them as potential weapons. Kate was watching Alexi hefting and swinging hand tools sure that he was going to try something. Suddenly the room had gone very cold and the black-eyed creature or one identical to it stood up from the mirror as if the mirror were a trap door it had popped up from. The creature's feet had not yet pulled free from the mirror, instead the creature rotated in place to look at Rue. "We are through the Gate and we have found a small farming community." The creature nodded to indicate it knew where she was talking about. "I will need you to find me allies in this place, those who can be bought with coin or flesh...or those who will aid me against those that guard Daniel." The creature nodded again adding a sharp-toothed grin of anticipation. "First I have need of your particular talents here, step through into the circle." The creature obeyed and stepped from the mirror into the containment circle and waited her orders.

Kate stared at the creature in horror and Alexi was mumbling something that was either a prayer or a long string of curses in Romanian. Rue ignored them both as she stared just above the creatures head and avoided the lure of it's dead gaze. "I need every living thing in this valley dead...except for us of course." Rue started to sketch the sign of dismissal in the air and froze "no wait, we may need hostages, save me five with wounds that will not kill them." Rue sketched the sign to release the creature and then watched with a smile as the creature cackled and sunk through the floor. It didn't take long for the screaming to start. Kate closed her eyes, her lips moving silently as if praying. Alexi froze staring at the locked door with a scythe in his hand, his knuckles white on the wooden handle. Rue waited a long while after the screaming had finally stopped until the creature had re appeared in the circle with a bow. "Five await you within the main building mistress, they will not die of their wounds..." the creature chuckled and Rue once again affirmed its vow of loyalty and obedience before rubbing out one side of the diagram and releasing the creature. The seeker moved off to the side and watched as Rue cleaned up the candles and scrubbed out the rest of the diagram. Alexi edged as far from the Seeker as he could and Kate merely kept her eyes closed as if willing this to be a dream. Finally when all evidence of magic had been erased, Rue unlocked the door and led her troupe to the main house. The fields seemed to be full of those who had tried to flee to escape their fate, their faces and bodies forever twisted in horror and pain. Blood made the path to the main building slick and shadowed lumps better left unknown sat just outside the reach of the torches that lined the now crimson path.

The moment the door opened, the wounded captives began whimpering and speaking to her in their strange language. Rue ignored the captives and looked around at all the fallen bodies laying like broken toys around the heavily laden table. "Seeker remove the bodies from here and dispose of them at the edge of the woods and return." The seeker rushed about like a cold, shadowy blur removing the bodies until only blood and viscera showed where the bodies had been. Rue next turned cold eyes on Kate "You will clean this room so that the smell of blood and offal do not offend me." The seeker let out a hiss of laughter and pointed a thin arm towards the door leading to the kitchen. Kate opened her mouth to reply and Alexi's hand clamped painfully on her arm as he mouthed the words pick your battles at her, to Rue he muttered "I'll help her then we all can eat yes?" Rue smirked and nodded "Yes Alexi once the place is clean you will both be allowed to eat." Kate followed Alexi into the kitchen and helped draw water from the corner cistern. Together it took them much less time than it would have for Kate alone, the bucket of 'parts' was tossed out the back door where Kate hoped it would not attract predators. While Kate and Alexi cleaned the room, Rue walked the perimeter of the building spreading a blue dust and reading from the leather tome she had kept at her side since she had discovered it in Romania. When Rue was done she smiled sweetly at the Seeker "Now Seeker, do as I bid you earlier and find me allies in this place that can be bought with coin or flesh or that have a grudge against those that house Daniel."

The Seeker let out another hissing laugh and bowed deeply before sinking through the floor. Rue seated herself at the head of the table and gestured imperiously for the others to join her as she loaded her plate with a little of everything, apparently her nausea had abated enough for her appetite to return. Alexi picked at his food as did Kate but either Rue never noticed or she was ignoring their loss of appetite. Alexi kept glancing into the far room where the wounded hostages huddled together in the corner. A willowy blonde Fae with ice blue eyes glared at Rue's back as Rue consumed their food. Finally sated, Rue stood and approached the hostages. All but the willowy blonde whimpered and tried to retreat further into the corner. The blonde woman was propped against the wall, her legs were completely shattered and though she must have been in sheer agony she never shoved any sign of discomfort. "you Elf, you understand my words?" The woman stared daggers at Rue for a moment that spat out a long string of syllables that flowed together and might have been beautiful if the tone behind them had not implied insult. The temperature of the room dropped several degrees and Alexi whipped his head around searching until he found the Seeker lurking in the shadows near the door. "Your allies come Mistress, they will present themselves at dawn." Rue starting quickly plotting, she would need to set up some surprises for her 'allies' just in case lest they think her weak and conquerable.

"You understand the language of these creatures Seeker?" The Seeker nodded and smiled its pointy-toothed smile at her. "I demand the ability to speak and understand all variances of their language." The Seeker crept forward still smiling at Rue "what will you give me for this ability Mistress?" Rue looked over her shoulder at the group of Fae cowering in the corner then turned back to the Seeker "you may have the small brunette to 'play' with as you please." The Seeker looked past her at the small fine boned brunette who closed her eyes in terror at the sight of him and nodded "done then Mistress." Extending one long ash colored finger, the Seeker touched Rue in between the eyes and Rue gasped as something deep in her brain clicked painfully. Turning back to the glaring Fae woman, Rue hauled back and slapped her across the face. The woman spat at Rue "As you give so shall you receive Daemon whore." Rue smiled brightly and replied in her language "call me a whore again bitch and I will wear your ears on my belt and give what is left to the Seeker to play with." The Fae woman's eyes widened as Rue replied in perfectly accented Sylvan. Rue starts setting up the boundary stones, the containment barrier springing up with each stone she set as she fenced the Fae into the corner. Before the last stone was set the Seeker darted in and dragged the brunette Fae out of the corner by her hair and then out the front door. Alexi listened to her screams fade as the Seeker took her into the woods to 'play' and hating that he was helpless to rescue her. Rue placed the last stone and the fence was complete. "Alexi go and fetch me 4 smooth fist sized stones from the yard." Alexi nodded and left without a word spoken, Rue next turned to Kate with an amused smile "from you I will take tea and do not think of adding anything 'special' to it." Kate narrowed her eyes at Rue before going into the kitchen and slamming the door shut. Seeing her companions otherwise occupied, Rue knelt on the floor and faced the Fae. "I know a human passed through here recently, tell me where he is and I may yet spare you." The blonde smiled sweetly revealing beauty that set Rue's teeth on edge with jealousy. "your fate was sealed the moment you ordered your Daemon to spill Fae blood, there is nothing more you can do to me and I will not damn an innocent man by turning him over to the likes of you." The blonde turned her back on Rue and pulled herself further from the barrier towards the others and whispered words of encouragement.

Rue's eyes were spitting sparks at the 'Elf's' audacity, how dare she turn her back on Rue as if Rue were of no consequence. Kate returned with the tea and set it on the table with a thump and a rattle of china. Alexi also returned and dropped the rocks on the table next to the teacup. Rue examined the rocks then ordered Alexi to collect them and follow her. Alexi sighed and re gathered the rocks and followed Rue out the front door. Rue examined the main house and pointed where she wanted the rocks. Alexi positioned the rocks as instructed and rue touched each one and the rocks flared flame bright for a moment before going dark. When Alexi reached out a hand to touch one of the rocks, Rue slapped his hand "unless you want to be scattered into a million pieces, I would avoid the rocks." Alexi stepped back and felt something squish under his feet, avoiding looking down he shakes his foot to the side and feels something fly free. Shuddering he heads back into the house being more careful where he stepped. Rue went through all the rooms and judged them 'pathetically Spartan' None of the rooms looked like anything other than a place to heal with narrow beds and un-dyed wool and cotton linens. Alexi was more than happy to sleep in a nice narrow bed underneath what appeared to be very comfortable blankets. Rue went through all the rooms and closets and gathered all the best clothing and linen for herself and carried the lot upstairs to the loft, which she claimed as 'her suite'. Alexi and Kate were all too happy to take the remaining blankets and each retreat to a room of their own.

Rue was awake with the dawn, which was a good thing since her visitors were already waiting at the end of the paved path on their horses. Kate whispered something about the riders looking like Tolkien wraiths in their black armor and astride their black chargers. Rue brushed and braided her blonde hair and changed into a Teal gown of Fae craftsmanship and suddenly she seemed taller and more mystical. Alexi wondered if it was the gown or a spell of Rue's that gave her the appearance of a true practitioner. Rue had Alexi and Kate walk flank her as she went out to meet their guests. Kate was wearing a flowing gown of pewter gray silk that complemented her 'collar', Alexi was wearing a white long sleeved shirt with a brocade vest and tight black leather breeches that laced up the front. Rue had even managed to find him a pair of knee-high boots that fit him as if made especially for him (pretty much the same outfit he had been wearing when Rue had met him). The riders were lined up at the end of the path, the closed helms revealing nothing about their guests. Rue stopped well back from the end of the path and well out of reach of the wicked blades strapped across each of the knights back.

As if a silent signal had been given, one of the knights clapped heels to his horse and rode straight at rue as if intending to run her down. Rue pointed to one of the stones as the rider's horse was passing it and the stone exploded and caused the horse to rear and panic. The horse reared and toppled taking its rider with it to the ground. The horse rolled off its rider and took off back towards the woods leaving the knight to slowly climb to his feet. The knight whipped his helm off with a colorful curse and tossed the helm to the side revealing a scarred Fae warrior with short spiky black hair. "You will pay for that Witch!" Rue laughed scathingly at him "I will be paid for the insult with your life if you take another step towards me whoreson!" The Fae warrior's face went a scarlet red and he slid what turned out to be a nasty looking serrated blade from his back and swung overhand at Rue. Had the swing made contact Rue would have been cleaved in two, as he started to bring the blade down the stone next to his leg exploded and took his leg off at the hip. The knight fell to the side with a scream of agony and a sudden fountain of blood spewing from the gaping wound, his sword fell from suddenly nerveless fingers as he hit the ground. Rue ignored the screaming man writhing on the ground and turned cold eyes on the remaining riders.

Off to the right a ripple in the air shimmered and a knight in silver and black etched armor appeared as if stepping out from behind a curtain. Rue turned slightly to keep ALL of her guests within her sight. The newcomer made a slicing motion with his hand and one of the black knights bowed his head indicating the new knight was their leader and dismounted. Rue watched the black knight unsheathe his sword and plunge it straight through the heart of his prone companion. The silence was absolute as the scream was abruptly cut off. With another hand signal the corpse was tossed onto the back of his executioner's horse and the knights remounted and turned their mounts back towards the woods and trotted off in that direction. The leader slowly came forward and dismounted in front of the trio. Rue gave a gasp as the knight removed his helm and placed it on his saddle. The face revealed was the epitome of male beauty. High cheekbones paired with a chiseled jaw and full lips. His long silver hair was pulled into a topknot that fell past his shoulders and eyes the color of the finest sapphires. The full lips pulled into an amused smile at Rue's reaction to his appearance.

The Fae inclined his head "I am Prince Marrat'hassar....and you are?" Rue felt her mouth go suddenly dry, she had never met a Fae Prince before. "I am Rue Bishop, a powerful sorceress of the human realm...these are my servants Alexi and Kate." Prince Marrat'hassar immediately dismissed Alexi and Kate as unworthy of his attention and focused solely on Rue. "May we enter your ...domicile and discuss the terms of our alliance?" Rue nodded and gestured for him to precede them into the building. The Prince entered and immediately made himself comfortable at the head of the table and gestured for Rue to join him as if he were granting an audience. Pointing a finger at Kate, he snarled "Wench! Fetch wine for myself and your mistress!" Kate stumbled over her own feet as she hurried to the kitchen to comply. Alexi had made to sit down at the table and stopped as the Prince's eyes fell on him coldly. "Do I share negotiations with servants now?" Rue scowled at Alexi "Go make yourself useful and help Kate in the kitchen." Rue apologized for her recently acquired servant and promised the Prince that Alexi would be beaten for his impudence later. This seemed to be the exact right thing to say as this restored the Prince's humor. "So Lady Bishop, what terms do you offer and what do you require of my people?" Rue thought carefully about how to phrase her request. "One of my servants stole something of great value to me and escaped to this realm,...he is being assisted my a different faction of your kind and I require your assistance to recover my wayward servant and property." The prince rubbed a hand across his jaw as he considered her words "Now I know what you ask of my people, but what do you offer up as payment?"

Rue stood from the table and gestured for the Prince to follow her into the other room. The prince stood to his full height and followed behind her, his eyes briefly widened at the sight of the captives. "You would purchase my assistance with these captives?" Rue turned to face him and laughed "You mistake my intentions your majesty, these captives are a gift for meeting with me...I offer my services as a powerful Sorceress in exchange for your assistance." The Prince gave her a slow once over then grinned, a greedy light entering his eyes "Then Lady bishop, we have an accord." Rue extended her hand to shake on it and after only a brief hesitation he took her hand and pressed his soft lips against the back while staring into her eyes. "I will open a Gate to the palace so that we may move the captives more easily." The Prince walked to the wall and began chanting and opened a door to what appeared to be an antechamber hewn from dark polished stone.

The Prince gestured and several servants stepped through the doorway. "Take these captives to the healers, we want them in pristine condition before we start their interrogations." The servants bowed and waited for Rue to dispel the barrier stones before striding across and hefting the captives as if they were sacks of grain and taking them screaming back through the doorway where the sound cut off immediately. Prince

Marrat'hassar took her hand again and stared into her eyes with that amused smile again "It would be my pleasure to have you join me for dinner...Lady Bishop." Rue forced herself to look confident as she curtsied. "It would be my pleasure to join you...and your wife for dinner your majesty." The Prince chuckled and placed his hand over his heart "I fear Lady Bishop, there will be no wife at my side tonight as none exists in my life but my father the King and my mother the Queen will be present." Rue inclined her head and blushed at being caught in her not so subtle inquiry. The Prince smiled and stepped through the doorway, three servants hopped back through the doorway to help her transport her things to the palace. Rue ordered Kate and Alexi to strip the place of anything of value and began packing crates and boxes and handing them to the servants who passed them through the barrier. When the servants had taken the last of their things through the portal, Rue turned to Kate and Alexi " Speak only when spoken to and remember your place or I will allow them to remove your tongues....or worse." Rue and the Prince walked arm in arm chatting like old friends while Kate and Alexi walked further back with the other servants. The Prince left her at the door to her suite and introduced her to Aly'ssia their 'Mistress of Maids' . Kissing the back of her hand he left her to go and inform his family of her presence.

Aly'ssia waited while Rue made up her mind what to request. Finally Rue let her know she would need a lady's maid for her hair and clothing and since she had no time to prepare for a formal dinner she would need the loan of proper clothing as well. Aly'ssia did not so much as blink when she nodded and clapped her hands sending maids to fetch clothing and accessories for Lady Rue and introducing her to Valerya who would be her Lady's Maid until such time as she no longer had need of her. Kate and Alexi were housed together in the servants' wing while Rue's suite was located in the Royal

Apartments. Valerya immediately took charge and stripped and bathed Rue with scented

water. After roughly toweling her dry, she gowned her in a shimmering forest green

gown with a plunging neckline and swept her hair up to fall in a waterfall of cascading

ringlets. By the time the servant came to escort her to dinner, Rue was gowned and

coiffed and her natural beauty had been enhanced with subtle cosmetics. Rue followed

the servant to the dining hall and waited outside the doors a few moments taking deep

breaths before nodding to the servant to open the doors for her.

The doors opened silently and closed again behind her with a muffled thump. Rue

found herself staring at the longest table she had ever seen laden with enough food to

feed several small countries, which was funny as it was only set for four people and three

were already present. Rue recognized Prince Marrat'hassar immediately although he had

changed out of his armor and now wore a form fitting pair of leather breeches and a blue

brocade doublet that matched his eyes. The Prince smiled at her as her eyes met his, then

her eyes skipped past him to fall on the next occupant of the table. King Melcindo'mien

shared the same silver hair as his son. While Marrat'hassar's hair fell past his shoulders,

the King's hair brushed his shoulders in a neat nearly military style. Also in contrast were

their eyes, the Prince had eyes of deepest sapphire and the King's eyes were dark and

fathomless pools that drew you in. A subtle cough brought her eyes to the only other

woman at the table. Queen Mo'readhiel had long blood red hair and eyes the same shade

of sapphire as her son. Rue felt a pang of jealous as she realized that the Queen's face and

form far eclipsed her own beauty and far more subtle curves. Like her men, Queen

Mo'readhiel was the epitome of beauty for her gender.

Rue made her way to the table with a tight feeling to her stomach and allowed a servant to seat her all the while wondering if she had gotten herself in over her head. Prince Marrat'hassar made introductions around the table and rue found herself the uncomfortable focus of three pairs of eyes. She smiled at the lust and appreciation in the prince's eyes ...until she found the same look mirrored in the eyes of both the king and queen as they contemplated her across the table. Rue shivered and wondered not for the last time what she had gotten herself into. Small talk passed the time as they ate, it was only after the servants had cleared the food and brought wine that the talk became serious. The King sat back and smiled at her "If we are to purchase your...wares Lady Bishop, I am afraid we will need a demonstration." Anticipating this Rue had brought a ring that she had added the controlling compulsion to and placed it before her on the table "I have the ability to enchant objects to gain absolute control over the wearers, it is one of my favorite but by no means my only talent." The Queen leaned forward, her large breasts threatening to spill from the top of her gown and an eager light in her eyes "absolute control you say?" Rue nodded "I can compel...violence or sexual desire in one under my control...complete obedience in all things in fact." The Queen purred as she sat back "I would like to see that demonstrated Lady Bishop." The king smiled in shared anticipation with his family before returning his smile to Rue. Rue glanced at each of them then nodded "I will need the use of one of two of your guardsmen and a maidservant.

A few moments passed as the King summoned the requested servants. The guardsmen were stripped down to tunic and trews and their weapons taken from them, the chambermaid stood to the side unneeded for the moment. Rue beckoned one of the guardsman to her, when prompted he responded his name was Jorkai, his fellow guardsman was named Denethor and the chambermaid was Lysstra. Rue looked both guardsmen over then slipped the ring on Jorkai's finger, then whispered in his ear and stepped out of the way as he suddenly lunged and attacked Denethor. The two guardsmen rolled around the chamber pummeling and tearing at each other until with a wet sounding snap Jorkai slammed a heel into Denethor's throat and snapped his neck. Covered in his companion's blood, Jorkai turned to Rue as if awaiting further instructions. Rue's eyes flicked to the horrified chambermaid and she smiled as she gave him permission to "take" Lysstra. Jorkai caught her as she attempted to flee and Rue turned back towards the table with a smile to drink her wine. The Royal Family watched the final demonstration and only when Jorkai had "finished" did they allow the servants to remove the sobbing chambermaid and Denethor's body. With a bow Jorkai deposited the ring on the table in front of Rue and left looking more than a little disconcerted.

The King and Prince both fell over themselves to assure her of their absolute interest in agreeing to her terms and closing the negotiations. Rue did not miss the look of anger that crossed King Melcindo'mien's face as his son was quicker to offer escort back to Rue's chambers. When they arrived at her chambers, it was obvious that the Prince expected to be invited in. Rue considered it for a long moment then decided it might look like she were too eager to ingratiate herself with the Royal Family, claiming to be overcome with the events of the day she stepped inside and with a smile of regret she closed the door. She heard him whisper "another time then Lady" before he returned back down the corridor.

CHAPTER EIGHT

Once again the days seemed to pass quickly as Daniel and Hart renewed their relationship as father and son and could even be found laughing and sparring with each other in the palace gardens. Hart and Daniel shared a love of 'The Princess Bride' and would laugh as they re enacted the great battle between Inigo Montoya and Wesley. Since most of the Fae had never seen the movie or read the book, the duel could be re enacted over and over again and look like it was an original production thought up between Hart and Daniel. On the third day Queen Sadronniel summoned them and once again the throne room was packed with all manner of creatures. If it weren't for the fact that the Consort was no where to be seen, Daniel would be having a horrible case of déjà vu. "Daniel Warwick, you presented your case in private audience before us and we asked for three days to deliberate." Daniel nodded to the Queen's announcement although it had not been a question. "During those three days we have learned that the one who summoned the Daemon that chased you has entered Underhill and has entered into negotiations with our foes of the Unseelie Court....why does this witch hunt you so obsessively?" Daniel shrugged and shook his head "I told you what I know, the one time I asked her that question she mentioned my half Fae parentage as a reason." Daniel gestured to Hunter who immediately hunched his shoulders at attention being drawn to him. "From what Hunter said, Rue was some Fae woman named Angelique's protégée'." Queen Sadronniel head snapped around so fast Daniel half expected it to fly off. "This witch was taught by 'the banished one'?" Hunter nodded and shuffled his feet like a chastised child. Queen Sadronniel sighed and gave Daniel an apologetic look. "This changes things I fear, Angelique was my sorceress and the crimes of her pupil are mine to answer for." There was a collective gasp from the onlookers. Queen Sadronniel was not one who easily admitted fault "I banished Angelique instead of execution for her crimes, I have learned that the witch has spilled Fae blood within our realm and so we will aid you Daniel Warwick and help you to bring the witch to justice." Her voice echoed in the now silent hall and she turned to her scribe who had until this moment gone unnoticed by Daniel and his companions, "So shall it be written, so shall it be done." Daniel hardly dared to believe that the queen had just announced before the whole assembled crowd that the Seelie court would ally with him against Rue and help bring her to justice.

Turning to Hunter and Lauren he whispered "Did she mean...is she offering to help us capture Rue and bring her to justice?" Hunter nodded with wide eyes and smiled. "Never thought I'd live to see the day when the Seelie Court would back a half-breed, ye got the Puck's own luck about ye boy!" Lauren giggled and then sobered "Sorry this is kind of like the night before the battle of Gettysburg, or before King Arthur charged across the fields of Camlann." Although Daniel was no history scholar he understood the references. "So we are going to charge in and take her from the other guys?" Queen Sadronniel chuckled "Hardly young Daniel, there is as much talking and negotiations in battles as there is fighting." Daniel gave her a very confused look and she shook her head. "First we send messengers requesting a parlay with the Unseelie court, then we will request she be turned over to us and state our reasons and they will decide if there is interest on their part in doing so." Daniel cursed under his breath forgetting for a moment who he was addressing. "So if they don't want to trade or barter her, then we are screwed?!?" Queen Sadronniel's eyes narrowed at the crude term "No we are not as you say 'screwed', everything has a price, we need to simply find theirs." Hart placed a hand on Daniel's shoulder "do not fret Daniel, ALWAYS will good find a way to persevere over darkness, ALWAYS there is light in the darkness." Daniel nodded wanting badly to believe that now that he had allies, Rue would be made to pay for her crimes. The Queen released them for the rest of the day as she went to her war room to draft a message to the Unseelie King and Queen and begin negotiations. Daniel needed air and declined yet another duel with Hart. Instead he headed for the Royal gardens on his own.

Hearing a crunching on the gravel walk behind him, Daniel turned and saw Lauren trotting to catch up with him. Lauren had taken to wearing her long red hair in a braided crown like the sylphs were seen in and it actually looked really nice on her. Lauren smiled as she caught up with him "mind a little company stranger?" Daniel shrugged and slowed his pace to make it easier for her to keep up with him. "So while Hart and I have been entertaining the masses with fencing duels, what have you and hunter been up to?" Lauren blushed "Hunter has been off with the other rangers doing whatever it is they do and I have been learning to dance and taking lessons on curing my clumsiness from the Flora Sylphs." Daniel smiled and went and sat on one of the stone benches just off the garden path. "I would love to see it, the sylphs shy away from Hart and I so I have not been able to see their dances." Lauren smiled and clasped her hands in front of her as she swayed to the music in her head starting with small steps and twirls and gradually becoming more expressive as she transitioned into a full Saltarello complete with high leaps and twirls as if she were a leaf on the wind. Lauren caught a glimpse of Daniel's enraptured face as she made a difficult spin and stumbled. Closing her eyes in anticipation of her tumble, she felt arms grab her and she landed on something other than the ground. Opening her eyes she saw Daniel's concerned face very close to hers and before she could think better of it she pressed her lips to his and felt warmth shoot straight to her core as his lips slowly moved on hers.

Daniel's eyes suddenly sprang open and he nearly dropped Lauren to the ground as he realized what he was doing and scooted back. Kissing Lauren had just felt so natural that he had just responded and not thought about it. Lauren was blushing furiously as she stood and brushed herself off. "I am so sorry Daniel, I just..." She shrugged helplessly at a loss to explain what had come over her. Daniel nodded his understanding, "this place seems to have that effect on people." Lauren smiled and took his hand tentatively "its not just this place, you are such a strong person and so much has happened since I met you..." Daniel gave her a teasing smile "Lauren are you trying to confess to falling for me?" Lauren's face went even redder and she crossed her arms over her chest looking embarrassed and took a defensive tone. "Well...is it so hard to believe someone might have real feelings for you?" Daniel stood and brushed his seat pants off, "Never really thought about it I guess, I am just a small town pizza cook and never really thought of myself as a babe magnet." Lauren grinned and nudged him playfully "Are you saying you think I am a babe Daniel Warwick?" Daniel rubbed the back of his neck and chuckled nervously as he realized the trap he had just stepped in. "Well yeah, curvy redhead with big green eyes...who wouldn't think you are a knockout?" Lauren grinned at him "So if you are not busy later...would you like to have dinner with me tonight...unless I am too much of a babe for you that is..." Lauren nudged him again playfully and he laughed and dropped into a theatrical bow. "Twould be my honor to share thy meal this eve m'lady." Lauren giggled and blushed "You have been spending WAY TOO much time with Hunter and Hart." Daniel stuck out his elbow and Lauren linked her arm with his as they walked arm in arm back to the palace.

Daniel and Lauren separated at the Royal Apartments, he to go to the suite shared with Hart and she to go to the one shared with Hunter. Daniel promised to be knocking at her door no later than seven and Lauren laughed as she hurried back to the suite to get things ready. Daniel went back to his suite and found Hart looking seriously troubled as he savored a cup of the ever present dark red wine. "What's got you looking so disgruntled?" Hart turned to look over the back of the chaise at Daniel and motioned for him to join him at the low table. "The Queen has made a tentative inquiry to the Unseelie Court in regards to a trade for your witch...they have agreed to meet and discuss the matter but nothing more has been promised and by the wording of the reply, they may not be interested in a trade at all." Daniel flopped onto the other end of the chaise and poured himself some wine. "So there is a chance I may be the root cause of the next Great Fae War?" Hart laughed "You put too much stock in yourself, the Seelie and Unseelie have been waging war against each other for thousands of generations, and I would be more surprised if we went more than a couple hundred years WITHOUT a battle." Daniel gave Hart an incredulous look "what are you guys still fighting over after so many years?" Hart took another swallow of wine and shrugged "The same things your people fight over, lands, slights of honor, insults, religious differences, imagined crimes against each other..." Daniel shook his head "Haven't you guys ever thought of marriage alliances or treaties to keep peace between the Courts?" Hart arched an eyebrow at him "Ever heard of Romeo and Juliet?" Daniel had just taken a drink of wine and found himself coughing and choking on the now burning wine as it went down the wrong way. Hart laughed as Daniel continued to cough And splutter. "Please tell me you are joking Hart..." Hart shrugged, "just as our bards make songs and stories of events of your past, so too do your poets and authors make stories from the events of our own world."

Daniel didn't know how long he and Hart sat and compared myths and stories from their worlds before he finally got around to asking the question that had been weighing on his chest. "So if these negotiations spark a war, how likely is it we will survive to see it end?" Hart saw the fear in Daniel's eyes that belied the cavalier tone and put a hand on his shoulder "If we end up on the battlefield, you stay on my six and do exactly as I tell you and we might both make it to the post war celebration." Daniel grinned as Hart once again surprised him with his adept use of human terminology. "Stay on your six...you picked up a lot of choice phrases while in my world, so when were you in the military there long hair?" Hart chuckled and set his now empty goblet on the low table before responding. "How better to study a world's warriors then to be one." Daniel set his goblet down next to Hart's and leaned back on the chaise. "You enlisted...didn't think they took hippies." Hart smiled as he took a deep breath. "Depends on the time and country." With a grand flourish he began the recitation of his military career. "In Assyria I was a general under King Xerxes, in Egypt I was a charioteer under Pharaoh Ramses the third." Daniel nodded and opened his mouth to speak when Hart continued. "During the French and Indian War I was an Indian scout with the 4th regiment's militia under Colonel

Winchester." Daniel smirked "Now I know you are lying, you aren't even Native American, so how were you a Native American scout?" Hart shrugged "your people see what they want to and who am I to dissuade them if they think me a native?" Daniel's eyes got wider and wider as Hart took another breath and continued listing his service. "I was recalled Underhill during your Revolutionary War but re emerged during the Civil War where I fought on the side of the union under General Grant." Daniel folded his arms "Is that all?" Hart smiled and shook his head "I also fought in WW1 and WW2, Korean War and Vietnam War...then I tired of my research and chose to go home for a vacation." Daniel felt like someone had slapped him upside the head with a shovel, Hart had fought in nearly all of the greatest wars and under some of the greatest commanders in history. Daniel whistled "If ever anyone deserved a vacation, it was you Hart."

Hart refilled his goblet and took a deep drink before looking at Daniel with a guilty expression on his face. "I would love to say that it was my altruistic nature that led me to fight in so many wars, but I was in a bad place spiritually and was seeking my own demise." Daniel nodded, after what he learned about the way things had gone down between Hart and his mother at the end...he understood the dark place Hart had found himself in. "I understand Hart, and shit you are still braver than I am." Daniel knew the moment he found himself on a battlefield facing hordes of angry Fae in armor, he would probably piss himself...if he lived long enough that is. Daniel glanced at the mantle clock and felt the blood drain from his face, it was five minutes to seven and he had not even changed. Daniel vaulted over the back of the chaise and sprinted into his room and started tossing clothes everywhere as he tried to find something decent to wear. Hart followed him and leaned against the doorframe watching for a moment before stepping in and tossing a light gray tunic and black doublet and breeches to him. "Take these and change in the bathroom." Daniel thanked him and ran into the bathroom slamming the door behind him. Hart tsked and began picking up clothes and draping them over his arm as he transferred them to the cedar wardrobe instead of the floor. It took Hart ten minutes to tidy the room, it was then that he realized Daniel had not emerged from the bathroom during that time. Walking to the door, Hart knocked lightly before swinging it open. Daniel stood half dressed staring at his own reflection. "Daniel are you alright?" Daniel's eyes shifted to meet Hart's in the mirror. "I don't know if I can do this, the last woman I was alone with was murdered for sleeping with me...what if?" Hart shook his head as he turned Daniel from the mirror and finished lacing the doublet and pulling everything straight. "If you spend your life asking what if, you will never live at all." Daniel took a steadying breath and shot Hart a grateful smile as he sprinted past him and out the suite door.

Daniel knocked on Lauren's door hoping she did not shoot him on sight. Hunter opened the door and whistled "five more minutes and she was going to come find ye and give ye a nasty piece of her mind boyo." Daniel gave a half smile and rubbed the back of his neck "I got talking to Hart and kinda lost track of time." Hunter nodded and stepped back to let Daniel in. Daniel slipped past Hunter and turned to say something further to him only to see Hunter heading out the door. Hunter paused in the doorway just long enough to give him a mocking smile and whisper 'have fun' before closing the door behind him. Daniel turned back towards the suite and noticed Lauren standing near decked out table with her arms crossed and an annoyed look on her face. Daniel noticed she was wearing an intriguing forest green gown that clung to curves he had somehow never noticed before, her hair was piled atop her head with a few stray curls falling loose to frame her face. Daniel's throat suddenly felt as dry as the Sahara desert. Daniel had never really 'looked' at Lauren before, he had been too busy trying to get away. The idea that this beautiful woman before him had gone unnoticed thus far made him feel like someone had once again knocked the wind from him. Lauren saw his guilty expression and after a tense moment of silence she started laughing. "You look so forlorn...I forgive you for being late, I am sure whatever kept you was very important." Daniel let out the breath he had been holding in a sigh of relief. "Hart and I got talking about things and I swear I just lost track of time...and then there was ..." Daniel shrugged and gestured to his outfit "I am at a loss with these clothes, I am a t-shirt and jeans kind of guy...all this froofarah is wasted on me."

Lauren laughed again as she gave his outfit a once over "Well I think you look sweet, I think the leather pants look is totally you." Daniel felt suddenly embarrassed and cast about for a distraction. "I appreciate you inviting me for dinner." He gestured to where a veritable feast sat cooling on the low table and Lauren took the hint and sat at one end and gestured for him to sit next to her. Daniel sat next to her and felt like a freshman at his first Prom as he poured them each a glass of wine. Lauren took pity on him and took control of the conversation, she made small talk and eventually steered the conversation to Hart and the conversation that had caused Daniel to be late. They both started laughing at Hart being mistaken for a Native American and laughed at each other's silly suggestions on what his 'Indian Name' would be. Lauren laughed, tears running down her face "Maybe it would be 'Makes toys For Santa." Daniel smirked and shook his head "How about tree dwelling cookie baker." Lauren snorted at the thought of Hart as a

Keebler elf then smiled "Maybe his name would be 'Shelf Sitting Santa Spy'." Daniel chuckled "You have a real thing for Christmas don't you?" Lauren wiped her eyes with the back of her hand "I am a big kid when it comes to Christmas, I love the lights and music and silly movies...especially the togetherness it brings out in people." Daniel took a big drink of his wine. "My mom was strict for Christmas, making me wear uncomfortable clothes and dragging me to church, I felt like a fake because Christmas and Easter were the only times we went." Lauren understood completely, her family had been ,much the same way. Something suddenly occurred to Daniel "I never got around to asking, what actually brought you to Bethesda?" Lauren's face went red as she thought back over her flight from her family which culminated with her falling down at Daniel's door. "I was taking some time away from my family, you see my fiancé Trevor and I...he was sleeping with my sister Shannon...I actually caught them in bed together and...I needed to get away." Lauren toyed with the skirt of her dress, her fingers twisting together.

Daniel felt like a rock had dropped into his stomach and suddenly the food and wine didn't seem quite so appealing. "So you are engaged to be married?" Lauren looked up at him quickly and saw the look of sudden comprehension cross his face. "Well no...not really, he slept with my sister so I hardly think that constitutes a healthy relationship." Daniel stood from the table feeling like an idiot "Does Trevor know the wedding is off?" Lauren bit her lip and suddenly realized how this must seem to Daniel, as if she were using Daniel to get back at Trevor. "No, not exactly...I mean I stormed out of there angry and they know that I know but, no...I didn't actually say the words." Daniel nodded and set his goblet back down on the table and bowed at the waist "I think I am going to call it a night, I need to get some rest for tomorrow." Lauren stood up and grabbed his arm "I meant what I said, I really do have feelings for you Daniel." Daniel gently removed her hand from his arm "I do not toy with other's affections and I do not get romantically involved with women who are married or even engaged to be married...the fact that you let me believe...I gotta go now Lauren." Daniel all but fled out the door, had he looked back he would have seen Lauren standing where he had left her with tears of agony running down her face.

CHAPTER NINE

Rue was pulled away from her pleasant conversation with Prince Marrat'hassar by Kate who was nearly hysterical. "You have to come with me, they are going to kill him!" Rue shook off Kate's clinging hands "What are you talking about Kate, who is going to kill who?" Kate avoided looking over at the Prince as she lowered her voice. "The guards are going to kill Alexi, one of the guards pushed us while we were bringing water to your room for your bath and the water spilled...Alexi punched him and then the other guards showed up and now..." Rue followed Kate as they headed towards the Southern Gate. When they arrived in the Southern corridor, the guards had formed a circle around Alexi. Alexi was sitting on a guards chest and bashing his face over and over into the marble floor. Rue screamed his name and the corridor went dead silent as the guard's loud jeers and catcalls abruptly went silent. Alexi turned to look at who called his name then slammed the unconscious guards head a final time into the floor and spit on him as he stood to his feet and turned to meet Rue. Alexi's once white shirt was now a mottled reddish brown and hung in tatters on him.

Rue turned to look at the carnage and realized there was not one but four downed guards in the circle of guards. Prince Marrat'hassar had followed Rue and barked orders for all but four of the guards to return to their posts. Rue glared at Alexi "How dare you disgrace me like this Alexi, you have attacked Royal Guards and threatened our tenuous alliance here." Kate opened her mouth to answer the accusation but was silenced by the look Alexi shot her before turning back to Rue with a grin "Always happy to disappoint you." Rue smiled and touched the side of his face tenderly "You will not and so your service to me will change...I will no longer require you for pleasure Alexi, merely hard work." Turning to Prince Marrat'hassar she smiled sweetly "Your majesty I beg the use of your guardsmen, please have them take my servant and flog him and when they are done with that I beseech you to have my servant gelded as well." Alexi cursed her in Romanian and lunged for her, a swift blow from the hilt of a guard's sword dropped him to the floor. The prince looked to his four guardsmen and nodded and smiled as they lifted the unconscious Alexi and carried him down the hall. Kate looked from Rue to the Prince and then glanced at the guard's retreating backs before dropping her eyes and muttering "better him than me." Rue ignored the comment and turned with a flourish to the Prince and whispered an invitation to join her in her room. Kate quietly slipped away as Rue and the prince made their way back to Rue's suite.

Rue giggled nervously as they reached her suite. Turning she wrapped her arms around the Prince's neck and pulled him into a passionate kiss. She felt his arms go around her and his hand found the latch, the door slid open behind her and suddenly she was swept up into his arms. Stepping inside he kicked the door shut behind him, never breaking from the fiery kiss and seemingly without looking carried her to the bed. Laying her on the bed he proceeded to strip, Rue felt her mouth watering as each delicious inch of him was revealed. Rue stood and turned her back to him "I am afraid I will need your assistance with this gown your majesty." With a quick tug he broke the laces and helped her slip out of the gown. As he turned her toward him he noticed her slightly rounded abdomen. Rue followed his eyes and bit her lip "Does the thought of my carrying another's child repulse you m'lord?" The Prince smiled and laid a hand on her belly. "Not at all Lady Rue, merely a surprise...children are rare for Fae and so every child is a blessing." Rue smiled uncertainly not sure she liked the light that came into the Prince's eyes when she had mentioned being pregnant. Laying her back on the bed, he lifted one of her long legs and brought it to rest on his shoulder his head turning to nibble her ankle and make her squirm. With a grin down at her he roughly shoved deep inside her, her back arching off the bed.

A cloud seemed to pass in front of the sun for a moment as she looked up at the Prince as he thrust deep inside her and she tensed as for a moment a dark skinned creature with glowing red eyes was grinning down at her, fangs showing between its black lips. The cloud passed and she was once again staring at the beautiful face of prince Marrat'hassar in all his fair skinned glory, the moment had shattered her pleasure though and she was forced to fake her enthusiasm lest she insult her lover. The prince came much later with a groan and a tensing of his taut muscles. Sliding onto the bed next to her, he kissed her bare shoulder and pulled her tightly against him. With anyone else she would have believed it to be a sign of affection, with the Prince it felt like a claim of possession as if he had just slapped a collar or a manacle on her. Eventually she felt him relax, his arm however remained as rigid as an iron bar, she did not remember implying she would like him to stay the night with her but there was no way to gracefully wake him and toss him from her bed. Besides, what if the vision she had seen was not just a trick of shadow, what if it was a true seeing and she had just bedded a nightmare. Rue shifted a little and winced as the arm tightened further around her and a sleepy hiss sounded from behind her as if she were laying next to a large snake. Rue settled herself in for a long night and just when she thought she would never get to sleep, she abruptly dropped off. When she awoke the Prince was gone and a servant was waiting nearby to help her bathe and from the smell of the tray, her breakfast was waiting as well. Rue could not believe she had slept so long or so soundly, normally she was a light sleeper. A glance out the window told her the sun had been up for hours, she really needed to figure out a way to set an alarm clock in this place. The servant helped her to bathe and dress and then sat quietly in the corner as she broke her fast. Rue watched her clear the dishes up and leave and found herself at a loss as to what do do with herself today. Perhaps she should go to the Chirurgeon and see how Alexi was doing after his punishment. That thought appealed to her and she quickly straitened her dress and headed in the direction of the Chirurgeon's office.

Rue arrived at the Chirurgeon's office in time to see them releasing Alexi, though he was pale beneath his tan and walked slowly, he seemed to be healed enough to return to work. Rue stopped him and smiled as his eyes spit fire at her "I will be bathing in my chamber later, you will bring hot water and fill the tub just after dinner..." Alexi nodded

and stepped past her to continue down the hall. The Chirurgeon came rushing out with a

small bag in his hands "wait, stop that young man, I have herbs for him to place in his tea

to alleviate his pain." Rue smiled and took the herbs "I will see that he gets them." Rue

tucked the herbs away and decided she would dole out the herbs only when Alexi did

something to deserve them. Alexi turned the corner and leaned his back against the cold

stone of the hallway, the stone felt good against the wounds on his back. Although all his

wounds had been closed, they still burned and caused him pain...he didn't want to think of

what else he was going to have to live with or more to the point without thanks to Rue.

Alexi sighed and pushed off from the wall and headed back to his room to lay down for a

couple hours before he had to start hauling and heating water.

CHAPTER TEN

Daniel returned to his suite to find Hart and Hunter playing some drinking

game using what looked like a chess board, shot glasses and strange looking dice. Both

Hart and Hunter looked up in surprise as he came in, he paused to say something then

changed his mind and went to his room and after stripping out of his clothes he went to

bed. Daniel heard Hart and Hunter having a hushed conversation before he heard Hunter wish Hart a good night and leave. Hart appeared in his doorway shortly after with two bottles of Siobhan's fire ale. Daniel pulled the blankets to his waist and propped up on his elbow. "I appreciate the ear and the beer Hart." Hart nodded as he pulled a chair up to the side of the bed and handed Daniel the beer. "I am here if you need to talk Daniel." Daniel took a cautious swig of the ale and sat up. "Why would a woman give you all the signs she was interested in more than a friendship then conveniently forget to mention she had already promised herself to another man?" Hart chuckled as he took a drink of his own ale. "Women are more mysterious than the most complex of magic Daniel, far be it from me to tell you what was going through any woman's head." Daniel took another drink of ale and decided to clue Hart in to what was going on with Lauren. "From what she told me, her fiancé Trevor was caught with her sister and she stormed out." Hart nodded and waited "I can understand her being angry at him, but if she didn't call it off...is the engagement over?" Hart smiled as he took another drink "only she and Trevor can say, maybe tonight was a good thing, maybe she will want to go back to your world now and talk with Trevor.. it would be settled one way or the other.' Daniel wished Hart had come with a more satisfying answer but maybe there was no easy answer for this. They finished their ales and Hart took the bottles and wished Daniel a good night as he left.

Breakfast was a quiet affair shared with Queen Sadronniel as she announced that Hart would be accompanying her to the meeting with the Unseelie court. Hart was outwardly calm but Daniel knew if he in Hart's place he would be feeling sick to his stomach at the prospect of meeting with an evil King and Queen. Hart nodded his acknowledgment then excused himself to see to preparations and without another word nor a backward glance, he was gone. Daniel had just started wondering if he should follow him when his attention was abruptly brought back to the matter at hand. Queen Sadronniel turned to meet first Daniel's eyes and then Lauren's as if making sure she had their complete attention. "There is a matter I must discuss with you two, our allies in your world have informed me that there is quite the disturbance over the disappearance of the two of you." Lauren and Daniel looked at each other confused. "Apparently Daniel's employer and your own family Lauren, have involved authorities involved searching for you...due in no small part to the crashed automobile on the part of Lauren's family I have no doubt." Daniel let out a quiet curse and saw Lauren drop her face into her hands with a sigh. The Queen cleared her throat to recapture their attention. "I must ask you two to briefly return to your world to let those looking for you know you are well and make your excuses, then you may return to us so we may finalize this distasteful witch situation with the Unseelie." The Queen made small talk until all of them had finished their meals, she then dismissed them to go and prepare themselves for the return trip.

Daniel's mind was spinning, he had not stopped to consider Angelo would come looking for him if he stopped showing up at work. Obviously he was going to have to come up with a good reason for just up and disappearing. His sudden disappearance would already look highly suspicious after the recent deaths of Hecate and Jason. Lauren's family was probably freaking out due to the wrecked car and the blood inside with no body. They had probably come to the conclusion that she had wandered off hurt and disoriented and was lying senseless in a field somewhere. Daniel entered his suite to find Hart packing, his hair damp as if from a recent shower. "So guess we are both going to be elsewhere, Lauren and I have to go back to our world to straighten things out with our families...guess there was a bit of a stir when both of us went missing." Hart nodded and stopped his packing and turned to look at Daniel. "I would go with you when you return to your world, as an escort if not a friend to guard your back." Daniel smiled and clapped Hart on the shoulder "I would be honored to have you at my back Hart." Hart allowed a brief smile before heading for the door, stopping with his hand on the door he looked back at Daniel "I will let the Queen know that I will be accompanying you and we can delay the meet until we are all safely back here." It occurred to Daniel only after Hart had left that he had looked almost happy at the prospect of delaying the meeting with the Unseelie Royals.

Daniel found a heavy bag in the closet, it felt like it was made from old carpets but had a wooden bottom which he discovered had a catch and was actually a small compartment. Shaking his head in wonder at Fae craftsmanship, he started packing clothes and anything he thought would be necessary. If shouldn't't take more than a week to get everything sorted and haul ass back here so they could finalize this business with Rue. What worried Daniel is that the Queen had informants in his world...might the other side have informants as well and would he and Lauren and Hart be safe back in their world even for so short a time? His turbulent thoughts were interrupted by a knock on the door. At first he expected to see a servant on the other side possibly summoning him to another meeting or meal, but when he opened the door it was Lauren. Lauren had dark circles under her eyes as if she had hardly slept last night. Her eyes briefly met Daniel's then flicked guiltily away "I just wanted to say that I am sorry, I realize that you were right...it was wrong of me to not tell you about Trevor and it was wrong of me to ....I will finish this thing with Trevor and maybe we could...." Lauren sighed deeply. "I would very much like it if we could try dinner again once we are back here again...if you still want to. Daniel knew he should be angry or hurt but instead he found himself pulling her into a hug. "I am sorry too, I should not have stormed out, and you have nothing to apologize for...I am just a little tense with everything that has happened." Lauren laughed in relief and he could hear how close she was to tears. Daniel pulled back and looked down at her "besides I would not be much of a friend if I dropped you the first time things got tense right?" Lauren smiled at him through her tears and looked past him at the bag sitting on the table. Her eyes got big "oh my, I forgot I have to pack too...I'll see you at the Gate." With a flurry of skirts she whipped around and jogged off down the hall to her own suite leaving Daniel silently laughing at her haste. Daniel was finished with his packing in next to no time and a servant came to take his bag to the staging area.

The Queen had arranged for them to take a different Gate back to their world, one that opened near an airport and transportation was waiting on the other side. When Daniel saw the black H2 sitting parked on the tarmac with a uniformed driver standing by, he wanted to hoot and cheer like a teen making a touchdown. Hart chuckled and Lauren gave a surprised laugh as he jogged around the shiny new car looking like a kid at Christmas. The driver stood with folded hands and a blank expression as if he were used to this kind of reaction to his fancy rig. The driver opened the back of the hummer and waited for them to toss their bags in the back before closing the back and sliding behind the wheel. Hart took shotgun and Lauren and Daniel slid into the back seats. After a brief discussion they decided to take care of talking to Daniel's employer first. The driver dropped them off at Angelo's and gave them a preprogrammed cell phone that had the car phone's number on speed dial. Daniel smiled as they walked in and the smell of garlic

and oregano wafted from the kitchen. Not surprisingly the restaurant was packed and the

mingling aromas was enough to make all of their stomach's growl. Daniel suggested

Lauren and Hart get a table and order some food while he slipped into the kitchen and

had a word with Angelo and his former coworkers. Hart was quick to agree when a

Chicken, mushroom and feta pizza passed beneath his nose on the way to its waiting

table.

Daniel waited until Lauren and Hart had seated themselves at a recently vacated

booth before heading for the kitchen. George dropped a pan of boiling water and cooked

shrimp covered the kitchen floor as Daniel came through the door. Suddenly Daniel was

caught up in a group hug from his kitchen crew amid loud shouts and exclamations of

surprise. Daniel started to give the concocted story he had come up with in the car when a

piercing whistle cut through the chatter and caused immediate silence. Angelo used a

wooden spoon to smack his employees out of the way as he approached Daniel. "six

months we had no word from you..." Suddenly Daniel was covering his head as the

wooden spoon came down again and again. "six months and you never called or came to

work...." the ranting continued in Italian and the other employees were trying to stifle

laughter as the tiny Italian owner smacked Daniel with the wooden spoon about the head

and shoulders. Daniel froze catching a sharp rap to the head as Angelo's words sunk in...

"six months...guess there is a time difference after all." Angelo looks confused "scusi?"

Daniel takes the spoon from his hand and tossed it over his head to George. "Look

Angelo, I just met someone and couldn't tear myself away from her, she was very...intense...I'm sorry it took so long to get back, time kinda slipped away from me."

Nothing he said was technically a lie. Angelo became silent a moment as he considered

Daniel's words and it seemed as if the whole kitchen held its breath to hear his decision.

Angelo nods and the collective sighs from the others nearly deafens Daniel who

chuckles as he glances at the relieved faces of his former coworkers. Angelo turns and

heads back towards his office "Very well Daniel, then you may return to work and we

will forget the long absence." Daniel cleared his throat nervously making Angelo freeze

in his tracks "Ummmm about that boss, I won't be returning...she and I are leaving and

we are not coming back..." The surprised gasps from the clustered workers nearly sucked

all the oxygen right back out of the room as Angelo turned in shock to face Daniel. "You

will not be returning...just like that, a woman turns your head and you will be leaving

gratzie very much!" Daniel sighed "I am sorry Angelo, but I cannot come back to work, I

am leaving Bethesda...I do not know if I will ever be coming back here." The kitchen

workers drifted back to their duties and the eavesdropping wait staff headed out with the

prepared food. Angelo was obviously still "Bene', you go, you do not come crawling

back to me, you leave and never come back Capisce?" Daniel nodded and winced as

Angelo slammed his office door shut.

Daniel left the kitchen, the fact that everyone now avoided his eyes as he left did

not escape his notice. Judgment had been pronounced and everyone would treat Daniel

accordingly. Daniel felt a piece of him die inside as he left the kitchen for the last time.

Hart and Lauren were currently enjoying a garbage pizza with loud exclamations of

delight. Daniel sat on the edge of the bench and watched them eat. It only took a moment

for them to notice that Daniel was not saying much. Lauren lowered the piece of pizza she had been about to tuck into. "So...did it go alright?" Daniel thought about it for a moment then nodded. "Yeah, I am no longer employed here...but that was expected." Lauren reached out and covered his hand with her own "I am so very sorry Daniel." Daniel nodded again and turned to Hart. "Did you know that there is a time distortion going through the Gate?" Hart shook his head "I really cannot say that I have ever noticed Daniel, how much time has passed since you left?" Daniel looked at Lauren and saw the shock on her face as he replied. "It has been six months since we left here....I'll need to go see my mom before we go take care of your family Lauren...if that is alright?" Lauren nodded mutely and stared at the pizza, she no longer had much of an appetite. Daniel signaled for the bill and they boxed up the pizza to go. Daniel paid the tab on their way out the door, turning he took one last look at the place that had been like a second home to him for so many years. Forcing himself to turn and walk away left him with an almost physical ache as he dialed the driver and left Angelo's for the last time.

The hummer pulled up in front and they piled in for the long drive to Daniel's mom's house. Daniel stared absently outside the window, the scenery outside flashing past in a blur as he wondered if he had done the right thing. Daniel had just burned bridges with a place he had once been happy. It seemed to take no time at all to pull up in front of the 'Martha Stewart Mansion' that was his mother's place. Lauren starts to offer to go with but Daniel taps Hart's shoulder and gives him a silent look of pleading. After a minute Hart nods and the two men slide out of the car leaving Lauren and the silent Driver to watch As they make their way up the walk. If Daniel had not already been aware of how much time had passed since the last time he had been there, he would never have know. The same semi wilted peonies in circular beds edged the walk, the same art deco wind chimes hung from the porch overhang. Daniel waited for Hart to join him on the porch and gestured for him to step to the side as he knocked. Lena waited several long moments before opening the door. The look of disdain on Lena's face as she stood in the doorway, a drink in her hand even though it was still early in the day was almost a physical blow. "So you are alive after all, the cops stopped by to tell me you were missing." He reminded himself that this was no longer his mother, but the woman who replaced the woman he had once been permitted to call mom. Lena took a drink from her glass, the ice cubes clinking gently. "Interrupted a very important garden party I'll have you know." Daniel bit back a sarcastic reply. "I am sorry mom....ummm Lena, I just came by to let you know I was alive and well." Lena sighed "You are not sorry, you are just like your father and Lord knows he never cared a wit about my feelings."

Before Daniel could stop him, Hart stepped into view. "Clearly I remember things differently." Lena's glass shattered as it hit the tiled foyer floor. With a gasp she stumbled backwards down the hall and grabbed the hall table for support. "NO! YOU CANNOT BE HERE...you...you." Hart's eyes were filled with sadness and longing as he approached her. "If you had let me explain that night, I would return after the battle and take you both with me." Lena shrieked and hurled a knickknack from the hall table at Hart's head, Hart cocked his head and it sailed past his shoulder and out the door. "YOU CHOSE YOUR SLUT QUEEN OVER ME!!!" Hart's normally impassive face went suddenly dark as he roared right back at her. " I CHOSE THE ONLY OPTION THAT WOULD ALLOW ME TO RETURN AND NOT HAVE MY FAMILY HUNTED DOWN LIKE DOGS FOR THE REST OF THEIR LIVES!!!" A shadow seemed to enter the room and Lena appeared to shrink in response to the full force of Hart's wrath. Then lights seemed to flicker and dim as if Hart's anger had taken physical form...then like the sun coming from behind a cloud, the shadow was gone and Daniel watched stunned as Hart briefly inclined his head to both Daniel and Lena and walked out the door. Daniel watched Hart return to the car with a stunned expression on his face. Daniel had never seen Hart upset or angry before, behind him he heard Lena clear her throat as she struggled to compose herself. "Now you see what I had to deal with?" Daniel gave her a scathing look as he turned to her. "You are not worth either of our times...I will not be bothering you any further with my obviously unworthy presence LENA...as far as I am concerned, my mother died a long time ago and I don't know who you are." Turning he thought he heard her whisper something as he walked away but he never stopped to find out what it was as he got back into the back seat and they headed to their next destination.

Hart was silent as they headed to Atlanta. Even with minimal stops it would take two days to make it to Lauren's parents house in Atlanta Georgia. Daniel leaned forward and placed a hand on Hart's shoulder. "I am so very sorry Hart...she wasn't always so...venomous." Hart shook his head "I was clinging to a dream Daniel, we would see each other and the love we once shared would be strong enough to bridge time and space itself and bring us back into each others arms." Hart chuckled at himself "we have both changed, we can never return to that time and that place...our time is over." Daniel sat back hurting for Hart and frustrated that he lacked the words to heal the wound. Lauren too felt Hart's pain as she leaned her head against the window. Silent tears slipped down her cheeks. Hart would never show the pain that this loss must surely be causing him and he would never let himself weep for what can never be recovered, so Lauren would weep for him.

The first night, they found themselves stopping at the same motel Lauren had stayed at. Lauren found herself glancing around as if she expected the 'hamlet witch' to come charging out of the shadows towards her. Daniel got two rooms, which would allow him and Hart to continue to bond and give Lauren her privacy. The two rooms were adjoining so they were able to leave the inner door open and visit with each other until by mutual agreement they decided it was time to call it a night. The next morning the driver was waiting for them out front, the minute they got into the car they were greeted with the smell of fresh coffee and McDonald's breakfast sandwiches. Lauren and Daniel greeted this thoughtful feast with loud exclamations of approval. Hart accepted the coffee but looked ill when offered his sandwich and gave it to Daniel instead. This half of the journey seemed more stressful than the first half and they took several pit stops to stretch their legs. When they were about an hour out from their destination, Lauren suggested they stop for the night even though it had only just gotten dark. When Hart asked her reasoning for the stop when they were so close she simply said "we will all feel much better after a shower and A good nights sleep." Since no one else was in a hurry to deal with the inevitable drama, it was agreed that a second night in a motel would not be too bad and they once again got adjoining rooms in a small wayside inn.

Once again morning found the car and driver waiting out front although the morning repast consisted of hot coffee and a dozen crispy creme donuts instead. Hart once again accepted the coffee but seemed to go green as he stared at the sugar glazed confections. Daniel was more than happy to eat Hart's portion. Lauren's mom Lanie lived in a forest green split level with a newly mowed lawn and two sun faded pink flamingo lawn ornaments looking forlorn in the front yard. Daniel had to fight back a laugh of relief that bubbled up from within. Daniel's mom lived in the cold "model homes" that you would see in a fancy decorator's magazine. Lauren's mom lived in the type of house that inspired visions of kids playing tag and weekend backyard barbeques. Daniel started to tell Lauren about his first impressions of her mom's house and noticed she looked like she was about to be sick. "Would you like me to go in with you?" Lauren immediately grabbed his hand as she nodded vigorously. "Would you please?" Daniel nodded and took her hand again as she came around the car and lead him up to the door. Daniel rang the doorbell and a few moments later Lauren's mother Lanie Campbell answered the door. Lanie was a petite brunette with short hair that seemed to be in perpetual disarray. As soon as Lanie's eyes alit on Lauren she gave out a shriek and launched herself into Lauren's arms where they both began sobbing loudly and clinging to each other. Daniel stepped to the side and averted his eyes, giving the women as much privacy as he could while standing less then five feet away.

Lanie sniffed loudly as she stepped back and suddenly noticed Daniel. "Oh my! Where are my manners, come in come in..." Lanie herded them up the stairs and down the hall to the living room. When they were seated in the living room Lanie again burst into tears "We thought you were dead Lauren!" Lanie gestured to the mantelpiece where Lauren's large picture sat front and center with a black ribbon hanging from the right corner. Lauren swallowed hard and opened her mouth to speak when Lanie suddenly stood and mumbled something about coffee before rushing to the kitchen, when Lauren stood to follow her Lanie waved her back down and rushed around the corner. Lauren looked around the living room, the place looked exactly as she remembered it with the exception of her condolence photo.

When Lanie re-emerged from the kitchen she was balancing three china cups and saucers which Daniel rushed to take from her and place on the glass top table. Lanie sat and twisted her hands, a stricken look on her face. "I know things were...rough when you left Lauren but really six months without a word?" Lauren discreetly squeezed Daniel's hand where it lay between them on the couch. Lauren then relayed the story she had vaguely discussed with Daniel on the way here. She told her mom about being upset and about the accident, stumbling away from the wreck and ending up at Daniel's house...she even mentioned how Daniel had taken care of her. Then the story left the realm of truth and entered the realm of fabrication. Lauren told her mother that Daniel's father was a specialist and that Daniel had taken her to him since Lauren had until recently had no knowledge of her own identity and that it had taken until now to fully recover from her head injury. When Lanie again questioned the lack of contact Lauren smiled and mentioned that she thought it would be better to tell her what happened in person instead of with a phone call. Lanie had to admit that did make sense. "I just wish you had called today dear, so much has changed since you have been away and..." Lanie started to say more when they all heard the sound of the front door being thrown open and a male voice that Lauren immediately recognized as Trevor's calling out to Lanie as he made his way towards the living room. "You were so right Lanie, it's a girl!" Trevor was grinning as he came around the corner to the living room and suddenly froze in place as Lauren stood up from the couch to greet him. Trevor's face showed nothing but confusion at first, then his confusion melted into elation as he charged across the living room and grabbed Lauren up in a hug and lifted her off her feet with a smile. "Oh my god you're alive!" Glancing nervously at Daniel, Lauren pushed at Trevor's chest until he put her down. Lanie on the other hand was watching this tender reunion with a pale, anxious face. "Lauren has been under the care of a specialist for a head injury due to her car accident Trevor, she only just recovered her full memories." Trevor turned to stare at Lanie for a moment and a dawning look came into his eyes as he slowly turned back to Lauren.

Trevor took Lauren's hands into his own and gave her a sad look. "Lauren sweetheart, you were gone and we thought you were dead...there were complications..." Once again conversation was interrupted by the arrival of another guest. Shannon waddled in wearing a flower print maternity blouse and was obviously pregnant, her once long dark hair sheared off into an asymmetrical pageboy. Grinning she started to address Lanie "did Trevor tell you the good news....FUCK!" Shannon caught sight of Lauren and her question to Lanie dissolved into an abrupt expletive. Trevor's attention went from Lauren, to Shannon and back to Lauren again. Lanie twisted her hands even harder and started quietly wheezing as if she were witnessing a potentially explosive situation. Lauren took her hands from Trevor and stepped back, "so this is the 'complication' you were telling me about...you got my sister pregnant?" Trevor turned and joined Shannon, his arm going around her. "Shannon became pregnant yes and you were...Shannon and I are married Lauren..." Shannon's surprised look changed to a triumphant smile as she held her left hand out and wiggled her fingers to show off her diamond studded wedding set. Instead of the anger or hurt that everyone seemed to expect, Lauren smiled and rushed over to hug Shannon and Trevor. "I am so very happy for both of you...you two truly deserve each other." Lauren then turned to hug Lanie and kiss her on the cheek. "I promise I will try to keep in touch mom, but you guys have a lot to celebrate and I really need to get some rest." Lanie nodded in shock, staring at Lauren as if she had never seen her before and even Shannon and Trevor only gave token resistance to her leaving so soon. Grabbing Daniel's arm she all but dragged him back out the front door and shoved him into the car as if she could not wait to be out of there. As they got back on the road Lauren regaled them with humorous predictions about what Trevor could look forward to as Shannon's husband. Daniel finally caught his breath long enough to interrupt. "Surely she CANNOT be that bad..." Lauren wiped her eyes and gave him a serious look. "Shannon cannot handle having anyone get more attention then her...when I was fifteen I broke my leg falling out of a tree, she was so mad she threw herself down the stairs and broke her arm and collarbone and suddenly attention was back on her again.' Daniel whistled and shook his head "I take it back....damn!"

CHAPTER ELEVEN

Rue secretly smiled as she watched the door to her suite close behind Prince. Marrat'hassar, he had become a frequent visitor to her rooms. The fact that time worked differently here and that she had already had to let her dresses out twice to accommodate her expanding belly, should have cooled his ardor but instead he seemed to be more aroused rather than less. The child growing within her seemed to be very active and she found herself wondering why she was not experiencing the sense of joy and wonder that she saw on so many pregnant women's faces. Instead of feeling euphoric, she merely felt impatient, she could not wait for this child to be born so she could have control of her own body once again. This unplanned burden was just one of the many things making her short tempered. Alexi's compulsions had to be modified again, he refused to speak to anyone unless compelled to do so and she had to add the additional command to eat and drink when Kate did or he would have starved himself by now. Honestly she was beginning to wonder why she kept him around at all, he was no longer useful in regards to her original intentions for him.

When Rue joined "the Royals" as she had come to think of them at breakfast, they were quietly discussing a missive received from their spies in the Seelie court. Apparently Daniel and the woman who had helped him escape were sent back to the Human world to tie up some loose ends and would then be returning to Underhill. Prince Marrat'hassar smiled over his glass at her. "The Seelie Court has been sending offers of negotiations for your release into their custody to face a trial for your 'crimes against nature' and 'perverse use of arcane energy', my oh my they positively make you sound like a scarlet woman Lady Rue." Rue smirked, though inside she wondered just how much of what she had done had not gone unnoticed by Daniel or how much he had figured out. Having Daniel back in the human world would make it easier theoretically to get her hands on him....her condition however would prevent her from going herself. The sudden silence at the table make her jerk out of her inner thoughts and realize a question had been asked. "I am sorry, my mind was elsewhere, what was the question?" The Prince tamped down his rising irritation at her attention being on something other than himself and forced a smile. "I said that it would be your choice to send someone to retrieve your wayward servant during this window of opportunity and avoid the politics or we can just barter for him with the other court once his assignment is over and he is back within our realm." Rue did not have to think long before the answer came to her. "I will send Alexi to retrieve my other servant I believe, but he will need some guards to assist him..." Although she had been speaking to Marrat'hassar, it was Queen Mo'readhiel that answered her. "Guards will be granted, is there anything else you may want...any other needs we may satisfy for you?" The Queen's question ended in a husky purr as she leaned forward on the table and gave Rue a very lustful look. Rue had not been unaware of the Queen's interest in her from the moment of their first meeting but the thought of being intimate with this amoral creature before was enough to make her gorge rise. Instead of the scathing reply that was on the tip of her tongue she smiled sweetly. "I am grateful for the loan of the guards your majesties, as to my own needs they are THOROUGHLY being met by your delectable son." Rue turned a sultry smile on the prince and was rewarded with a smile filled with promise in return. Neither of them noticed the look of disgust that the Queen shot both of them before settling back into her chair with a feigned look of boredom. Beside her King Melcindo'mien chuckled and patted her arm. "Now dearest, Lady Rue may not be interested in your enviable talents but perhaps she might lend her maidservant to you instead." Both of them turned their questioning eyes to Rue and it did not take more then a second for her to nod in the affirmative with the stipulation that her maidservant would not be permanently damaged upon return to her.

Queen Mo'readhiel smiled as she agreed to Rue's terms and excused herself immediately. Rue turned her attention back to Prince Marrat'hassar and his father as a new discussion started up regarding a masked ball to celebrate their new alliance. Queen Mo'readhiel left the dining room and went immediately to her private chambers. She quickly changed into a tight black bodice and an extremely short skirt, thigh high boots complemented the outfit. Her garments were all of the deepest black to prevent bloodstains from showing. Pulling the tasseled rope hanging next to her bed, she summoned a servant and ordered the Human maid 'Kate' be brought to her. The servant bowed low and left to fetch Kate.

It took more than a few moments for the servant to return with Kate. Kate bowed low and started to ask why she had been summoned when the Queen interrupted her "Stand there chambermaid and be silent!" The other servant had walked into the room and waited until the Queen nodded at her before rolling the carpet back revealing rings with attached manacles attached to the stone floor. Glancing at the ceiling she noticed identical rings set in the ceiling above, the servant went to the oak armoire in the corner and removed manacles secured with a length of chain and attached them to the rings in the ceiling. Kate was starting to realize the reason she had been summoned. By the looks of things Rue had displeased the Queen in some way and Kate would pay the price. Kate glanced at the door as if measuring the distance and the likelihood of her making it through said door before being stopped. As Kate turned to ask yet another question of the Queen she saw the statuette descending and got a close look at the base right before it connected with her forehead and the world went black.

When Kate came to she was aware of two things, she was naked and she was hanging from the wrists...okay three things...her feet did not touch the floor. Opening her eyes blearily she looked down and noticed wrist and ankles were far enough apart that she was hanging spread-eagle in the center of the room. The Queen's chuckle broke the silence "good you are finally awake." Kate opened her mouth to reply and the same servant rushed over and tied a gag around her mouth before retreating and resuming staring at the floor. The Queen's eyes gleamed with malice as she circled Kate examining her as if she were a horse for sale. "You are far from a perfect specimen...too skinny...oh well, you will suffice as merely a whipping girl for your mistress." Kate yelled a denial against her gag but the Queen only laughed and turned to the oak armoire in the corner.

The Queen sorted through her 'toys' looking like a professional dominatrix as she flicked various whips as if testing their weight and balance. Kate felt sick as she saw the multitude of rods, knives and whips in various sizes and colors revealed by the open doors of the cabinet. Finally she nodded at a red leather cat o nine tails. "Your mistress made the stipulation that I cannot permanently damage you...but its amazing what my healers can heal and re-grow." Kate barely had time to catch her breath before the cat was whistling through the air, the leather tails leaving searing pain in their wake as the Queen brought the weapon down across her back and shoulders. The sight of the blood trickling down Kate's thin body seemed to excite the Queen as her breathing increased until she was positively panting, apparently so did Kate's muffled screams. Again and again she heard the whistling as the tails descended on her and tore away more of her skin from her back. Kate was only aware of the fact that she had passed out several times when the servant would toss a bucket of water in her face to awaken her. Distantly through her fog of pain, Kate became aware of the sound of the door opening and for a brief moment she clung to the hope that whoever it was had come to rescue her. The King's voice tutted at the Queen "awww, you started without me..."

Kate heard them whispering behind her and then a bare hand swiped across her ravaged back causing Kate to cry out and feebly jerk against her chains. "mmmm, her blood is sweet my love, I wonder..." Kate's eyes nearly bugged as she heard the sound of tearing cloth and then the unmistakable sound of two people having sex. If ever Kate felt hate in her heart for Rue, it was now as she hung in limp agony from her restraints and was forced to listen to the King and Queen having sex in the spreading pool of her blood. Much later Kate was released to stumble down the long dark corridor to the small room that she shared with Alexi. Alexi had already been told he would be returning to the Human world with a contingent of guards to take hold of Daniel and bring him back here. When Rue had announced to Kate and Alexi that details of Alexi's mission, Alexi's despondence had vanished. Alexi had confided in Kate that he intended to find Daniel and those helping him and make a plea of Sanctuary in exchange for insider information on Rue and the Unseelie court. Kate immediately thought of several large holes in his plan, not including the 4 armed Fae guardsmen that would be coming with him.

Once Alexi was finished packing, he hung around their tiny room biding his time until he could get going. Kate brought bread and cheese for them to sup on and wished she were going with him, not for any need to be near Alexi, but so that she could be away from Rue and more importantly Queen Mo'readhiel. Kate watched Alexi for a few minutes as he settled back on his bed and stared at the blank wall, then shook her head and curled in her blankets. The skin across her back felt tight and itchy from where the healer had used magic to replace the missing flesh. Kate wished the wounds to her heart and mind could be fixed as easily as they had fixed the wounds to her body. Kate would never have believed Rue capable of tossing her aside so callously to be used by the King and Queen, but Kate would never have believed Rue capable of collaring her either and clearly that had already had happened. Kate fell into troubled dreams and slept so deeply that she never heard the guards when they came to escort Alexi to the portal. Rue was standing near the portal with a small silver blade when Alexi and the guards showed up. With a grin Rue nodded and the guards shoved Alexi to his knees before Rue and held him down as she opened his shirt and began carving a new rune onto his chest. "That symbol will prevent you from speaking to anyone belonging to the "bright court", just in case you have any ideas of switching sides or betraying me to my enemies." With another nod the guards let him up and he was roughly shoved towards the portal. Rue saw Alexi hesitate and clench his jaw before stepping through, the guards following closely behind him.

CHAPTER TWELVE

The group consensus was once again to stop for food before heading back Underhill. They pulled off to the Country Roadhouse Restaurant which promised "real home cookin." They surprised their driver 'Bill' by inviting him to dine with them. The atmosphere was light and filled with the sound of laughter and in Lauren's case snorting as they enjoyed bill's stories about some of the famous people he had been hired to chauffeur when he was living in L.A. "And then she told me to come back and pick her up in an hour from Versace and the car better be PINK because she ONLY rode in PINK cars!" Lauren snorted and hid her red face behind her linen napkin as she howled with laughter, Daniel and Hart were wiping their eyes and slapping the table in identical expressions of mirth as Bill adopted a high pitch nasal tone of voice to mimic his former client. When Lauren could catch her breath she asked "so what did you do?" Bill wiped his eyes and took a drink from his water glass before continuing. "The only pink car I could get on such short notice was Edgar Hamm's stretch..." Daniel groaned "you mean Edgar Hamm owner of the Hog Heaven Restaurant chain?" Bill nodded and started laughing again. "Imagine her surprise when she came out with all her bags to find a bright pink stretch limo with 'Hog Heaven' painted down the length in bright purple letters." Hart choked on the bite of cheeseburger he had just taken and coughed several times before he could ask a question. "Whatever did she say to THAT?" Bill finished his own burger before replying "not a thing, she got in and kept silent all the way back to the airport." The waitress came by twice to refill their drinks, remove their empty dishes and ask them to lower their voices so as to not disturb the other diners.

Finally when all the dishes had been cleared and the last glass emptied, they decided to get going before they were all too drowsy to move. The backside of the airport where the private aircraft were kept was dark and silent as they pulled up and parked near the woods edging the tarmac. They all slowly filed out of the car, every one of them feeling ready to call it an early night and sink into a food coma. Bill popped the trunk and walked to the back of the car to unload the bags and Daniel went to help him. Daniel was just swinging his duffel out of the trunk when he suddenly realized how quiet it was. Slowly Daniel lowered the duffel to the ground as he strained to hear any of the normal night noises you would expect to hear from the woods. Daniel had just turned to ask Bill a question when Bill suddenly made a gurgling noise and something warm and wet sprayed across Daniel's face. Daniel's head whipped around to look at Bill and he stared at the black fletched arrow that pierced Bill's throat, it had entered just under his chin and jutted half a foot out the back of his neck. Bill's eyes rolled towards Daniel as if in disbelief before he dropped to the ground. Daniel let out a yell and Lauren dropped to the ground next to the front tire and started keening. Hart whipped a short metal rod from his jacket and slashed it through the air, the rod lengthening to the size of a quarterstaff as he charged the woods where Daniel could see a single Fae firing arrows in their direction. Lauren was rocking back and forth and staring at the spreading pool of Bill's blood. Daniel slid over to her and shook her arm to get her attention. Pointing towards the covered hangar he gives her a shove "run to the hangar, I'll be right behind you!" Lauren nodded and took off like a shot, an arrow whizzing past her head as she sprinted for the hangar. Daniel hesitated looking from Lauren's retreating form to where Hart now faced off against not one but two Fae with identical quarterstaves. In the end he realized he had no weapon and would be more of a liability then a help to Hart if he were to run in unarmed.

Lauren had just reached the hangar door and looked back to reassure herself that Daniel was following before disappearing inside and letting the door swing shut behind her. Daniel was nearly to the door when a shadow detached itself from the parked truck to his right and charged towards him. Daniel had enough time to throw his hands up before the shadow bowled him over. Daniel found himself looking up at an attractive man with long dark hair who seemed to be frantically mouthing words at him. At first he thought he had gone deaf, the man seemed to be silently screaming at him and growing more and more agitated. Finally a look of dawning realization crossed his features and mouthing what looked like the words 'fuck it', he grabbed Daniel's head in both hands and slammed it hard against the ground. The world disappeared in a white explosion before going black.

Hart brought the end of his staff down on his opponent's wrist causing his opponent to drop his weapon before bringing the end of his own quarterstaff around to connect with the side of the other Fae's head and dropping him like a rock. Spinning he lunged toward the second Fae only to find the second Fae had disappeared. Hart glanced in the direction of the nearby hangar and saw a dark haired man toss Daniel's limp body in the passenger seat of a black pickup truck before getting behind the wheel. Hart charged across the distance screaming denials as the truck peeled out leaving him coughing in a cloud of exhaust. The sound of Lauren's terrified scream alerted him to the fact that while Daniel was taken, the danger had not yet passed. Throwing the door to the hangar open he saw a dark haired Fae grab Lauren and jerk her back to his chest, a piece of serrated metal pressed against her pale throat. The Fae guard opened his mouth to speak but Hart had had enough tonight and threw his staff like a javelin. The staff entered the Fae's shoulder just under the collarbone and pinned him to the wall behind him. The pinned Fae's weapon dropped from nerveless fingers and allowed Lauren to jerk out of his grasp and rush over to stand behind Hart.

Hart approached the Fae angrily. "Where have you taken Daniel?" Hart ignored the gasp from Lauren and focused all his attention on the Fae guardsman struggling to push himself off the wall. Hart and the Unseelie guardsman spoke rapid fire Eldritch, the guard cursed Hart and all his ancestors who apparently fornicated with livestock. Finally when he had heard enough, Hart gave the quarterstaff a twist and dug it deeper into the Fae's flesh. The Guardsman was suddenly a lot more helpful and began confessing the plan entailing killing all but Daniel and bringing Daniel back to the Unseelie court. Alexi taking Daniel and leaving was never part of the plan. Hart ripped the javelin from the guard's shoulder and struck him a blow to the temple. The guard dropped to the floor with a sickening thud and Hart turned to face Lauren. "One of the witch's people deviated from the plan and abducted Daniel, where he took him and for what purpose we have no idea." Lauren's eyes filled with tears and she wrapped her arms around herself as if to keep from breaking into a thousand pieces. Hart frowned and grabbed Lauren by the shoulders. "Do not start mourning him as if he were already dead, we need to get these guards back to the Queen and let her know what has happened." Lauren nodded and helped him search the hangar for something to haul the unconscious guards in and after a brief search they located a rolling scrap bin half filled with broken pallet boards. Hart and Lauren emptied the bin and dropped the unconscious guard into the bottom of it with a thud.

Hauling the bin behind him, Hart headed towards the car and the other unconscious guard. As soon as they rounded the front of the car they noticed that the spot where the guard had been laying was empty. Bill's body and the bags were added to the bin, then with much pushing and pulling they managed to take the bin through the portal. Hart immediately explained the situation to the perplexed portal guards. The bags were handed to servants to deposit in their owners rooms, then bill's body was turned over to the priests for proper burial and finally the Unseelie guardsman who had just started to struggle was taken off to be interrogated. Lauren stood near the portal looking lost as Hart took charge of the present servants and guardsmen. As if he had suddenly remembered Lauren was there, Hart came over and patted her arm with a smile. "Our boy is not gone yet, lets go talk to the Queen and see how we can bring our boy home again ok?" Lauren started to nod when she saw Hunter standing near the doorway and just like that she was across the room hugging him and finding herself bursting into tears as she filled him in on everything that happened. Lauren had become close friends in the same way that Hart and Daniel had become close. Hunter had become the father that she had yearned for growing up in a single parent home.

Hunter rubbed Lauren's back and looked up as Hart reached them. "Has the Queen been told of Danny boy's abduction?" Hart shook his head "we only got back and brought an Unseelie guardsman back with us for interrogation. Hunter nodded. "There have been new developments since ere ye left Hart...but it is no my place to say so we will go and speak with yon Majesty and let her drop that brick on ye head." If Hart was curious to know what Hunter was talking about, he said nothing as the three of them headed to the Throne room to consult with Queen Sadronniel. The Queen looked up from where she sat at the end of the long table that had been brought in to seat the full war council. Hart looked surprised to see a war council had been called. Queen Sadronniel turned her impassive face first to Hart. "We have been informed that Daniel has been taken by agents of the Unseelie court, is this true?" Hart nodded and bowed his head. "The fault is mine your majesty, I let my guard down and he was taken during an ambush near the portal." The Queen rubbed her temples. "No Aelon I fear the fault is mine, I have learned that my former consort Lithaldoren has defected to the Unseelie court." Hart's face was blank as she continued " We can assume our meetings are known to our enemies."

Hart led Hunter and Lauren to empty seats at the table and the war council resumed its previous conversation. A councilor dressed in the color shifting leather of a ranger cleared his throat before he spoke. "The Dark Court has agreed to a parlay at the Temple of Kierkunnos at sun's zenith tomorrow." The Queen nodded her thanks "Thank you Councilor Gethrau, were there any other terms or conditions for the meeting?" Councilor Gethrau nodded and cleared his throat again. "Yes your majesty, they also state that we are allowed a delegation of no more than six." The rumble of sudden conversation sounded like rolling thunder as the councilors presented arguments and counter arguments for whom should be included in the delegation. Finally the Queen stood to her feet and the abrupt silence that followed was almost deafening. "We have heard your arguments and we beg your patience as we make our decision, may we please have our guests join us in our Royal Suite." Without waiting for an answer she turned and exited through the door behind the throne. It was only at that moment that Lauren realized the second throne had been removed.

Hart could count the number of times he had been to the Royal Suite on one hand. Silently he led Hunter and Lauren through the maze of corridors that led to the Royal Apartments. The Queen was sitting sipping tea from a crystal cup while an older maidservant tutted and fussed over her. The Queen immediately rose as they entered and handed the cup to the maid with a dismissive gesture. The maid frowned but took herself from the room with a brief curtsy. The Queen directed her questions at Hart which left Lauren to look about at her sumptuous surroundings. The suite was decorated in white with pastel blue undertones and trimming as if the rooms were encased in perpetual winter.

Lauren turned her attention back to the conversation in time to catch the fact that she and Hunter would be staying behind and only Hart would be going with the Delegation. Lauren opened her mouth to object when she felt Hunter pat her arm sympathetically. Leaning close to her, Hunter whispered "ye can no help in this girl, ye best leave it to those what can." Lauren nodded, her heart was heavy as she silently acknowledged the wisdom of Hunter's words.

CHAPTER THIRTEEN

Rue was surprised to learn not only would the "royals" be attending a parlay with the Seelie court, but Rue was required to attend as well. Prince Marrat'hassar was becoming increasingly possessive of her time and attention. The Prince had even gone so far as to give orders that only female servants were to attend to her needs. Things were going to come to a head very soon, after all she could hardly have a harem of exotic lovers if she was tied to a possessive not to mention extremely jealous Fae Prince. Rue's appetite for food had increased again although her cravings seemed to be limited so far to fruit and cheese. Prince Marrat'hassar was only too happy to bring her gifts of exotic fruits and cheese as an excuse to check up on her...constantly. Rue's chambermaid had finally started piling all the "gifts" in the adjoining room.

Rue's maid Valerya had been packing her newly expanded wardrobe from nearly the moment that it had been announced that Rue's presence would be required. Valerya had just finished with the last of the packing when the sound of tapping was heard from the door. The maid opened the door and stepped back to let a Royal Guardsman into the suite. "The lady Rue's presence is requested in the dining chamber by their Royal Majesties King Melcindo'mien, Queen Mo'readhiel, and Prince Marrat'hassar." Rue nodded and ordered her maid to go through the bags and make sure that nothing was forgotten and then followed the Royal Guard to the dining chamber feeling as if she were marching to her doom. Her feeling of doom was only heightened as she entered the dining chamber and saw the unsmiling faces of the "Royals". A pompously dressed blonde Fae man sipped from a crystal goblet and grinned at the Queen "Have we a bargain then?" The Queen tapped her chin as if considering then nodded, guards seemed to appear to either side of the man as he stood. The Queen looked to the guards "Bathe him and box his head up for the Seelie queen, make sure the container is fit to travel. The man looked shocked.. "NO, WAIT, YOU CAN'T...I HAVE MORE TO TELL YOU!!" The blonde man was quickly dragged from the chamber still screaming his denials and pleas for mercy. The Queen imperiously gestured for Rue to enter and be seated. "I am afraid lady Rue that your servant has deviated from the plan and absconded, his departure from the plan has caused the capture of one of our own servants and brought the attention of the Seelie court upon us." The King cleared his throat and picked up where she left off. "Now we are to meet with the Seelie court to discuss our relinquishment of both you and your servant Daniel." Once again as if the whole meeting was scripted, the Queen picked up the thread of conversation. "Clearly they have no idea that you have completely lost control of your servants and haven't the faintest idea where they are...and we have no intention of telling them either." Rue opened her mouth to defend herself "I'll have you know..." she was cut off by the Queen's upraised hand.

"Normally a blunder of this magnitude would cause me to be out of sorts and I would behead you immediately and send your servants with your rotting head directly back to the Seelie court, but my son has taken a fancy to you and has requested a second course of action." Queen Mo'readhiel turned with a fond gaze on her perfectly coiffed son. Prince Marrat'hassar turned with the indolent smile of a satisfied cat towards Rue. "You will marry me within the week and the babe in your womb will be fostered once it is born with our Dark Elf Cousins in the sacred art of the assassins, we will reclaim your servants and hand Daniel over to the Seelie court while Alexi will be executed, and Kate will belong to my mother." Rue stood from her seat, her chair nearly toppling as she shoved herself to her feet. "If I refuse?" All three Royals smiled with anticipation but it was Queen Mo'readhiel who answered. "I would love for you to refuse my Lady Rue, I will personally dole out the consequences...." Turning Rue left the room and slammed the door behind her as she returned to her room. The Queen turned to her son and stroked her hand along his jaw. "Go and see that your betrothed is prepared to travel within the hour and advise her that she will speak nothing of her loss of control over her servants." Prince

Marrat'hassar kissed his mother's hand and inclined his head to his father before leaving the room. Rue was pacing angrily, her fists thumping against her thighs as she worked herself up into a froth, her maid standing by helplessly. The Prince entered without knocking which only fueled her ire. "You DARE enter my rooms unannounced and uninvited?!" The prince smiled and waived the maid out the door. " Uninvited perhaps, but must I announce myself like a tax collector when only moments ago our betrothal was announced?" Rue clenched her jaw. "I never said I accepted your 'proposal' m'lord." The Prince nodded as he tossed his jacket aside and came further into the room. "You have no choice in this, you care too much for your own life and you would not find my mother a gentle persuader...she does so love the sight of blood." Grabbing Rue roughly he shoves her back against the wall his hand around her throat, her hands clawed at his tightening fingers even as she saw black spots start dancing in front of her eyes and felt his other hand shoving her skirts up, his knee pressing her legs wider. His hand fumbled at the front of his trews and was only cut short by the knock on the door. A single guard entered and turned his eyes aside at the scene he had interrupted. "Her majesty asks that her son attend her in the Royal stables, the Royal coach is being prepared." With a bow the guard retreats out the door and the Prince turns back to Rue with a grin. "Know this my soon to be wife, no locked door will keep me from what is mine and I will take you anytime and anywhere I choose...you are my property to use or discard as I choose...get used to the idea." Placing a cold kiss on her cheek he steps back and straightens his clothes before leaving her bruised and angry and sends her maid to "repair any damage to her apparel".

The Prince found his mother and father waiting in the courtyard, his mother loudly complaining at the servants as they loaded the Royal coach. Behind the coach no less then twelve Eldritch knights were already mounted and waiting. Cocking his head he turns to his father. "I thought the dictates stated that we were only allowed a six person delegation?" King Melcindo'mien smiled. "Those guards are not strictly speaking part of the delegation, they are merely the Queen's escort..." Both men chuckled at the Queen's clever loophole. When Rue joined them they could all see the darkening hand shaped bruise around her throat, she was silent as she climbed aboard and sat as close as possible to the window and stared blankly at the passing scenery outside. The Queen gave her son a satisfied smile and patted his hand, it was about time he let the 'Human' woman know how things stand in the Fae realm. The Temple of Kierkunnos was large and made of ancient dark stone delved deep from the mines of their dark Fae cousins. A silver chased coach was already parked beneath the sweeping boughs of an ancient willow nearby. Four horses showing the royal insignia were tethered to the rear of the coach showing that the Seelie Court had not found the loophole and had followed the letter of the terms. The "Royals" smirked at the naivety of the Seelie court as their full contingent descended on the Temple. Rue's arm was caught up in the Prince's iron grip as if he thought it likely she would slip away during the meeting. Rue knew before the end of the night she would have an armlet of purple bruises to match the collar he has already gifted her with. If the seated Seelie delegation were at all surprised at the number of guards the Unseelie had brought with them, it did not show on their impassive faces. When both sides were seated, the Kierkunnos' high priest stepped forward and tapped his staff three times on the floor. The large chamber echoed, the feast length table and accompanying chairs were the room's only furnishings aside from tall candle holders and torches affixed to the wall.

Rue looked up at the vaulted ceilings that were so high that the roof was lost in velvety black shadows. "We join each other here today as in ages past in this place of peace to negotiate the terms of barter and treaty. Queen Sadronniel, you as first arrival will make the opening offer."

Queen Sadronniel stood, her velvet gown a pristine white that should have been impossible to keep clean in this dust covered chamber. Rue sneered at the Seelie Queen's perfect blonde curls and small waist, she was so busy picking apart her appearance she barely heard her as she spoke. "This Human witch you bring with you has used magic taught her by my former protege Angelique and perverted it in order to enslave men of her race for her carnal desires, we ask that the Half blood Daniel be returned to his father Aelon Dryearghym, furthermore we request that you turn over the witch known as Rue Bishop for trial charged with crimes against her fellow man and misuse of magic." Having said her part, Queen Sadronniel returned to her seat. Queen Mo'readhiel stood, a haughty smirk stretching her full lips. "I happen to know from a 'close' source of yours that you are in no fit condition to battle us for the life of our witch." Queen Sadronniel thrust herself to her feet angrily "I know very well where you have gotten your information but I am sad to say his information is flawed, he rarely paid attention to anyone or anything but himself, and where is this 'informant' of yours?" Queen Mo'readhiel grinned wider and gestured her guard to present the beautifully wrapped package in his arms to the Seelie queen. With a wary glance at her opponent Queen Sadronniel lifted the lid of the box and glanced inside before handing it to her own guard with a whisper in his ear and the box was removed from the room. (Burning with curiosity, the guard would open the box himself and rush to the nearest corner and be violently ill at the sight of Consort Lithaldoren's severed head). As if nothing untoward had occurred, arguments went back and forth on what Rue should be tried for and whether the charges were even valid since the only witnesses were not present. Rue finally got up and peeled Prince Marrat'hassar's bruising grip from her arm and walked outside for some fresh air, she was only alone for a moment when the Eldritch knight who had been seated next to Queen Sadronniel stepped out the door and joined her. He nodded at her and extended his hand. "I am Hart, and you are Lady Bishop?" Rue nodded warily "I have been called such, what can I do for you 'Hart'?" Hart nodded acknowledging she was not going to indulge in small talk but would rather cut to the chase. "I would like for you to drop your claim on Daniel and order your servant Alexi to return him to us, Daniel wants no part of you...clearly you are a beautiful and seductive woman you have no need of spells and artifice to gain bed partners..." Rue snorted and crossed her arms her dress pulling tight across her abdomen and she smiled as hart's eyes dropped to her swollen abdomen. "I have more claim to him than as simply a bed partner and what I do or do not use my spells for is none of your business, Daniel is mine!" Hart smiled and shook his head. "You cannot own another person, this is against nature itself, just as the spells you weave were never meant for the way in which you use them and there is always a price for power." Rue turned her back to him. "Daniel will be mine until the day I have no more use for him, then I will slide a dagger between his ribs and toss him into the nearest river to feed the fish."

Hart grabbed Rue's arm and jerked her to face him just as Prince Marrat'hassar came out the entranceway. "DEFILER! YOU DARE LAY HANDS ON MY BETROTHED?!?" Hart jerked back, his hand going to his empty scabbard at his waist.

Weapons were forbidden during peace talks. The Prince's yells brought the others out at a run. Both delegations stood in the doorway overlooking the scene. Finally the High Priest stepped between Hart and the Prince. Prince Marrat'hassar spit at Hart. "You will never have my betrothed for your petty trial and her servants are her own, so if it must be war then so be it, we will see you on the Field Of Blood three days hence at dawn." He turned towards his parents and they nodded their support in his proclamation. Hart looked to Queen Sadronniel who sighed and nodded as well. Looking back at Prince Marrat'hassar he nodded "so be it, three days hence." The Unseelie Court were the first to leave with their company of guards. When they had gone Queen Sadronniel approached Hart with a look of supreme sadness. "I was hoping to avoid another war with them, but this is what the fates will I am seeing." Hart nodded and started to apologize but she shook her head. "They would have found a way to goad us into it, it is a small matter." She turned and directed the servants to reload the coach and they were quickly on their way back to their own court to announce the imminent battle.

*****

Daniel smelled stale cigarettes and old urine, he cracked an eye open and found himself face down on a hideous paisley bedspread. Rolling onto his back he looked around at the cheap motel room and wondered how he had gotten here. Slowly the memory of the dark haired guy shouting silently came back to him and he looked around until he found that guy sitting in a corner chair watching him. "Don't suppose you want to enlighten me on why you kidnapped me?" The man stood and approached the bed, once again his mouth was moving but no sound emerged. Throwing his hands up with a clearly read expletive the man sent the small table crashing to the floor and turned to Daniel with clenched fists. The man took a deep breath and tore his shirt open showing a chest full of runes and lines carved into his chest with what appeared to be a dull blade. The man pointed at the scars on his chest then to Daniel's cuff and finally to his own mouth. The man repeated the gestures three times before Daniel made the connection. "Wait a second, Rue carved those into you?" The man nodded and dropped to his knees with relief. Daniel stood and took a step towards the door only to see the man leap to his feet in a single motion and clench his fists. "OK, I get it, you need me for something." Daniel knew he had a choice to help this guy or to bolt out the door and hope he could escape and leave this guy to fend for himself.

Even as he thought over his options, he already knew it was really not a choice, if someone had not come along and helped him he would still be under Rue's power. There was always the possibility that Rue was controlling this guy but at the same time Daniel had the strange feeling this guy had dragged himself up through Hell itself to be here today. Daniel made a decision and moved away from the door, he passed Alexi and sat on the bed farthest from the door. Alexi relaxed his tense stance as Daniel moved away from the door. Still wary, Alexi seated himself cross legged on the bed opposite from Daniel which had the added advantage of being between Daniel and the door. Daniel reached over and grabbed the message pad and pen from the bedside table and started to write before stopping as a thought suddenly occurred to him. "Um no offense but you CAN read and write right?" Alexi cocked his head and rolled his eyes at Daniel as if he could not believe Daniel asked him that. Daniel laughed and held his hands up.

"OK, sorry about that, well guess we should start with names since I can't keep calling you 'hey you'." Alexi motioned for the pad and quickly scribbled his name on it before handing it back. Daniel looked at it for a moment then tapped the pen on the pad thinking. "Alexi... that sounds Russian." Alexi sighed and started to verbally correct Daniel then as if remembering the reason why they were using a notepad, he got up and walked into the bathroom.

Daniel had just started to stand when Alexi came back from the bathroom with a towel tied around his head like a pirate, his hands caressed the air as if looking deeply into a crystal ball. Daniel laughed at the theatrics and gestured for Alexi to retake his seat. "My mistake, you are a gypsy which would be...Armenian? No...um Romanian right?" Alexi gave him a thumbs up to let him know he had guessed correctly. Daniel hands the pad back to Alexi as he asks his next question. "So how did Rue capture you?" Alexi stared at the pad for a moment, then looked around the room as if thinking of how to start, then he scribbles a quick sentence and hands the pad back to Daniel. Long story, too much writing. Must be a better way to communicate. Daniel tosses the pad onto the bed beside him and considers for a moment. "Do you happen to know which of those painful marks on your chest prevents you from speaking to me?" Alexi gives a quick nod and points to the freshest of his wounds.

Daniel touched the wound experimentally and apologized as Alexi stiffened in pain. Daniel was once again thankful he had gotten away with nothing more painful then the cuff on his wrist. Rue was apparently upping her game and choosing to make her control over her 'pets' absolute. Thinking out loud Daniel studied the mark. "Maybe if we were able to mar the rune, it would lose power." Alexi pushed Daniel back and started pacing the room looking about at the sparse furnishings as if judging and discarding the various objects as useless to help in the situation. Alexi suddenly turned and studied the large mirror hanging above the dresser. Daniel had a sour feeling start in his stomach as he watched Alexi study the mirror. Without another word Alexi tore the towel from his head and wrapped it around his fist before punching the mirror and sending glass flying as the mirror shattered. Daniel cursed loudly and questioned Alexi's sanity as Alexi knelt in the broken glass and chose a long 'dagger shaped' shard which he then wrapped the towel around for a handle. Alexi grabbed Daniel's hand and shoved the 'dagger' into it, Alexi then closed his hand over Daniel's and increased the pressure painfully as Daniel tried to pull his hand back. "You can not seriously expect me to..." Daniel's words were cut off as Alexi used Daniel's hand to shove the dagger against his ribs and open a shallow gash across the rune. The rune flared briefly then went dark, the blood dripping down Alexi's side further blurring the lines of the wound.

Daniel stood there in shock as Alexi stumbled backwards and laid on the bed with his eyes closed. It was the sight of the blood pooling on the bed that shook Daniel out of his shock. Running into the bathroom he quickly grabbed a small first aid kit from under the sink and several towels and rushed back to the room. Alexi was sitting up, the blood now staining the waistband of his jeans. "Alright lay back again and we can at least clean that wound up a bit." Daniel waited until Alexi had complied then poured a generous amount of peroxide on the wound then pressed a clean towel onto it and had Alexi place pressure onto the towel to stem the bleeding. "How do you feel, you're not going to die on me right?" Alexi clenched his teeth. "Mă simt ca și cum cineva mi-a tăiat cu o bucată de gaura fund de sticlă!" Daniel stepped back as the harsh syllables flowed audibly from between Alexi's clenched teeth. "I would say that worked though I have no idea what you just said." Alexi's chuckle sound harsh as if from lack of use as he reached over and gestured to the roll of medical tape.

Daniel bound the towels tightly to Alexi as Alexi answered Daniel's earlier question. "I said I feel like someone cut me with a piece of glass...asshole." Alexi looked embarrassed as he translated his earlier rant including the insult he had tacked on the end. Daniel laughed and shrugged. "Ask a stupid question, get a stupid answer I guess." Alexi rose from the bed and went to study the rest of the runes carved into his chest in the bathroom mirror. "Do you think the same can be done of the others?" Daniel stepped behind him and looked at the runes over his shoulder and shook his head. "I am pretty sure you would bleed out with all the cuts we would have to make to ruin those runes big guy." Alexi scowled fiercely and stepped past Daniel back into the bedroom. Silently he sank down on the bed and closed his eyes wearily. Daniel knew the hopeless rage that was twisting Alexi up inside, he had felt it himself not too long ago. If it had not been for Lauren's fortuitous car accident he would still be enslaved by Rue and locked within the confines of his own home. "Don't give up man, we will figure out a way to free us both, we just need to get back Underhill and speak with the Seelie court." Alexi looked up at Daniel skeptically "I am her minion, branded and commanded...why would they help such as I?" Daniel wished he had a more definitive plan for helping Alexi and even himself get free of Rue and her twisted desires but all he could come up with was a shrug and a feeble "because that's what they do...."

Alexi's look was disbelieving, yet deep down he maintained a spark of hope that maybe Daniel was right and they could find a way to free themselves.

CHAPTER FOURTEEN

Daniel and Alexi argued back and forth. Alexi was of the mind that since they were mostly free of Rue and he was reasonably sure she was unaware of their location, they should continue running and never look back(after all she could not possibly control them from halfway across the world could she?). While Daniel could understand Alexi's logic, he could not agree with his plan. If Daniel and Alexi disappeared now, Lauren and Hart and the rest would believe them dead or worse and search for them for who knows how long. Daniel could never be so cold and callous to the person who had helped free him from his prison, nor could he in good conscience abandon the father he was only now truly getting to know. Daniel argued that if they went to the Seelie court with the knowledge Alexi had garnered while under Rue's spell, he could very well buy his sanctuary and give "the good guys" the opportunity to study and perhaps break the hold that kept him obedient to Rue's "whims". Daniel shoved his hands through his hair in irritation. "Look Alexi, all I am saying is that we should go to the Seelie court and let them take a look at the runes and hear what you have to say and THEN if you want to run, you have the choice to do so." Once again Alexi shook his head. "What is the difference between the 'Seelie' and the 'Unseelie', you say one is good and one is bad.

Maybe they are both bad and you have seen only one side of them just as I saw only the side of Rue I wanted to see, short a time as that was." Daniel lost what little patience he had left, while he was arguing with Alexi on the proper course of action, people were undoubtedly searching for them. "NO YOU STUPID THICK-HEADED GYPSY BASTARD, 'NOT ONE IS GOOD AND ONE IS BAD'. MORE LIKE ONE IS GOING TO HELP YOU AND ONE IS GOING TO KEEP YOU ENSLAVED!!!" Alexi threw himself to his feet and Shoved Daniel's back against the wall, his forearm pressing against Daniel's throat. "I LOST EVERYTHING BECAUSE OF THAT CRAZY MAGIC USING WHORE, MY BROTHER, MY CLAN, I WILL NOT GO QUIETLY INTO HER HANDS AGAIN!!!" Daniel brought his knee up sharply, Alexi stumbling back with a gasping groan as his testicles were driven suddenly upward from the force of Daniel's blow. As soon as Alexi's arm was no longer across his throat Daniel grabbed Alexi's head with both hands and slammed his face against his knee. Daniel felt Alexi's nose break against his knee and Alexi dropped to the carpet with a muffled thud. As Daniel went to step past Alexi, Alexi's hand shot out and gripped his leg. Daniel felt Alexi tug and suddenly his balance was gone. Daniel's head hit the edge of the dresser with a wet sounding thwack before he found himself face down on the thin carpet. Alexi kept his grip on Daniel's leg and starting pulling himself closer to Daniel with a murderous glint in his eye. Rolling to his back, Daniel slammed his heel into Alexi's face. Once. Twice. Three times until Alexi dropped back to the carpet his grip on Daniel's leg going slack.

Daniel slid his leg out from under Alexi and stood over him breathing hard. Deciding he was done trying too reason with this asshole, he crossed to the door, opening it he found himself looking at a short, hunched old woman with skin the color of old leather. The woman stared up at him from a wizened face surrounded by wildly curling white hair and wearing what looked like either a ratty old brown bathrobe or a burlap monk's robe. Her piercing blue eyes seemed to bore into him and he felt himself compelled to step back into the room. The old woman followed him into the room, the door seeming to snap closed on its own. The woman curled her lip at the sight of Alexi laying bleeding on the floor, then turned cold eyes upon and Daniel. Daniel felt great power and great displeasure coming off the old woman in waves. " A fool with my help I have bought, a fool to bring harm where healing is sought!" Daniel started to interrupt her and was silenced as she gestured at him. He opened his mouth to speak and nothing came out, his lips moved without sound. The old woman stalked up to him until he was forced to sit on the edge of the bed, then with an age roughened hand she grabbed his chin and forced him to look at Alexi's still form. The witch gestured at Alexi and Daniel watched as the blood vanished, his bruises vanished and with a sickening pop his nose righted itself.

"Travel to the Fields Of Pain,

if thy freedom thee would gain.

Confront thy witch where blood nurtures   field,

With her actions, her fate is sealed."

The hand holding Daniel's jaw tightened and he winced from the ache in his jaw, he closed his eyes and suddenly the hand was gone. Jerking his head around, he found the spot where she had been standing empty. The door was still closed yet he hesitated to open it lest he find another unwanted guest on the other side. Taking a breath he threw the door open and found the walkway empty, not a breeze stirred the empty parking lot beyond. Closing the door he thoroughly searched the room, stepping over Alexi in his haste to reassure himself that the woman was indeed gone. The closet and bathroom were empty and only dust and stained carpet were hiding beneath the beds. When he had reassured himself that she was indeed gone he dropped to the floor between the beds and put his back against one of the beds. Daniel had never liked riddles, but if anyone might be able to explain the mad rantings of a vanishing crone, it would be Hart.

Alexi awoke feeling disoriented. Alexi opened his eyes slowly to find Daniel staring down into his face with a worried expression. Though his brain felt foggy, memories of the brief scuffle seeped through. Rather than feeling a renewed sense of anger, he just felt...tired. Alexi was tire of fighting, tired of pain and tired of being controlled by some sex crazed witch. Alexi reached up to wave Daniel back and noted how Daniel flinched as Alexi's hand came near. With Daniel's help he was able to sit up and put his back to the end of the bed. Daniel stood and stepped away and Alexi attempted a smile "so now that we have tested each other's mettle, we can move on and figure a plan da?" Daniel chuckled and scrubbed a hand through his hair before sitting on the floor across from Alexi and proceeding to relay all that had happened while Alexi was out.

The ride back to the portal seemed to take longer than their previous trip, but then Daniel had been floating in and out of consciousness at the time. The portal remained in the same place, an almost unnoticeable glimmer in the air between two trees.

There was no sign of the altercation that surely must have occurred once Alexi had grabbed Daniel. In fact there was not a soul to be seen working at any of the hangars. Daniel looked to Alexi who merely shrugged and lead the way toward the portal. Alexi gestured for Daniel to precede him.

Daniel knew something was different the moment he emerged from the portal. The antechamber was cold and the guards were absent. Alexi stepped through behind him and nearly collided with Daniel's back. Daniel stared incredulously, the antechamber was empty! Even the throne room beyond seemed absent of life. Daniel jogged into the throne room, his voice echoing eerily through the empty chambers. Alexi's head whipped around at the sound of a door slowly creaking open. Daniel ran back into the room and grabbed two ceremonial spears from the wall, tossing one to Alexi they both crouched and prepared to meet their visitor. The maidservant, arms loaded with buckets and mops came through the door and screamed at the appearance of two warriors in what had just been an empty room. The clattering of the buckets echoed as she dropped to her knees and began rapidly pleading for her life. Daniel set the spear on the floor and with open hands slowly approached the maid in an attempt to calm her and show her they meant no harm. Alexi turned away from the babbling servant and began to notice the not so subtle differences in the two courts. The high pitch please from the servant were staring to resound in Alexi's temples. He slowly made his way deeper into the chamber.

The walls of the portal antechamber were rough cut and twined with flowering vines in jewel bright tones. The Seelie court seemed to focus more on designing their dwellings to appear in harmony with nature while the Unseelie court was decorated with dramatic colors and Gothic statuary. Alexi looked over his shoulder and noticed the maidservant upon seeing no harm was intended for her had gone from pleading to scolding and Daniel was forced to apologize several times before she stormed back the way she had come. Daniel shrugged as he approached Alexi. "There has to be someone here who knows where they all went." They both made their way into the throne room and Daniel once again located a servant and began questioning him in hushed tones while Alexi was left once again to admire his surroundings. The Seelie Great Hall had slender living trees ringing the perimeter of the room and extending hundreds of feet above his head. The boughs of the trees met in a woven canopy where brightly colored birds could be seen flitting amongst the emerald canopy. Daniel trotted back past Alexi into the antechamber and returned with his dropped spear. "Everyone is out at the battlefield, apparently war has broken out while we were....elsewhere." Apparently the servant had given Daniel directions to the battlefield because Daniel lead them unerringly to yet another portal that would take them where they wanted to go. Before Daniel could step through the portal, Alexi stopped him and gestured to their spears. "You do know how to use one of those things right?" Daniel gave Alexi a crooked grin "what's to know, the pointy end goes in the other man." With a mock salute Daniel leapt through the portal leaving Alexi wondering what he had gotten himself into.

Daniel stepped through the portal and shivered as a cold breeze cut through his thin shirt. The sky above was filled with roiling gray clouds and sheets of rain obscured his view. The battlefield below was briefly lit by white streaks of lightning, thunder shook the hillside he found himself on. It seemed Nature itself raged at the spilling of Fae blood.

Further down the hill and to their right was a large white pavilion. Here sat the Seelie court, their eyes locked on the bloody battle commencing on the field below. The pavilion walls snapped in the wind and the ropes creaked as the wind sought to tear the very structure down and cast it away. Daniel and Alexi made their way to the pavilion and after a brief conversation with the perimeter guards, were allowed to pass into the pavilion. Daniel's sudden appearance was greeted with loud exclamations of surprise and delight. When Daniel had finally succeeded in convincing his friends that he was fine and quieted them, he slowly told them what had occurred since his capture. Despite Daniel's assurances of Alexi's good intentions, the entire court was looking with thinly veiled mistrust at the large Gypsy standing quietly in the corner. Daniel nudged Alexi toward Queen Sadronniel. The Queen's guards crossed their pikes before her as Alexi approached. With out being prompted Alexi dropped to his knee, his dark head bowed before him. Kneeling before Queen Sadronniel Alexi vowed eternal fealty to the Seelie throne and any knowledge he possessed of the Witch Rue and the inner workings of the Unseelie court in exchange for the sanctuary and clemency of the Seelie Court. Several long moments passed as Queen Sadronniel made up her mind. Daniel could see the tension in Alexi's back and shoulders and as if someone whispered in his ear, he had a sudden revelation. Here was a man who had been the leader of his clan and if even half what he had told Daniel was true, this was a man who until Rue had appeared had never been made to kneel or grovel before anyone in his life. It made Daniel cringe to realize how very much Alexi had lost because of Rue. Daniel knew he and Alexi had wounds to their flesh that would heal, but how would anyone ever heal the wounds to Alexi's soul? How do you heal wounds so deep you wake screaming in the night...when do you begin to trust again? Gently the Queen rose from her seat and taking the three steps to where Alexi knelt and laid her hand on his head. "Our protection is extended to you warrior, rise and join your allies." Alexi slowly stood and was quickly pulled to the side to be introduced to the circle of people surrounding Daniel. Hunter gave him a wary nod of welcome while Hart clasped forearms with him and thanked him for returning Daniel to him. Lauren hesitated after being introduced to Alexi, then pulled him into a hug and thanked him for bringing Daniel back to her. Alexi was stunned by the sudden acceptance of him. Alexi patted her back awkwardly as she started to sob into his shoulder, stepping back with tears in her eyes she quietly thanked him again before pulling Daniel into a tight embrace.

Hart gestured Alexi over to the side where he and Hunter stood watching Lauren and Daniel and discussing their next step. Lauren's shoulders shook as she released her pent up emotions and sobbed into Daniel's chest. "I ...I thought you were dead, I thought I would never see you again and..." Her voice fell silent choked with emotion. Daniel wrapped his arms around her, his head resting on the top of hers. "Alexi asked me to leave with him, back when we were at the motel." Lauren's fingers gripped his shirt harder. Daniel stroked her hair as he stared at where Alexi, hunter and Hart stood talking in hushed tones. "He wanted to just get in the truck and run, go so far away that Rue's power would never be able to reach us." Lauren tilted her face up, her swollen eyes meeting his. Daniel cupped her chin in his hand as he smiled down at her. "You were my reason for coming back, I could never live without my heart." Lowering his head he pressed his lips to hers in what started as a tentative kiss. Lauren slid her arms around his neck and pulled his lips more firmly against hers. The heat from the kiss left them both breathless as the world around them faded away.

It took several exaggerated coughs and clearing of throats to bring Daniel and Lauren back to the world. Lauren was blushing furiously as they stepped apart to face their friends. Hart gave them both an apologetic look before gesturing to the battlefield below them. "Rue is somewhere down there on the battlefield with her Champion Prince Marrat'hassar." Daniel turned to look at the battlefield as if he could pick her out of the hundreds of battling Fae. Looking down on the carnage below he could almost hear the ringing sounds of steel meeting steel and the deeper sounds of steel meeting flesh. Shaking his head he once again heard only the sounds of the wind and rain assaulting the pavilion roof over his head. Staring into the storm he muttered just loud enough for the others to hear. "She chose to be a witch, she sealed her fate when she chose to be evil." Turning to face his friends he saw shock, anger and confusion mirrored on each face. Hart's eyes burned fiercest but it was Hunter who spoke first. "Are ye telling me that being a witch means ye're evil?" Daniel started to confirm his belief but something made him pause. Hunter shoved forward and glared up at Daniel. "Then I 'spose ye will be saying next that yer Da and I are nawt but evil as well aye?" Daniel stepped back, the rain leaking from the roof edge nearly as cold as the looks from his friends as they suddenly realized the extent of his ignorance. Hart waved Hunter back and joined Daniel at the edge of the Pavilion. "True we do not worship your Christ, but that makes us no more evil than the nature we revere." Turning Daniel to once more face the battle he pointed to where the battle seemed fiercest. "Down there are those who worship and respect nature and seek to live in harmony with it, they battle those who would rape our Earth mother and reap her bounty to sate their selfish desires." Turning Daniel away from the fray, he faced him, water running into both their eyes as they stood exposed to the elements. "Angelique opened Rue to the ability to use our magic in a way it was never meant to be used, but it was Rue's choice to continue to use the magic in such a way too cause harm that makes her evil." Alexi had also stepped out of the shelter to join them and clapped Daniel on the shoulder. "Witches are good or evil by their actions and not their beliefs little brother."

It was with dawning realization that Daniel understood he had been barreling through life long before Rue appeared. Daniel never stopped to truly think about what he believed, he had contributed to the same ignorance that sparked wars in his world for hundreds of years. Daniel started to apologize but didn't know where to start. Hart nodded as if the words were written in the air between them. "I am not angry at you Daniel, but...there is more."

Daniel slid again in the mud as he clumsily sidestepped Hart's swing. "You move as if you think this is a game, do you think the Fae on the field will pull their blows because you are human?" Hart was shaking with restraint as he fought not to yell at Daniel. It had been Daniel's idea that Hart give him at least the basics on how to use the sword to defend himself. Daniel would lead a small group of Fae onto the battlefield with orders from the Queen to capture Rue and bring her unharmed back to the Seelie Court. After Rue had given birth to Daniel's child she would stand trial for her crimes and Daniel would be free to raise the child free of Rue's influence. Alexi whistled sharply from the edge of the training field. "Perhaps he needs to be seeing what he should be doing Hart." Hart cocked his head as if in thought then nodded and tossed a blade to Alexi. Alexi made a couple of practice swings then took Daniel's place across from Hart. It was obvious from the first few strikes that Alexi had been born with a blade in is hands. After a few minutes Alexi and Hart were even laughing and taunting each other. Daniel laughed in admiration, this was like watching one of his old movies. He could swear it was Basil Rathbone and Errol Flynn dueling before him in the wind and the rain. With one blade Alexi was amazing, when Hart tossed him a second, he proved unstoppable. It was decided that Daniel would lead the strike party onto the field to capture Rue and Alexi would keep him alive long enough to do so.

The realities of war were suddenly made abundantly clear to Daniel as he led his group onto the field. The rain kept him from smelling the blood as he stepped over and around the fallen, but nothing could stop the images from being burned into his brain. This was no gore heavy film being watched safely from the comfort of your living room, this was real. Daniel moved to step over a group of corpses when one of the corpses moaned. Startled, Daniel turned back to the pile of bodies and realized several were staring at him in silent agony. Daniel hesitated only a moment before ordering his guardsmen to start carrying the wounded back to the healer's tents. The guardsmen immediately began untangling the living from the dead and escorting the wounded away from the battle. Alexi grabbed Daniel's arm as he turned to continue in the direction of the Unseelie army. "Without the guardsmen you have no back up." Daniel shoved wet hair out of his eyes. "I cannot assume that we are going to win this battle, hell I can't even guarantee we are going to survive our encounter with Rue!" Alexi gestured at the retreating guardsmen vanishing like ghosts in the rain. "Then why would you send them away?!" Desperate to make his new found friend understand, Daniel grabbed Alexi's shoulder. "Every life I send to the healers, is one more Fae who can continue this battle if we fail...now do you get it?"

Alexi stared silently at Daniel for several long moments with only the sound of the rain and the thunder around them. "You would make a great King Daniel." Daniel laughed. "Lets hope it never comes to that." Turning they both began once again to trudge through the ever deepening mud.

CHAPTER FIFTEEN

A circle of guardsmen surrounded both Rue and Prince Marrat'hassar.Rue was throwing her head back and laughing as she pointed seemingly at random toward the groups of battling Fae and caused rocks to explode. Every explosion sent bits of Fae and debris showering on the those nearest. Those caught in the explosions either fell where they were too wounded to continue fighting, or were tossed like ragdolls from the force of the explosion. Not all of those wounded and tossed were from the enemies army, it seemed not to matter to Rue who was in the area when she ignited her spells. The storm seemed to be going around Rue and the prince, the rain stopping a few feet above their heads as if an invisible umbrella were held above them.

The Royal Guardsmen tightened their formation and presented an impregnable wall of bristling swords and solid shields as Daniel and Alexi approached. Daniel stopped short of the blades and raised his voice, timing his request between the thunder so as to ensure he would be heard. "We seek an audience with the Lady Rue Bishop." For a moment it seemed as if the world held its breath, as if this moment was a turning point or a deciding factor on the fate of what would come after. Alexi pulled his cloak more firmly around him, concealing the twin blades in his hands and prayed to whatever gods were listening that they were not about to be disarmed. Rue's eyes met Daniel's across the distance and her full lips pulled into a triumphant smile. Rue gestured for the guards to let them through, but it was not until the gesture was repeated by the prince that the guards moved aside and allowed the humans entry. Once Daniel and Alexi stepped through, the circle closed once again behind them, the guards now facing the visitors. Daniel watched something dark flare behind Rue's eyes at the response of the guards. It disappeared so quickly that if Daniel had not already known the evil that lived in Rue's heart he might have thought he had imagined it.

Rue stepped past the prince and approached her visitors, stopping just out of reach she beamed triumphantly again. "So you two have nobly decided to surrender yourselves and end the needless slaughter of your allies have you?" Rue's tone was mocking as she smirked at Daniel and Alexi. Daniel stared briefly at her swollen belly and sighed before once again meeting her eyes. "I am beseeching you Rue to please come back with Alexi and I to the Seelie Court and after the the child is born stand trial for your crimes against humanity and the Fae, I am further offering to plead leniency on your behalf at your trial." Rue stared at Daniel before walking directly up to him and shoving him hard in the chest so that he slid in the mud. Daniel threw his arms out but managed to regain his balance as he once again forced himself to meet Rue's enraged gaze. Rue had stepped from beneath her weather shield, her blonde hair turning dark with the rain. "You really expect me to just turn myself over to your pitiful allies and allow them to pass judgment on me?" Daniel found himself shaking from more than the cold as he continued to meet Rue's eyes. Standing so close to her once again he watched memories of what he had suffered at her hands flash through his mind, his breath caught as the familiar fear and helplessness closed in on him. When he spoke his voice shook and he had to force the words past the sudden dryness of his mouth. "I am asking you to think of the child you are carrying, I am appealing to the goodness that I know resides in the hearts of all people, even your heart must have some goodness in it Rue...please Rue do the right thing and come back with me."

Rue tilted her head and started to answer when she was suddenly shoved aside. Prince Marrat'hassar tore his helm from his head and tossed it without looking to one of the watching guardsman who caught it deftly as if this was a long established routine. Striding to within arms reach of Daniel he pulled his blade, his attractive features ruined by the angry scowl on his face. "I have had enough of this talk of judgment and surrender, you humans were amusements that should have been disposed of long ago."

Rue regained her footing and shoved against the prince's back. "No! They are mine and I forbid you to kill them!" Thrusting his arm behind him, the prince shoved Rue away from him and whipped around to face her. A small flicker of fear lit Rue's eyes when she saw the pure wrath reflected on the prince's face. Looking past Rue, he saw his mother Queen Mo'readhiel approaching the circle of guardsmen. Doubling his fist he hit Rue in the breastbone, just above the swell of her stomach and send her stumbling backwards to drop in an ungraceful heap amidst her tangled skirts in the mud. "You forbid me nothing WHORE, you and all you own belongs to me and when I am done here I will teach you to know your place!" In one fluid movement the prince spun back towards Daniel and brought his sword up in an overhand strike. Time seemed once again to slow and Daniel knew he would never get out of the way in time, closing his eyes he waited for the blow.

The breath went out of Daniel and he was suddenly shoved to the side, the ring of metal on metal sounding nearby. Looking back at the prince, he saw that Alexi had dropped his cloak and caught the prince's descending blade on his own crossed blades. Alexi laughed and yelled something in Romanian at the prince. While the prince may not have understood the words, the tone was unmistakable. Tossing his long hair out of his face, Alexi shoved the prince back and dropped into a defensive stance, his two blades at the ready. Daniel barely had time to roll out of the way as the prince charged past him. Alexi and the prince met in the middle of the circle, blades flashing in the uncertain light. Again and again they attacked at each other, neither giving quarter, both masters of steel. Daniel was mesmerized by the deadly dance, the flashes of lightning reflected off the swinging steel. Daniel glanced over at Rue and saw that she was equally enthralled by the swordplay, she had regained her feet, a sword loosely clenched in one fist and hanging at her side. The look on her face was one he hoped never to see aimed at him. The evil spark he had glimpsed behind her eyes at the Guards slight had settled in whole upon her visage, her beautiful face was twisted with such intense hate and fury that one was left with the feeling they were staring at no less than pure evil. Daniel turned back to the battle and a movement to his left brought his attention to the guards. One of the guards had managed to slip a rock into his hand, his eyes trained on Alexi's back. Daniel threw himself up out of the mud and charged the guard, the rock left the guard's hand as Daniel slammed into him. Daniel yelled a warning to Alexi but the warning went unheard as once again thunder roared across the plain. Daniel did not hear the rock reach its target but he saw its affect. The rock impacted the side of Alexi's turned head and he stumbled. The prince used the distraction to sweep Alexi's blades aside before shoving his sword through Alexi's shoulder. Alexi cried out in pain and dropped to his knees as the prince ruthlessly tore the blade free. The prince nodded at the guard even as Daniel shoved away from the guard and ran to where Alexi sat, his blades dropping from his hands. Daniel saw blood running from Alexi's temple, Prince Marrat'hassar's blade had entered just below Alexi's collarbone, the front of his chain shirt was covered in blood. There was pain and defeat in Alexi's eyes as he looked up at Daniel. Daniel stepped in front of Alexi as the prince approached. "I am the one that Rue sought after, I am the one you want." Daniel gestured at where Alexi knelt behind him in the mud. "You have already defeated him, he can do no more harm, if you need to take vengeance on someone take it on me." The Prince sneered and spat at Daniel. "I will slay both my whore's pets, then I will teach her a whore's place once and for all!" Prince Marrat'hassar raised his blade, a triumphant smile on his face, once again Daniel found himself instinctively closing his eyes to block out the sight of the blow that would take his life. Daniel's last thought was of Lauren, *I never got to say goodbye...I love you Lauren...* Daniel's eyes jerked wide as the Prince screamed in pain. Two feet of steel had suddenly burst from the Prince's chest. The prince looked down at the blade extending from his chest and his own blade dropped from nerveless fingers. He started to turn towards his attacker but dropped instead to his knees, his eyes wide in disbelief as he saw Rue standing there smiling. "I am no man's whore and these are MY pets!" The prince dropped to the side, the light going dim behind his eyes. Rue started to speak, a wailing from behind them interrupted her as Queen Mo'readhiel shoved past them and dropped into the mud next to her son, cradling his head against her ample breasts. "My baby! What have you done to my baby!?!" Tenderly she wiped the mud from his pale face with her silk skirts, true tears of grief slipping silently down her cheeks. The guards closed in around the humans. King Melcindo'mien staggered to a stop next to his queen, his armor as battered and blood stained as the wicked mace in his hand. Dropping the mace to the ground, he seemed to age more than a thousand years in a second as he gazed at the lifeless eyes of his only son. Gently he bent and pulled his wife to her feet, the price's head dropping silently back into its muddy resting place. The dim light behind the queen's eyes suddenly flared to life as she caught sight of Rue surrounded by guardsmen. There was no sanity in those eyes as she shoved away from her husband and marched towards Rue with deadly intent.

"You filthy bitch, you killed my baby, I will peel the skin from your living body and wear it as a dress!" Grabbing a sword from one of the guards she shoved herself in Rue's face. "I will bathe in your blood witch!" The guardsmen were shunted aside as Queen Sadronniel stepped forward and caught her rival queen's eye. "No Mo'readhiel.

The witch Rue carries a child of Seelie descent, when the child is born Rue will stand trial for ALL her crimes, including the death of your son." Queen Mo'readhiel looked uncertain as sanity slowly returned to her eyes. Sadronniel stepped closer and laid a hand on the arm still clutching the sword as if to use it on Rue. "I swear by the laws of of our courts and may nature herself bear witness, Rue will face judgment that will be agreeable to both our courts." Queen Sadronniel's proclamation rang out over the suddenly silent battlefield and once again the world held its breath. After a long silence, Queen Mo'readhiel nodded and dropped the sword from her hand. King Melcindo'mien with nary a glance at the Seelie queen, enfolded his wife in his arms and led her and their guardsmen off the field. The seelie guards pulled Rue's hands roughly behind her and as a precaution she was also blindfolded and gagged before being led through the portal. Daniel was shocked into silence when Queen Sadronniel knelt in the mud near himself and Alexi and smiled. "What you have done here will echo long into the histories of even our long lived people, you have truly saved our people Daniel, we are in your debt...we always repay our debts." With help from her servants she stood and made her way to the portal leaving only Hunter, Hart and Lauren to assist Alexi and Daniel. Daniel gasped in pain as Lauren socked him in the shoulder, her eyes brimming with tears. "You stupid ass, you nearly got yourself killed." Before he could respond, she grabbed him around the neck and pulled him into a hug. Daniel could never understand how women could both laugh and cry at the same time.

Lauren captured Daniel's lips in a fierce kiss before stepping back embarrassed. Hunter and Hart had helped Alexi to his feet while a healer bandaged Alexi's shoulder. Alexi grinned "we won today yes?" As if in answer the rain lightened then stopped altogether and the dark clouds began to dissolve like mist before the dawn. Suddenly the sky above was alight with glittering stars and a full moon shone its pale light upon them. It was Hart that renewed the shadow on their hearts as he spoke. "I believe what we did here was a good thing, but I fear it is not over yet." Daniel felt the truth in Hart's words and could only agree.

CHAPTER SIXTEEN

Rue expected to be deposited by the guards in some damp drafty dungeon where rats would feast on her living flesh. Instead she was brought to what appeared to be a well furnished suite with an adjoining room for a servant or maid. The furnishings were straight out of a fairytale complete with curtained four post bed big enough for an orgy and plush carpeting that you sank into with every step. The color scheme was blue and silver, perhaps this was supposed to have a 'calming effect' on her. Regardless of the rich surroundings, it was still a gilded cage and her time here was only temporary. Rue now understood the trepidation a prisoner on death row must feel, knowing that the end loomed ever nearer. Unlike a death row prisoner however, her only regret was that she had not been able to finish what she had started. When the guard asked if she was in need of anything else to make her stay comfortable she had only one response. "Bring me my maidservant Kate."

Within the hour a scowling Kate was deposited inside the door and the door firmly shut and locked once more behind her. Kate turned to face Rue with genuine hate in her eyes. "Even now, you cannot help but keep me near you, not out of love or loyalty or friendship...so why Rue!?" Rue smiled at Kate's impotent fury. "You are my slave, where I go thither you also go...get used to it, I am sure when I am dead you will return to Queen Mo'readhiel's tender ministrations." Kate paled and she shivered. "You don't know...they have brought me to the brink of death only to bring me back...they touch me and they..." she shook her head, unspoken horrors lurking in her dark eyes. "You could make them free me, you could release me and let me go...if you ever loved me Rue, please let me go." Rue turned and strode to the wide window overlooking a pleasure garden. The garden was bisected into four perfect squares, each square was locked eternally in a single season. The winter garden showed crystalline sculptures and snow covered trees. Well worn paths showed the frequent passage of visitors. The spring and summer gardens were in full bloom and Rue could almost imagine the heady scent of the many blossoms filling the air like perfume. The autumn garden should have been as beautiful as the rest but somehow she found it the hardest to look at. Like her own life, she was at the autumn of her life, the blooms had come and gone and soon the cold of winter, of death would embrace her and she would know no more. She had not answered Kate's entreaties, but then no answer was necessary. If Kate knew anything at all, she knew Rue would never willingly let go of anything that was hers. Kate would serve her in the beyond as she had served her in life...whether she wanted to or not.

Kate jerked awake at the sound of Rue's stifled cries. They had been here barely two weeks and Rue had gone into false labor several times this week alone. Kate started to roll over and go back asleep but something about the frantic way Rue was trying to muffle her cries told Kate that this was the real thing. Leaping to her feet she went to Rue's bedside and dragged the covers from the bed. Rue was muffling her cries into her pillow, her knees bent, and the bottom of the bed soaked with fluid and blood. Kate ran to the door to the chamber and pounded on it until the guard shoved it open, a naked blade at the ready. Kate gestured at the bed. "Her water broke, the baby is coming...there is blood!" The guard nodded and assured her the healer would be here shortly before closing the door in her face. The bolt shooting home had become so familiar, Kate barely heard it as she she turned back to Rue and wrapped her arms around herself. Once the baby was born, they would have a three day reprieve, then they would stand trial. Kate stumbled forward as the door was thrown open against her back and guards rushed in to secure her. Once she was pressed against the wall, a mailed arm across her throat, the healer entered. This was not the usual healer, this was some ancient crone. By the deference she was shone by both servant and guard alike, she must be someone very important. Kate never got a chance to ask, as soon as the healer had knelt at Rue's side and seen that the labor was not false, Kate was escorted to her adjoining chamber and the door shut firmly in her face once again. She could hear the sounds of the labor progressing and found herself pacing her small room anxiously.

Knowing that any day now Rue would give birth to his child and he would become a father in truth hung like a cloud over his head. How did someone know if they were ready too be a father, if they would be a good parent. The conversation around the table had suddenly ceased. Daniel looked up from the food he had been absently pushing around on his plate to find all eyes on him. "I'm sorry guys, I just... was lost in thought." Lauren laid her head on his shoulder and took his hand in hers beneath the table. "We are all worried about what is going to happen next, but you seem to forget that we are all in this together sweetheart." Daniel swung his arm up and around her and pulled her against his chest as he kissed her hair. "What can I say, I am a work in progress." Alexi grimaced as he lifted his goblet in his right hand and quickly switched it to his left. "We all are my brother." Hart and Alexi spent a lot of time in the sparring room training with different weapons and fighting styles. If Lauren had not been keeping Daniel equally as occupied, Daniel might have been jealous of Alexi's unintentional usurpation of his father.

Hart and Alexi had just stood and excused themselves to go back to the sparring chamber, when a guard came hurrying forward and whispered in Hart's ear before heading back the way he had come. Hart turned to the table with a grim look on his face. "Lady Rue has given birth to your Child Daniel, she has rejected it sight unseen and the healer asks for you and Lady Lauren's presence." Daniel stood feeling nervousness and excitement warring within him. Daniel took a moment to look each of his friends in the eye, it was Alexi that broke the silence. "Go my brother, we will be here when you return." Daniel smiled his thanks, and taking Lauren's hand hurried down the corridor the guard had taken. Even without guards along the way to give directions, Daniel would have know where to go by the sound of a baby crying loudly. Lauren pulled up short when she saw a familiar ancient crone of a woman holding the crying baby wrapped in a thick woolen blanket. "I know you, you did something to my car...at the hotel." The crone nodded and gave her a gap toothed smile. "Ye were what we were looking for, but nearly did we miss ye...needed a push to get ye there in time." Daniel looked from Lauren to the crone and back again. "I feel like I am missing something here." Lauren gestured to the crone. "She cast a spell on my car, it got me to you faster than should have been possible, but then the storm hit and ....the accident, was that you as well?" Lauren turned her questioning eyes back to the Crone. The crone smiled and laid a finger alongside her nose. "Bright as buttons ye are lass, and aye...we were what created the storm, twas necessary...and now I will ask thee to finish what we started." The baby's cries had started to sound pitiful and weak. Lauren approached the crone, her eyes on the swaddled babe in her arms. A small red face, screwed up in misery with a cap of dark hair peeked around the edge of the blanket. Lauren felt tears swim in her eyes as she held her arms out for the baby.

The Crone looked over at Daniel who nodded silently before laying the crying babe in Lauren's outstretched arms. The baby must have sensed a change, the cries quieted and a pair of deep blue eyes opened and stared up at Lauren. Lauren bent and kissed the baby on the forehead and cuddled it closer to her. The crone touched Lauren on the shoulder to gain her attention. "A fine strong son yer man will have if we find one to nurse the boy...so here be my question lass." Lauren nodded to show she was listening. "Will ye help[Daniel to raise this man child as yer own, will ye raise it to know its roots, and will ye carry that what it needs to feed as if ye were its mother in truth?" Lauren understood about raising the child with Daniel, but she was unsure what the crone meant by 'carrying what it needs to feed as if she were the mother in truth.' Lauren slowly shook her head. "I am not sure what you mean, I am sorry." The crone gestured impatiently to Lauren's chest. "What it needs to feed, would ye nurse the babe lass?" Lauren looked confused. "I can't nurse him, I have no milk for him, I am not lactating." The crone smiled "and if ye could, would ye?" Understanding dawned on Lauren's face, this crone could cause her body to lactate as if it had been she that had given birth. This child may carry Rue's genes but it would not learn evil at Rue's breast. Lauren nodded with tears in her eyes. "Oh yes, please, I would nurse him as if he were my own." She suddenly turned to Daniel who up unto this point had been content to let the women speak. "If that is ok with you, he is your son." Daniel smiled reassuringly at Lauren. "I can think of no one who would make a better mother than you." Lauren beamed at him and the crone led her to a quiet room to do whatever it is she needed so that Lauren could feed his son. Daniel started to follow but the crone was suddenly back. "To you I say this, in three days, those twain in there will face judgment before the bright and dark court, if you would speak to them then this tis the time." The crone left him standing outside Rue's chambers, a braver man might have entered and thanked her for the life of his son, promised to speak for her at the trial and maybe find a way to forgive her for the sake of their child. A brave might have done these things, but Daniel was not feeling particularly brave and turned aside to join his friends instead.

When Daniel returned to the dining chamber, Lauren was tucked in a comfortable chair in the corner with a blanket draped over her shoulder. Every so often Lauren lifted the edge of the blanket and looked beneath it before re adjusting it and leaning back with a bemused smile on her face. Daniel hesitated a moment before joining her, he wanted to give her this peaceful time with their son. Just the thought of Lauren's face as she agreed to be mother to his son caused an ache in his chest. Daniel was beginning to believe in miracles. This beautiful woman risks a witch's wrath to break him out of prison and continues to help him long after they are free. Somehow in all this merry chase, she snuck into his heart and despite all the problems he had brought into her life, she wanted to stay with him and raise another woman's child as her own. As if she knew his thoughts, Lauren smiled at him and held out her hand. Daniel took her hand and stepped closer to her. Lifting the blanket edge, he gazed down at the cap of dark curls lying thickly atop his son's head. He felt tears pricking at his eyes as he realized for the first time that his family was now complete. He was reunited with his father, he had his son with him, and the woman of his dreams.

Kneeling down next to the chair, he cupped Lauren's chin in his hand and turned her face to him. "I know it's probably a little late to ask, you agreeing to mother my son and all...Lauren, would you marry me and make me the happiest man on earth?" Tears welled up in Lauren's eyes as she silently nodded. So intense was the happiness on her face that the others silently excused themselves to give the couple this moment alone. Daniel pulled one of the rings from his keychain and slipped it onto her left ring finger. "It's just symbolic you understand, I plan on getting you the biggest diamond you can handle on the real thing." Lauren laughed. "I neither need nor want anything so pretentious as a diamond Daniel, a simple ring will be fine...besides I am marrying you for you and not for what you can buy me." Hart had re entered the room without either of them noticing and discreetly cleared his throat to gain their attention now.

"Perhaps I can help in regards to a suitable ring." From his pocket Hart produced a beautiful opal ring. The band was silver with lacy filigree. The opal was smooth and rounded and showed the blue of a summer sky with threads of sunset gold and rose pink. Clustered around the opal were small chips of amethyst. Lauren gasped as she saw it and could not take her eyes off it as Daniel removed the keyring and slipped the beautiful opal ring onto her finger. Daniel stared at how right the ring looked on Lauren's hand and turned back to Hart. "Thank you so very much, how much do I.... Hart held up his hand to Halt Daniel's offer of payment. "The ring was to be a gift to my son when he reached his manhood so that he might present it to the woman who captures his heart. So was it stated in the will of my grandmere, your great great grandmother." Daniel hugged Hart tightly before returning to Lauren's side. The baby had gone quiet beneath the blanket shield. When Lauren peeked beneath, the baby was sound asleep. Carefully she rearranged her blouse and laid the sleeping baby in a nest of blankets in the chair beside her.

It was Lauren's turn to hug Hart and tearfully thank him for everything, especially the beautiful ring. Daniel stood grinning like a fool as he looked from one to the other. A sudden thought struck him. "Don't we need like a priest or something to make a marriage official, and don't women want lots of lavish gifts and gowns and things for their weddings?" Hart raised an eyebrow, laughter sparkling deep in his eyes. "In our world, it takes two people to announce their intentions before two witnesses and they are married until before two witnesses they state their intention to part." Daniel looked at Lauren and solemnly took her hands in his. "Lauren Matthews, it is my intention to have you as my wife, to comfort and hold, to love and cherish. I swear to honor you and your ways so long as you will have me." Daniel was never sure where those words had come from, though later Hart had told him it was an ancient vow spoken by the first Seelie King to his human consort. Lauren stared deep into Daniel's eyes as she recited the vows back to him, her voice breaking a bit as she forced the words past a throat gone tight with emotion.

Daniel pulled Lauren into his arms and kissed her deeply, as with every other kiss they had shared, time disappeared and they were aware of only each other. Hart cleared his throat several times before the newly weds became aware once again of his presence. "Although he cannot yet speak, I am sure my grandson will agree to act as the second witness in this private ceremony." Lauren and Daniel both turned to look and noticed the baby had woken at some point and was staring at them with big blue eyes, a half smile on his cherub lips. Daniel lifted his son and cradled him against his chest for the first time. Looking down into those beautiful depth less eyes he could suddenly recall something he had once heard, he found himself murmuring it now in wonder as it suddenly made sense to him. "If you ever want to see the face of God, look into the eyes of a newborn, for they were just with him." Lauren smiled and hugged Daniel's arm as she peered over his shoulder at the beautiful baby staring at them in silent wonder. Daniel smiled at Lauren and Hart. "Guess I should get around to figuring out a name for this little guy huh?" Lauren suggested several names, but it was finally to Hart that Daniel turned for suggestions. "My uncle who was the one who gave me my sense of honor, was named Leucathius...that might be a little unwieldy for such a small soul though." Daniel looked down at the boy and smiled. "Leucathius...but we can call him Luke until he is older."

Luke's tiny smile widened and a small chuckle escaped from him as if he approved of his new name.

Chapter Seventeen

Truly miracles were afoot, the two courts who never agreed on anything, agreed to push back the trial a full week. The trial would be held just three days shy of the feast of Samhain. The courtroom was on neutral ground. The court itself looked exactly as Daniel had pictured it might if the trial were to be held in a gothic fantasy movie. Tiered rows of bench like seats looked down upon a sunken stage. The accused would be forced to stand tall as the weight of a thousand eyes looked down on them. The accused would actually be chained and sitting in a hard, ugly wooden chair. A bright light focused upon them so that they were blinded to the identity of their accusers. The seats would be filled with the silently watching witnesses to the trial and the accused would answer questions called out to them from the dark. Daniel could imagine the feelings of fear and isolation that past accused must of felt as they sat in the chair, the chains ringing quietly as they sought a more comfortable position.

Daniel had scarcely given Rue a second thought since the night he had stood outside her door and realized that he was not brave enough to face her. Rue was brought in under guard, she had been given a long white robe like gown that somehow seemed like a uniform. The seats had filled early with both Seelie and Unseelie alike, mortal enemies sitting shoulder to shoulder as they waited. Daniel handed Luke to Lauren and after a whispered word in her ear, he made his way down the steeply carved aisle and stopped before Rue's guards. "I need a word with her for a moment." The guards had not been given orders to stop anyone from speaking with the accused, only to stop anyone from harming her, so with military precision they stepped aside to allow Daniel to pass. Rue turned hard eyes on Daniel, she had no illusions as to the outcome of her trial. Daniel hesitated before stepping closer to her as if loath or afraid to do so. "I promised I would speak on your behalf, I have spoken to the courts and the Seelie court has agreed to grant you clemency in gratitude for my son's life." Rue made a scoffing noise and looked down at her dirt edged nails, cracked and badly in need of a manicure. "Say what you came to say and be gone, I have no more desire or use for your presence." Daniel nodded, "I just came to tell you that I kept my promise, despite..." Daniel's voice trailed off, when he met Rue's eyes he was again stunned into silence by the depths of the pure hate in her eyes. "Am I to suddenly care if you 'kept your promise', you are pathetic and I was a fool to think you would ever be worthy of my attentions...go back to your scarlet whore and that pitiful parasite I was forced to give life to." Rue turned her back on Daniel, her hated filled eyes scanning the dim figures in their seats.

Daniel returned to Lauren's side and at her concerned look, he shrugged. He could not explain to her let alone top himself why he felt the need to visit Rue and explain that he had spoken to the closeted court and tried to ensure her life imprisonment instead of her death. How successful he had been was still left to be seen.Rue was led to the chair and chained securely to it arms and legs. Queen Sadronniel, King Melcindo'mien and Queen Mo'readhiel entered from the right, though Rue would not be able to see them past the blinding spotlight. It was Queen Sadronniel who spoke first. "Rue Marion Bishop, you stand accused this day of crimes against Humanity and Fae, how do you plead?" Rue turned her head in the direction of the queen's voice with a mocking smile. "Not guilty of course, I refuse to acknowledge the right of a bunch of shriveled and archaic imps to judge me for my actions." Her words caused gasps and murmurs to fly around the room. Queen Sadronniel had to raise her voice several times before silence fell upon the echoing courtroom. If anything the disruption had delighted Rue, her smile was filled with amusement as Queen Sadronniel turned once again to her.

"Know this Rue Bishop, we do not need your acknowledgment of our rights to judge you, for judge you we will." Rue kept her delighted smile on her face and shrugged as if was no matter to her what they decided. "Rue Bishop, when offered a trial and the ability to defend your actions, you refused so today we do not come here to hear evidence. All evidence was heard and examined in a closed session of the courts. During our deliberation, Daniel Warwick has come to us and pleaded your case, that we might give you a lesser sentence...The Seelie court has agreed to grant you clemency and drop our charges against you in gratitude for the life of the baby henceforth known as Leucathius Warwick." Rue laughed out loud and mumbled what sounded like "poor kid." Queen Sadronniel sat down and it was Queen Mo'readhiel who took her place now. The Unseelie Queen seemed to have aged a decade or more in the week since Daniel had last seen her. Her flawless pale skin was now marked with the signs of strain and fatigue. As she stood up from her bench, the fire in her eyes almost succeeded in reversing the signs of her grief. "Rue Bishop, though the Seelie court has seen fit to clear you of charges, the Unseelie has not...For taking the life of my son, I call the Wild Hunt upon you, you and your maid who was complicit in your crimes." Daniel was not sure what the Wild Hunt was but the reactions of those around him, horror from the Seelie and delirious excitement from the Unseelie told him it would not be something good.

Rue tried to push herself to her feet but was kept seated by the chains attached to the chair. "How dare you judge me, you fat bloated hag!" The sound of a thousand angry Fae surging to their feet and yelling was enough to cover whatever response the queen might have answered and once again it took several long moments for order to be restored. Queen Sadronniel once again took the lead as she stood and faced Rue. "In three days the moon will be full and the Hunt will be ride, you Rue and your maid servant Katheryn Anne Rochester will be present." Rue looked around her as if expecting to see Kate lingering in the shadows. "Why is my maidservant not present at our trial?" It was the previously silent King who answered her. King Melcindo'mien stood looking as if he too had aged greatly since the death of his son. "Your maid was given the choice to be here and face judgment with you or to be tried separately from you. She chose to be tried separately, her sentence was for her ears alone and she has accepted our sentence and prepares herself for her fate." The room held its breath as if waiting to see if rue would have any further outbursts or questions. When it appeared there was nothing else to say, Rue's guards unchained her and returned her to her rooms to await her fate.

Daniel sat quietly as those around him stood and left the room, the spotlight having been turned off and the room now brightly lit. It felt unreal, Rue's trial was over but he was filled with questions, what was the Wild Hunt and why were the reactions by the two courts totally opposite each other?

Chapter Eighteen

The moon was full and overhead as the procession made their way out of the disguised portal. The portal hidden in an abandoned mine somewhere in the outskirts of Poulsbo Washington State, brought them out into a heavily wooded area. The woods were mostly old pines and firs and a circular glade had been made not far from the mine's entrance. Daniel got the feeling as the procession formed a circle in the glade, that this was the purpose of the glade, a meeting place perhaps. Daniel pulled Lauren closer against him as if and looked at Hart. Hart's face was impassive as he took his place in the circle. Alexi had chosen not to join them, he would await their return, he simply stated "I know what is coming, I have no desire to see it in the flesh." The mood was appropriately solemn as the two Queens stood before Rue and Kate. Kate was paler than usual but there was a manic energy about her, she seemed to be barely controlling some strong emotion, whatever it was she was feeling, her features gave nothing away. Rue by contrast let no one mistake her mood for anything less than black rage. Queen Mo'readhiel held her hands palm up to the moon above her head and her voice took on the cadence of one reciting a long memorized speech. "Rue Bishop and Kathryn Rochester, for the crimes you have committed unto Fae and humanity alike we sentence you to the Wild Hunt." A shorter Fae in velvet garb adorned with a stylized red ram emblazoned on his tunic stepped forward and pulled from his belt a long curved horn. Taking a deep breath he blew deeply into the horn and the sound that emerged made cold shivers run down Daniel's spine. Lauren shivered against his side and Daniel knew she felt as he did, something evil had been loosed into the world.

The slight breeze that had been rustling the branches above silenced and as before, Daniel got the feeling that the world was holding its breath. Hart turned his back to the circle and gently lead Lauren back towards the portal with a whisper in her ear. He turned to look at Daniel. "You may not want to see what is coming Daniel..." Daniel shook his head. "I'll stay, I need to see this thing to the end." Lauren jogged back and pulled him into a tight hug before allowing Hart to lead her back to the portal. Daniel watched them until they vanished into the shadows. Turning back to the circle he noticed all of the Fae had retreated, the circle widening so that Rue and Kate stood unquestionably alone in the center. As if this had been the signal the world had been waiting for, the winds picked up and hair and clothes were whipped about their owners at the force of the gale that suddenly tore through the glade.

A black swirling rift in the air suddenly appeared and from within it the sounds of horses and unearthly hounds emanated. Daniel would never forget what came through that rift that night, he could never unsee the horrors and wished now that he had stayed behind with Alexi. The creatures were in full armor from head to foot, cruel curving horns rose from their helms and their gauntlets ended in curved claws. It was the eyes, red glowing eyes that pierced Daniel to his very soul that made him start to shake. Huge black boarhounds with crimson eyes that matched the dread riders wove around the legs of the steeds. The steeds like the hounds were large and black, but in their eyes the very flames of hell seemed to be reflected. The eyes were not merely red as were those of the riders and hounds, true flames seemed to be crackling behind their lids, as if the eyes were mere windows to someplace Daniel never wanted to see. The largest of the riders approached the two women standing alone in the center of the glade. The jingling of harness and the creak of leather sounding loud even over the fierce winds. The steed snorted, its breath touching the women and they both began to shiver. Rue straightened her spine as she looked up at the rider as if denying the fear she must surely be feeling. It was Kate that the rider turned to and a voice rolled out sounding like the mingled voices of a thousand damned souls. Daniel shuddered at the sound, he could not understand a word of it, but somehow Kate was able to understand and nodded. A cruel smile lit Kate's face as she stepped away from Rue and slowly began to undress. Rue stared at her as if she was mad, but the other riders seemed to be enjoying the show immensely. When Kate stood naked and pale in the moonlight, her black lace collar her only adornment, the lead rider gestured to her.

Kate's body began to shudder as if she were having a fit, her mouth opened in a silent scream as she sunk to her hands and knees in the grass. Kate's bones seemed to be twisting and writhing like snakes beneath her pale skin, then suddenly her skin split wide and dark fur shoved through as if an animal were forcing itself from within her. The human skin sloughed off in bloody tatters until amidst the gore stood a large crimson eyed hell hound twin to its companions. A black lacy collar hanging about its neck was all that set it apart from the others.

Rue's look of horror drew a chuckle from the lead rider and once again the voice spoke this time to Rue. Whatever was said made Rue go pale for the first time and without another word she turned and dashed into the forest. The riders inclined their heads at the watching Fae and a second rider pulled from his belt a black rams horn. Three long blasts from it caused the steeds to move restlessly, then the hounds with Kate in the lead let out a chorus of unearthly howls and charged into the forest following Rue's path. The riders spurred their dark steeds and in a moment the glade was empty of the Wild Hunt. The wind died as the dark vortex closed, there was no sign of of what had occurred in the glade. The flesh that had been Kate had been accepted by the earth and not even a dark spot remained behind. Daniel shuddered as the distant baying of hounds echoed in the night air. The circle broke as the Fae made their way back to the portal. Hart, Alexi, Hunter and Lauren all sat at the table in the great hall drinking steaming chalices of Hunter's best mead. Daniel could not stop shivering long after the warming drink had filled him. Looking to Hart who seemed to be having the same reaction, he forced himself to ask. "What will happen to Rue now?" Hart paused as if considering how much to say. "The rift which brought them here will emerge further afield and they will herd her into it, if she is able to evade the Wild Hunt three nights in their own territory, she will be offered her freedom..." Daniel took another sip and wished he did not feel compelled to ask, but he did. "Does anyone ever win their freedom from the Wild Hunt?" Hart stared into the polished depths of the table for so long that Daniel thought he would not answer at all. His voice was soft when next he spoke. "Only one in the last five thousand years has done so...and now I must take my rest, I suggest you all do the same." With a servile bow of his head, Hart silently stood from the table and left. Hunter stretched and let out a groan so loud both Daniel and Lauren jumped. "Weeeell I am t'bed and best ye two be doin the same." Hunter grinned at their startled expressions and headed towards his room. An awkward silence followed Hunter's departure.

Finally Daniel stood and as gallantly as possible, held out his hand. "My beautiful wife may I accompany you to our room?" Lauren giggled and kissed him lightly on the lips as she stood and allowed him to lead her to their room. Since the wedding, Hart had moved out of the room and rumor had it, his room now adjoined the Queen's chamber so as to better protect her of course. Lauren excused herself into the adjoining bathroom as soon as they entered. Daniel noticed that the room had been moved about, the bed was larger and was festooned with rose petals. Scented candles had been lit about the room with a spicy scent reminiscent of cinnamon and vanilla. The room looked to have been prepared in anticipation of their arrival. A thought occurred to Daniel as he looked about the room. "Sweetie, where is Luke tonight?" The door behind him opened and Lauren stood in the open doorway wearing a lacy purple negligee and matching thigh high stockings. "Hart and Queen Sadronniel have offered to keep him tonight." Daniel sat down on the edge of the bed, his body responding to Lauren's slow seductive walk even as he asked the question. "Are you sure you want to...we can take this slower sweetheart.." Lauren pushed him slowly back on the bed and kissed him, her tongue plundering his mouth and no more words were spoken.

Daniel woke to the delicious feeling of someone's arms wrapped around his chest. He could feel Lauren's naked body pressed against him from behind. Suddenly Lauren sneezed, her forehead bouncing against his back and he chuckled as he turned over. Pulling her head onto his chest, he kissed her forehead and whispered "morning beautiful." Lauren smiled and stretched, the satin sheets falling away to expose her rose tipped breasts to the golden sunlight streaking through the curtains... The sun was much higher in the sky before they made it out of the room.

Breakfast was as usual a loud informal affair where scads of food were loaded onto the groaning table and everyone talked at once to their neighbors or calling down the table to others. What was surprising was that Queen Sadronniel who seemed up to now to want to keep her distance from the humans, had deigned to join them and instead of her formal dresses, had come wearing a long tunic and divided skirt as if she had been out riding. Daniel realized he was staring when Queen Sadronniel turned to him and smiled, lifting her glass in a silent greeting. Daniel glanced at Hart who seemed to be much more relaxed today and could only shake his head in wonder as Hart and Queen Sadronniel sat laughing with each other looking like friends or lovers rather than Queen and servant. Lauren had begged off breakfast saying she needed to feed Luke and promising to join him later. Daniel turned to his left and noticed Alexi had also found a "friend" last night. Daniel recognized the Fae woman next to Alexi as one of the chambermaids who cleaned the royal apartments. Alexi was nibbling some sliced fruit and giving the woman a heart stopping smile as she twirled a lock of Alexi's hair and leaned close to whisper in his ear. Alexi only chuckled and shook his head, the woman went back to work, her back a little straighter as if his refusal had been only mildly offensive.

Daniel realized as they all sat at the table joined together by camaraderie and food, that it was time to start thinking about what comes next. Underhill was a beautiful place, but Daniel wanted to raise his child as a human, in a world that Daniel understood. Later when the food had been cleared away, Lauren sat nearby. Lauren was rocking Luke in a willow rocking chair that had been covered with a foot of dust when it had been discovered for her convenience in some forgotten nursery. Once the chair had been cleaned thoroughly, it had become Lauren's favorite place to nurse their son. Daniel walked to the wide windows casting golden sunshine upon his wife and son and looked out onto a beautiful city filled with bustling Fae. Carts drawn by horses and other "mythical" beasts going who knew where. Fae dressed in outfits common only at a renn faire going about their daily lives. So much magic and beauty existed here, but there was a home shaped hole in Daniel's heart and he was feeling the ache of homesickness. Turning he knelt next to the chair, stroking one callused fingertip down his son's velvety cheek and causing Luke to emit a gurgling laugh. He kept his eyes trained on the smiling face of his cooing son as he asked Lauren the question and dreaded what she might say. "Lauren...this place is beautiful and magical and...I miss our world, I miss knowing what to expect every morning and knowing what law apply...I miss things making sense to me...I am homesick. I love you and I do not want to take you from this place if this where you want to make our home...I'll live wherever you want." A drop of moisture appeared on Daniel's wrist and he looked up to see Lauren smiling with tears in her eyes. "You idiot, I love you too and if you want to go home, we can leave this minute, as long as I have you and Luke I am have all the magic and beauty I need." Daniel hugged Lauren hard, Luke complaining at being squished between them.

Daniel laughed and stood, too excited to remain kneeling. "I'll go tell Hart, ...are you...is there anything I can?..." Lauren laughed and shooed him off with a smile. "Go on then you crazy lout, make preparations, our son and I will sit here and bond." Daniel smiled at them again before trotting in the direction of the practice yard, his heart so light at the thought of going home that he felt he could fly there. It wasn't until he had reached the edge of the practice yard and stood staring at Alexi and Hart sparring against each other that he realized he might be leaving them behind. Daniel's elation evaporated like fog before the dawn. Daniel approached his father and friend, his light steps suddenly feeling mired in drying cement. Hart called a halt as he caught sight of Daniel approaching. Alexi pulled his swing and with a clap on Hart's shoulder, took the blades to the weapons rack. Hart's eyes took in Daniel's expression and turning him, led him to where Alexi was dunking his sweaty head in the rain barrel. Daniel had to laugh as Alexi flipped his long wet hair behind him looking like a shampoo model. Alexi grinned and shook water from his ears. "You look as if you have ought on your mind my brother, what causes such a long face on you?" Daniel looked from Alexi who grinned from ear to ear, to Hart who looked pensive. "Lauren and I decided we are going to raise Luke in our world...instead of Underhill." Alexi laughed. "You owe me fifty dollars Hart, I told you it would be today." Daniel looked from one to the other, confusion written across his face. Hart chuckled and washed the sweat from his face and neck. "Alexi bet me that it would be today that you would talk to Lauren about leaving and that she would most likely be more comfortable in your world as well." Alexi clapped Daniel on the shoulder in the same manner he had done to Hart earlier. "Truthfully I thought it would be sooner, no offense my brother but you and Lauren fit in here like geese amongst swans...your culture is so different from here that you have no grounding, you are a ship without a rudder."

Hart cocked his head as if weighing the examples Alexi had used and seeing them valid he nodded. "Alexi means no disrespect Daniel, but he is right...his people are more familiar with us, while in America most modern people think of us as myths and stories with no basis of fact." Daniel understood what they were saying but it did not make it any easier to hear. " So you guys are not mad that we are leaving?" Alexi grabbed a water skin from a nearby bench and took a long drink before answering. "Not at all, and just in case you are worried about what will become of Alexi, have no fear...Hart has offered to take me on as his protege and help train the guards in the ways battle as my people know it." Alexi leaned close to Daniel to whisper. "Truly I think he is looking for lessons in seducing certain royalty...as we gypsies are masters of seduction this is a good bargain for him da?" Daniel chuckled and Hart shot them both a withering glare. Apparently the stories of Fae hearing were not exaggerated. Hart gathered Alexi and Daniel to him like a father with his two sons and as he walked them back to the palace he told them of a beautiful wood built house he owned just outside of Chimicum in Washington State....

Rue's house had been searched and Angelique's 'gifts' reclaimed and taken Underhill. A certain black tourmaline was gathered with a mix of fear and awe by the seelie court and Daniel heard one mention "burying it where none would find nor waken it again." With a lot of help from the Fae and a good portion of Hart's wages which he termed "back child support", Lauren, Luke and Daniel were settled into as beautiful split level home on 30 acres of old growth forest. The house had a beautiful view of the mountains and was close enough to a little used portal that Hart and Alexi could still come visit, although the leaving was bittersweet, it was not really goodbye..for there are never really 'goodbyes' among family and friends, only 'good journey until we meet again'.

Daniel closed the leather journal on his desk and looked up startled as the door creaked open and light fell upon him. Lauren stood in the doorway, her hair sleep rumpled. " Daniel, is everything alright?" Daniel smiled at his beautiful wife as he slid the journal into his bottom drawer and dropped the pen back onto his desk with a sigh. "Everything is wonderful sweetheart...just finishing up something I needed to do." Walking to the door he took her gently in his arms and slid his hands beneath her robe feeling bare flesh beneath. "Lets get you back in bed shall we?" Lauren's chuckle was muffled against his neck as he led her back to their room and closed the door on the dark office.

Made in the USA
Middletown, DE
27 May 2017